Readers love
Tales from the Gemstone Kingdoms
by AMANDA MEUWISSEN

The Prince and the Ice King

"I desperately hope we get to see this cast of characters again because it wasn't just our two leads I fell in love with…"

—The Cozy Reading Corner

Stitches

"I loved the first book in the series, and I love this one as well! It's very creative, the characters are all great, and the story has many twists and turns to keep you on your toes!"

—Bayou Book Junkie

The Bard and the Fairy Prince

"A story full of amazing creatures and stunning magic, with lighting and smoke, whirlwinds, elements working their power…all excitingly written, it started with an easygoing pace but accelerated the further the journey came."

—Love Bytes

Void Dancer

"There is something captivating about a series of books that focus on gemstones being the defining object and force behind a kingdom and its people—and Meuwissen has an engaging, easy style of writing it."

—Paranormal Romance Guild

By Amanda Meuwissen

Coming Up for Air
Their Dark Reflections

DREAMSPUN DESIRES
A Model Escort
Interpretive Hearts

MOONLIGHT PROPHECIES
By the Red Moonlight
Blue Moon Rising
Wane on Harvest Moon
By Cold Moon's Night

TALES FROM THE GEMSTONE KINGDOM
The Prince and the Ice King
Stitches
The Bard and the Fairy Prince
Void Dancer
The Dragon and the Emerald King

Published by DSP Publications
After Vertigo

Published by DREAMSPINNER PRESS
www.dreamspinnerpress.com

THE DRAGON
AND THE
EMERALD KING

AMANDA MEUWISSEN

Published by
DREAMSPINNER PRESS

5032 Capital Circle SW, Suite 2, PMB# 279, Tallahassee, FL 32305-7886 USA
www.dreamspinnerpress.com

The Dragon and the Emerald King
© 2023 Amanda Meuwissen

Cover Art
© 2023 Kris Norris
https://krisnorris.com
coverrequest@krisnorris.com
Cover content is for illustrative purposes only and any person depicted on the cover is a model.

Trade Paperback ISBN: 978-1-64108-666-0
Digital ISBN: 978-1-64108-665-3
Trade Paperback published November 2023
v. 1.0

Printed in the United States of America
∞
This paper meets the requirements of
ANSI/NISO Z39.48-1992 (Permanence of Paper).

CHAPTER 1

THE BLAST was startling, but it only erupted for a moment and then imploded on itself to collect the debris.

"This thing is a godsend," announced the foreman as he approached the pile where one of the newly minted Dragon's Glands, the stone it had blasted, and the ore they were after could all easily be sifted through.

"More like *king*-sent," chuckled one of the workers.

Mining in the Ruby Mountains had never been easier. They had more workers, too, because the danger was far reduced between new explosives and light sources. To mine the most coveted of materials, they could go deeper into the mountains than ever before, even past the Ruby gemstone.

They were mindful of the catacombs for the dead, of course, but there were many other caverns once thought impossible to excavate. Now they could, with the hopes of building more homes and discovering even more resources for those in need. The recently appointed Ruby King, Enzario "Enzo" Dragonbane, was an inventor as well as a man of the people, determined to correct the disparity between classes.

What the workers didn't realize, however, nor the king, nor anyone else in Ruby or the other kingdoms, was that in a few decades time, the mining would reach the last slumbering dragon—his platinum scales already rippling with anticipation within the safety of pleasant dreams.

THIRTY YEARS LATER

THAT MARVELOUS rumbling that had been tickling Pax's scales the past few decades had finally reached the cavern where he'd lain dormant all these centuries. In some ways, it hadn't been enough time to heal his aching heart, but he was done sleeping and longed to return from what had finally become nicer dreams to an indulgent adventure or two that would help him forget the day he let himself be buried once and for all.

"What are those? Some new kind of crystal?"

"Metal maybe?"

"It feels like the most polished and pristine armor I've ever seen."

Why thank you, Pax thought as he felt the strangers' hands on him. He was still curled up, and given his size, likely looked like a wall in the cavern to these unsuspecting men.

One of them tugged a little too harshly, but it felt quite nice, like getting an itch scratched that Pax hadn't known he'd needed.

"It won't come loose. We may need another Dragon's Gland for this."

Dragon's *Gland*? What an apt name for whatever device they'd used that had shaken the mountains. Pax preferred his glands to be utilized in better ways, but it had been ages, and he very much looked forward to becoming familiar with that again.

Although the last time he'd indulged, he'd forgotten his rule and ended up here.

Only dalliances this time, he told himself. Just for fun, no attachment. Surely, he could find someone in the Gemstone Kingdoms to strike his fancy until he was ready to move on from these lands. It seemed wrong to leave without granting one final mortal his scales.

Which of his brethren he would choose to follow, he didn't yet know. Would he take to the skies? Through one of the gemstones itself to join his closest kin and the wild magic folk? Perhaps he would chase the final adventure and choose to never wake again.

For now, he needed to stretch.

"Go back and get some while I work on this. I can't tell if these be metal or diamonds or what. What *are* they?"

Pax rippled his scales to an exclamation of surprise, unfurled his long neck from how he'd been coiled into a tight ball, wings extending from how they'd folded against his back, and turned his head to blink down at the dwarven miners.

"They're scales, actually," he said with a rumble as potent as their bombs.

They screamed, clutched each other like they might stay frozen in terror, only for one to find his feet and drag the other behind him as they sprinted from the cavern.

No matter. Pax got to his feet to give chase. Surely, they were headed toward the main cavern of the Ruby Kingdom, and from there, he knew every crevice that opened to the skies. He hadn't changed forms since he'd started to slumber, but it took only a mere whim to grow smaller or larger, depending on how he best fit into even the tiniest of tunnels.

The miners screamed once more when they saw him barreling after them and hastened their steps. Pax didn't mean to frighten, but he doubted they'd listen if he stopped to explain, and he was eager to be out of the mountains' grasp.

He tore into the next cavern, which halted him with a ring of familiarity. The Ruby gemstone, nestled in the rocks, glowed pinkish red in the darkness that wasn't as dark as it might have been, for torches had been set into the walls to line the way for the miners. Pax paused upon seeing it, fat on the natural magic of the lands and beautiful as ever.

"Hello, friend," he said, and the gemstone pulsed in answer.

They weren't sentient in the normal sense, but living embodiments of the earth, able to cast their will from time to time through the magic they were birthed from. Beyond the Ruby, down other tunnels blocked with ropes and bearing signs telling the miners not to trespass, were the burial chambers for royals and heroes.

Pax wondered if....

No. It didn't matter where *he* had ended up. What mattered was escape and putting as much distance between himself and this kingdom as he could.

Hurrying into the next tunnel, Pax shrank further to better fit. At the optimal size, he overcame the pace of the miners in no time, nearly on their heels when they burst forth from the final tunnel into the largest cavern of them all.

Pax leapt over their heads, returning to his true, glorious size as the new space allowed him to grow and grow, and he roared at how good it felt to finally spread his wings fully. Reaching the skies would feel even better, and he didn't want to look down upon the kingdom and see how it might have changed. He wished the people no ill-will, for they had freed him, but he needn't stay in the place that had wounded him most when that day was something he longed to forget.

Forget he would and find someone worthy of his attention and scales before he left these lands forever.

"Dragon!" rang up from the people below, as Pax flapped his wings toward the nearest opening out of the mountains.

Yes, he was.

And he was finally awake.

"I'M AFRAID the protesters have returned, Your Majesty. Both sides."

One month as king, and Bertram still wasn't used to being called that. "Thank you, David. I'll be down in a few minutes."

David, Bertram's personal guard, an elf who had been personal guard to all the recent Emerald monarchs, bowed and took his leave.

Not for the first time, Bertram wondered if he'd made a mistake accepting the Emerald throne when his Uncle Reardon's father, King Henry, passed away. Henry had declined an extended life that he might have been granted with visits to the immortal lands of Sapphire, or even Diamond and Amethyst. He didn't want more than a normal human lifespan before joining his wife in the next world.

In truth, Henry had been regent these past thirty years, only ruling when Reardon and his husband, Jack, Bertram's blood-related uncle, were in Sapphire. The Emerald and Sapphire Kings had ruled the two nations jointly ever since they were wed, but never apart, and so Henry had been regent here in their absence, and the now Queen Josephine, Bertram's mother, had ruled Sapphire when they were here.

Bertram had grown up surrounded by authority, with royal blood in his veins, but tempered by his father's "peasant" blood, as Barclay himself called it, to never act as though he was superior to anyone. Becoming king certainly didn't make Bertram feel superior. Quite the opposite when comparing himself to his mother, his uncles, or the pseudo-grandfather Henry had been to him.

When Reardon and Jack asked Bertram to present himself as a candidate for Henry's successor, he'd happily accepted. He'd been happier still when the people voted him in. He hadn't known then that a change in rule would coax dissenters from the city's woodwork, bringing up age-old aggressions and disagreements about magic. It would have been easier if he'd had Reardon and Jack to turn to for guidance, but they'd yet to be heard from since leaving the Gemstone Kingdoms to seek adventure.

Emerald hadn't only lost one king when Henry died, but three. Reardon wanted to get away after burying his father, understandably so, and Jack had used the opportunity to finally ask if he was ready to give up the throne and spend a bit of their long lives doing something other than ruling. After all, Jack had been king of the Frozen Kingdom, now Sapphire again, for over two hundred years. No one begrudged them a reprieve from their responsibilities.

If only they'd waited a few months for Bertram to settle in, but then, if Reardon and Jack were around, he might have begged them to take the crown back from him. He'd already thrown away half a dozen pieces of parchment that morning, changing his mind as to how to update his parents on how he was faring his first month.

The rejected letters said everything from bold lies—*everything is splendid!*—to desperate petitions for mercy. So far, the currently acceptable letter merely said: *Dear mother & father.*

Pushing the parchment aside, Bertram rose from his desk. The king's chambers were more modest here than in Sapphire, which remained dormant with Reardon and Jack gone, since Josie and Barclay had their own rooms. Here, there were high ceilings and a four-poster bed, as well as a separate room at the back with a bath and other plumbing of convenience, but there was no antechamber for an office. Bertram's writing desk was in the bedchamber itself, and since he often worked here, he kept his door open to interruptions throughout the day.

It wasn't as if he'd had bedroom visitors of another nature since becoming king. When would he have had the time? He'd rarely had time for such activities back home, having taken on most of the steward responsibilities in lieu of Zephyr, who'd originally had the role, but was traveling with his lover, Nigel. Part of the reason Reardon and Jack had asked Bertram to try his hand at being king was because he'd basically been helping run a kingdom since he was a boy.

Of course, Josie had often chided him for being too focused on duty and neglecting to nurture friendships and courtship, but having grown up on lands that stopped him from growing older after coming of age, Bertram knew he'd have time for such frivolities later. Duty was immediate.

The actual monarchs and regents couldn't handle every affair and settle every dispute, and so, when no one was available one afternoon to assist a squabbling pair of neighbors concerning a tree on their property line, 'twas a fourteen-year-old Bertram who'd pulled them aside and talked them through a compromise. They could each take the fruit from only their side of the tree, and another tree would be planted beside it, so that once it was mature, each family's property would have their own to pass down.

His mother loved telling that story, proving her son's supposed brilliance in governance. Little good that did him now when he couldn't settle the current dispute filling Emerald's streets.

"Magic for the masses!"

"Unchecked power corrupts!"

He heard the competing mantras filtering in through his open doorway as he crossed the room to leave. He'd heard the stories from Reardon and his father, Barclay, about how magic was outlawed in Emerald when they were boys. Elves and others with magical ability had been forced to hide themselves to avoid being given as tribute to Jack, then called the Ice King, like some offering to a cruel god.

People feared magic, and rightly so. It could be dangerous. But most people had some magic within them, with only a few having more powerful abilities like especially attuned elves and mages. Even fewer were as potent with magic as the wild magic folk, two of whom had returned from their world across the veil and ruled kingdoms peacefully—the Fairy Queen in Diamond and the Shadow King in Amethyst.

Bertram wasn't blessed with any special magic, not like his father who could see visions of the past, present, and future when he touched things. It was Barclay's power of prophecy that had gotten him sent to the Frozen Kingdom, where he met and fell in love with Bertram's mother.

Barclay had always said he couldn't see anything clearly where it pertained to Bertram. Perhaps because Bertram was his son, or because he was young, with too many unknown opportunities before him that could lead in different directions. Bertram, however, often wondered if his father was simply withholding the truth. He'd certainly looked like he had a vision when Bertram hugged him goodbye the day he left Sapphire, but when Bertram asked, he'd simply said:

"Surprises can be a good thing. Even frightening ones. You are going to do wonderful things, my son."

When?

Bertram paused on his way out the door to cast a glance at his reflection. As much as he wasn't yet used to being called Your Majesty, he was less used to having green eyes. Henry never had green eyes. Not that he wasn't worthy, but he'd always been a placeholder, waiting to pass the throne to Reardon, since it was Reardon's mother who bore the crown when she was alive. But Bertram was meant to be a true king, not split between kingdoms, not a regent—*king*. The moment the crown was placed on his head, his formerly brown eyes changed, and everyone watching had exclaimed it was a sign they voted right.

Apparently, the Emerald gemstone was as blind as Bertram's supporters.

He had his Uncle Jack's straight nose, high cheekbones, and firm jaw, but the darker coloring of his father. His skin was brown, wavy hair almost black, which he kept short, and a dusting of dark stubble adorned his cheeks. He was average in stature, but taller than Barclay, and had surpassed both parents in height by the time his voice began to change. He was average in build as well, between his father's compactness and mother's lithe grace. Handsome, he supposed. He'd certainly been told as much by courters and lovers—and by his mother.

Josie had gifted him a beautiful doublet that she'd made for his coronation, which he wore again today. It was rich in color with alternating panels from blue to teal to green, meant as a bridge between kingdoms so he never forgot where he came from.

He looked weary otherwise, but presentable. He hadn't been sleeping well, but even after a bad night of insomnia, he still looked closer to twenty than thirty. He was twenty-nine, in fact. He'd aged a little from travel to other kingdoms, but barely more than a year's worth in appearance since turning twenty-two.

He knew it bothered his parents that his aging would continue like any normal human while he ruled Emerald, but he was sure to be long-lived enough that he hadn't hesitated to answer Reardon and Jack's summons, even knowing it shortened his life. It was how one lived that mattered, not how long.

He started to leave his chambers but had to pivot back. He'd forgotten to retrieve his crown. 'Twas the same one passed from Henry to Reardon, Henry having worn a princely coronet while regent. It still sat too heavily on Bertram's brow, gold with inlaid emeralds, but when addressing one's people, a king needed to be *king*, even if he still had no idea how to rule them right.

Some citizens were calling for a return to when magic was outlawed. Most didn't mean it to the extent it had once been, but that it should be forbidden outside the home, and that children should be shackled with magic-blocking limiters until they came of age.

It was far too extreme for Bertram to accept, but he also understood why they demanded it. As magic had become more accepted in Emerald, more people lived openly, more were moving here from other kingdoms, and overuse of magic had become a problem, spilling unchecked onto the streets, and even used during minor arguments. Something needed to be done, but *what* wasn't an easy answer.

Bertram nodded to the castle guards he passed along his way to the central foyer, all of whom bowed. They were a good sort but inherited from the previous reign. He knew they must doubt him, given the unrest that had erupted only days after his coronation. He had so many plans he'd wanted to focus on. Like the establishment of a council that had proven so beneficial in Ruby. But who to put on that council when such a contested issue was stirring? He wanted to expand the city walls as well, enough to allow more businesses to be built, given the booming trade, but without taking too much farmland or private property.

He even wanted to open more trade hours with use of the Veil Curtain, a device combining alchemy and magic invented by the Fairy Queen and since passed to all five kingdoms. It allowed instant transportation to anyone who used it. Some said that the Fairy Queen's personal device could take her literally anywhere, but the ones in other kingdoms only connected to each other. Even so, trade had never been more fruitful now that days' long travel was no longer required to exchange goods.

The Veil Curtain in Emerald was in a parlor room on the lower level of the castle, rather than being accessible at all hours to the public, for fear of children stumbling upon it.

Or the inebriated.

The parlor was one of the final rooms Bertram passed as he made his way to the castle doors. There was a long line of those desiring to travel through the Curtain today, like every day. Too often it was all Bertram could do to keep from fantasizing about sneaking down to the device at night and escaping to another kingdom. He'd half expected his parents to come through at some point, but they'd been respecting his wishes to not loom over his shoulder. Never mind how much he wanted to visit them, but if he ported home every time there was an issue, he'd have used the Veil Curtain every day since he took the crown, some days twice.

The large double doors at the front of the castle were open to be welcoming but were currently blocked by guards, preventing anyone new from entering.

"Make way for His Majesty!" David announced, bowing as Bertram approached. His cry caused the guards to part, allowing Bertram to pass through.

"Magic for the masses!"

"Unchecked power corrupts!"

"Enough!" Bertram cried, raising his hands to emphasize that the chanting needed to stop. There were two groups in the castle courtyard, both sides with familiar faces, since it was always the same ringleaders stirring discontent.

Penelope on the anti-magic side was from a tailor's family, a young human woman with little to no magic herself, and her family the same. Her brother had been caught in a terrible accident, where a bunch of foolish teenagers were playing with magic and set half the tailor's shop on fire. Her brother made it out, but not without extensive burns that healers were still trying to soothe. Some of his scars would be permanent.

Dain, an elf who looked as young as Penelope but was decades older, helmed the pro-magic side. He'd been forced to hide his lineage during the dark years of the Emerald Kingdom and was adamant against any return to those days, especially having married a human woman, with several half-elven children.

"Both sides have valid concerns," Bertram said as he often did when addressing these protesters. "But no decision on such an integral aspect to most people's lives can be hastily made—"

"Then form the council you promised us!" Penelope demanded. "Let the people vote on who speaks for us."

"We *did*," Dain argued, "and the people chose Bertram, of royal and magical blood that originated from this very kingdom."

"Yes, and that makes him so impartial," she shot back.

"Please!" Bertram raised his voice to hush them. "While I appreciate your sentiment, Dain, I do indeed wish to see a council formed, and the members should be chosen by vote. But," he pushed on when Penelope smirked, "I worry about doing so now, when tempers are hot and the issue so heavily contested. The people are clearly split, just as you all prove. If equal members on both sides are voted in, won't it lead to the same stalemate and heated debate inside a council chamber as we are seeing in the streets?"

"So you'll continue to do nothing?" Penelope barked.

"No, that is not what I'm saying. I want you to be patient with me while I find some common ground between your demands. Then, when the people have calmed, you can make more sensible decisions on voting—"

"Like when they voted in you?" Penelope scoffed. "So sensible! You'd have us wait here forever, continuing to put people at risk, because you can't make even one decision!"

"Bah! She'll never see reason!" Dain yelled right with her and moved to the side of his followers so he and Penelope were dangerously close. "Some children get out of hand, and you'd see us all burn for it?"

"Out of hand? My brother could have died!"

Diplomacy was so much easier when it wasn't attempted before a hostile crowd. Others joined in the argument, all yelling over each other, without a single thought to seeing the other's side. How could Bertram call for votes on council members when the people were this divided? But he had no idea what compromises would ease them long enough to—

Sparks caught his eye from the middle of the cluster of magic users. Lightning? A fireball? Even if merely illusion to scare someone, tempers flaring was about to become a brawl, and sunlight reflected on sheathed daggers and swords that several people were inching their hands toward.

"Listen! Please, I beg of you!" Bertram tried, but just as he was certain he'd have to call for the guards, a scream echoed over the quarreling, and a whoosh like some great beast flying overhead caused everyone to look skyward.

Bertram had never seen anything so beautiful, enormous, or equally terrifying as the *dragon* that soared over his kingdom from out of Aurora Wood. Its massive shadow covered the entirety of the expanse of courtyard and streets that he could see, its scales glimmering in the sunlight so brightly that it almost seemed to glow.

It was silver. No, gold. No… prismatic almost, with every color glinting within the guise of metallic shimmer. Its four legs ended in sharply taloned feet, with similar talon-like spires on its wings. Its head and tail were crested almost like the top fins of a sea creature, and from its cheeks were similar fin-like appendages. Four great horns sprouted from its head, two almost straight up from its brow, and two more flanking them, arching outward to the sides.

It was a storybook or tapestry come to life, its wingspan double or triple the mass of its body, and its tail twice the body's length too. Its maw when it opened it to roar was filled with razor-sharp teeth that could have snapped up a grown man in a single bite, and the sound shook Bertram's very bones.

"Dragon!" A fresh scream cut the silence, and the courtyard and surrounding streets erupted in panic.

"Wait! Stay calm—" But Bertram was no match for hysteria.

People scattered, fleeing to seek shelter, when surely the safest place was behind Bertram inside the castle. Yet the crowd fled the courtyard, filling the already crammed streets with more chaos.

"We have to keep people calm, or someone is going to get trampled," Bertram ordered his guards. "Help them get to safety and make no attempt to attack the dragon."

Several of the guards stood gaping, but there wasn't time for fear or awe. Bertram sped from the castle doors to leave the courtyard like his citizens and do whatever he could to help them.

"Majesty, wait!" David cried after him, but what else could Bertram do? Hide within the castle while his people were under threat?

A few foolish spells could be seen fired into the sky as the dragon flew out of sight, people running with no order or thought to which direction might be safest. Bertram tried to ease those frozen with fear, urging them to take shelter, and helped move those smaller, especially children, out of the path of the stampede, even handing the occasional child to a floundering parent, who'd lost them in the throng.

The dragon whooshed back overheard like it was circling, and every moment it was within view, Bertram feared an expulsion of fire might set ablaze the buildings and very people until they were nothing but cinders.

"You see!" Penelope's voice reached Bertram from wherever she'd fled to. "You see what havoc their magic has wrought!"

Urg. Of course she'd take that stance, and far too many others would listen.

Why did a dragon have to appear now? Why here?

"This way!" a nearby voice called, and Bertram spun, finding a group of men ushering two young women into an alleyway. Once the women bolted ahead, Bertram saw the men who'd summoned them break into sinister grins.

Without knowing the extent of the threat, Bertram hurried after them—and would swear he felt the dragon's shadow looming.

"The door? But it's locked!" one of the women cried, trying the back entrance into a shop with a signpost just outside. It was shaped like a lamppost with a sign dangling where the light would have hung, bearing the familiar name Jafari's, a long-established family store.

"Pity," one of the men said. "Guess there's nowhere to go."

"Except that way," said another, gesturing behind him without looking, where he might have spotted Bertram, "but I think you'll need to be relieved of some of your valuables to make the trip."

"I think not!" Bertram announced himself.

The men turned, and the two women clutched each other, realizing the danger they'd been in. The men had weapons, but none had drawn them yet, and they hesitated upon seeing Bertram's crown.

"If it isn't the boy king," said one. "And without guards?"

"I'm twenty-nine, hardly a boy, and I trust you are not career thieves but simply foolish men making a bad decision during a worse situation. Walk away, and I shall pretend I never witnessed this transgression, since you have yet to break the law."

Another man scoffed. "You've no weapons, no strong magic to speak of. And I doubt you'd recall our faces after a day."

"Then by all means, strike your king dead, and see how far you get." Bertram spread his arms, giving whatever opening they might want, but he could see on their faces that these were no killers. Their weapons looked more like those of craftsmen. "Or see reason, and I won't clap you in irons."

One blessing was the dragon's shadow seemed to be gone and the din in the streets had quieted as people found their way indoors.

"I told you this was a stupid idea," one man muttered to another, and with shamed, embarrassed glances, the would-be thieves raised their hands to show they remained empty and moved past Bertram to leave the alley.

"Go on," Bertram encouraged the women. "Try Jafari's front door. I'm sure the owner won't turn you away.

"Thank you, Majesty!"

"Thank you so much!"

They bowed before hurrying past him too, still holding each other close.

"Volatile protesters, wannabe bandits made of what should be honest men," Bertram grumbled, turning to face the mouth of the alley, yet uncertain of what to do next. "And now a dragon? Where in the skies did it go?"

"I'm impressed."

Bertram whirled back around, surprised to see a young man hanging upside down from Jafari's sign.

"And I am rarely impressed." He grinned.

He had to be an elf, given his long, pointed ears and unique coloring. His hair was white, but with a shimmer to it like it might have had strands of silver, and dangled long and straight toward the ground. His eyes were such a soft blue, they almost looked silver as well, and his skin was as pale as any Bertram had seen, practically white, with only the faintest pink blush to his cheeks. He was a beautiful youth and would grow into a handsome man, but he couldn't be older than sixteen. Elves aged like any human until they were grown.

His outfit was simple, well-made but not embellished, with white trousers, dyed gray leather boots, and a long-sleeved teal tunic, covered in what would be a knee-length white vest, if the bottom half wasn't also hanging upside down.

"You stepped in to defend your citizens with no recourse to defend yourself other than hope of common sense. The mark of a good king, I dare say. And a handsome one too."

"You tread dangerous ground." Bertram winced, though it was his own best guess whether from being called a good king when he hardly felt like one or because a child was flattering him.

"For calling you handsome?"

"I do not fraternize with boys not of age, and you have a few years of maturing to do."

The elf dropped from the signpost, flipping backward to land gracefully on his feet, and proved to be no taller than Bertram, maybe an inch shorter. His willowy figure spoke of someone who could have been an apt thief himself, for he'd landed without making a sound. "Decent all around, then. I'm liking you more and more, Your Majesty."

"I don't have time for this. You better not have been part of that band of aspiring thieves or thinking it a laugh to join them. I do try to be decent, and decency is one of the few virtues I ask of my people. How else can we thrive as a kingdom when unexpected terrors arrive? Or did you fail to notice that, aside from the magical chaos in the streets of late, we also have a damn dragon to deal with?"

"*Damn* dragon?" the boy repeated. "You don't like dragons?"

"I don't like not knowing what one might consider its next meal or homestead to burn."

"Silly king." He laughed. "Platinum dragons don't breathe fire."

"You got a good look at it?" Bertram took more interest in the boy. "Platinum? That's why its scales were so radiant...."

"Radiant, you say? Did you find the dragon beautiful, Your Majesty?"

"Of course it's beautiful, and likely twice as deadly."

"While that is true, I assure you...." He reached back to grip the pole of the signpost and spun himself around it, finishing, "I have no intention of razing your city, even if you hadn't opened with flattery."

Dread sunk into the pit of Bertram's stomach. "You... what?"

"My sincerest apologies for the commotion caused by my massive wingspan, but you handled it so very well." He spun around the pole again. "I just needed to stretch my wings and clear my throat, you understand. Sounds like things are calming out there, though, and in no small part because of you. I caught a glimpse of that glittering crown and had to get a closer look. You didn't disappoint. Do you know what my kind used to offer for being impressed by a mortal?"

"*You're* the dragon?" Bertram stared. "You can't be...."

"Would you prefer to see my other form?"

"No! You'd never fit."

The boy—dragon—spun again, looking decidedly more devious. "I can fit just about anywhere, Your Majesty, but I don't mean *that* form. This one is less oppressive when meeting new people, you see, disarms and relaxes them if they think I'm more child than man, but my preferred mortal form is a bit more...." He spun around the signpost yet again and somehow, when he appeared from around it, skinny though it was, he was a different creature altogether.

And breathtaking.

The boy version had been lovely, but *this* was a man. In some ways, he looked identical to the younger version, at least related, but he stood half a foot taller, broad and well-muscled, which was easy to notice with how the tunic beneath his vest had vanished, displaying most of his smooth chest. He wore sandals now, and his trousers had vanished as well, leaving only the long vest to cover him with a loincloth-like flap over the front, showing powerful thighs and even the slight hint of his rear through the slits in the sides when the fabric billowed.

"Better?" He leered, and his voice was deeper too, evoking that same rumble from the dragon's roar that had made Bertram's bones shake.

Bertram could merely gape.

"I'll take that as a yes. Pax." He moved from the signpost finally to approach Bertram and bowed. "At your service, King…."

"B-Bertram."

"A pleasure to meet you, Bertie." Pax stood upright and his now towering height reminded Bertram that this was a dragon, who could be far, far larger when he wanted to be. And said dragon, in the form of the most beautiful man Bertram had ever laid eyes on, was looking him up and down with interest. "A promising leader, handsome, and with an appraising eye when other beauty stands before you. I'd say that calls for the usual three scales. But as tradition dictates, we'll start with one."

He reached for his thigh, stretching a leg outward, and as he touched it, his form changed yet again. He was still a beautiful adult elf, but now he had swaths of scales over certain parts of him, and he plucked one right from below his hip.

The colors were as Bertram had seen when the dragon flew overhead, but even more dazzling, catching the sun and shimmering between silver and all the hues of the rainbow. *Platinum.* They covered some of his exposed chest, his shoulders, and the backs of what were now taloned hands. They were there on his outer thighs where he'd removed the scale and over his knees. His feet were nearer to the dragon's form too. Scales even highlighted his cheekbones and lined his returned tail, which would have been long enough to touch the ground if it wasn't hovering with undulations and flicks.

Most impressive were his horns, exactly as they'd been in the sky but smaller to fit this body, two from just above his brow pointing upward and two flanking them, curving to the sides. They looked just as shimmering metallic as the scales, and his smile showed longer eyeteeth like fangs.

There weren't wings, but Bertram wondered if that could change in a blink like the rest.

"Take it." Pax held the scale out to Bertram, which in this dragonkind form was about the size of a coin. "There is enough magic in this small scale to grant any wish your heart desires. You merely need speak it."

"I-I...."

"Think on it, Bertie." Pax took another step forward and grasped Bertram's hand, placing the scale in his palm, and closed his fingers around it without his talons leaving a scratch. "I'll return once you decide. The only things off-limits are the usual caveats—no killing, no resurrecting, and no hearts or minds changed. Aside from that, anything you desire I can grant." He grasped Bertram's chin and tilted it upward, just as gentle with his talons as before. "Anything at all."

Bertram was too shocked, too captivated to speak. He hadn't felt such a stir of want and wondering in his belly since he'd last dallied with a willing partner back in Sapphire.

"I'll be listening, and do accept my apologies for the trouble. I will gladly make it up to you in any way you ask." Pax winked, released Bertram's chin, and circled around him, only to vanish when Bertram turned to follow. There was no whoosh, so he couldn't have flown, unless he could do so invisibly, but he was gone.

And so was Bertram's crown.

THE STREETS had indeed calmed, and Bertram made a proclamation to be passed through the city by his guards that the dragon was gone and of no lasting threat. He doubted most would believe him, but he wasn't certain if he was allowed to speak the truth, or if he'd be believed any more readily if he told his citizens that he'd chatted with the dragon in an alley.

And was given a scale that could grant any wish.

And had basically been propositioned.

Maybe. Possibly. The heat that flushed Bertram's cheeks was a rare occurrence, but then, it had never been caused by a dragon before. Bertram only knew stories, and not enough concrete details, especially about platinum dragons, to be sure he knew anything at all. He'd never heard of wish-granting scales. He knew dragons could speak, had heard of them shapeshifting and that they commanded some of the most powerful magic on earth.

They were also supposed to be extinct, or at least had long since left these lands with no plans to return. No one had encountered a living, breathing dragon since the originator of the Dragonbane line drove the last of them from the Ruby Mountains.

Thankfully, the protesters didn't return. A dragon sighting was cause for staying indoors the rest of the day, it seemed, and gave Bertram the chance to think. He had so many decisions to make, so much work that needed to be done, but he spent a good several hours after the chaos had been quelled staring at the platinum scale, wondering what he should wish for.

No killing, resurrecting, or changing of a person's heart or their way of thinking, just like in stories about djinns, but that left so many possibilities. Could it be as simple as wishing to be a better king? That felt like cheating, disingenuous to the calling.

Could he wish for a solution that would satisfy all sides in the raging debate about magic? That too felt wrong. He'd chosen this path because he believed in himself to do the job well, and if he cut corners now without working his way to the answer on his own, how else might he fail in the future when no scale was there to help?

He certainly wasn't going to wish for a night of passion with the dragon.

Pax.

That would be... far too foolish, wasteful, and indulgent.

But then what?

Finally, when Bertram knew David and the other guards might be worrying over his seclusion, having shut his bedchamber door, an answer came to him. He sat at his desk, surrounded by crumpled-up failures of notes to his parents, and held the scale between both hands, saying:

"I wish... I could see ten years into the future whether everything would be better if I'd never agreed to become king."

"Granted."

Bertram turned, catching the brief sight of Pax lounging on his bed, wearing *his* crown and grinning in apparent approval, before the room vanished and they were suddenly somewhere else.

CHAPTER 2

TEN YEARS LATER—IN ANOTHER LIFE

AN INTERESTING wish to be sure. Both selfish and selfless in different respects, which proved to Pax even more that he had chosen well for this last adventure.

He could have whisked them away to anywhere given the power in Bertram's wish, but easiest was to end up where Bertram would have truly been had his life gone differently and he never became king, now ten years later.

The room was a bit plain if Pax was being honest.

"I'm home...." Bertram whispered.

No longer in the elegant multihued doublet, he now wore a plainer dark blue one without sleeves, his arms still covered but by an undershirt tunic in white. He looked much the same otherwise, with short dark hair, rugged stubble, handsome features, and not a year older, even with ten years gone. Although his green eyes were now brown.

Seeing as though they were in another room with a bed, Pax dropped down onto it to lounge like before, in his larger elven form. He watched Bertram gaze into the mirror above the washbasin. The chamber was a single room, with a privy and bath separated from the rest by a partition. There was a wardrobe in one corner, a desk, a candle clock on the wall, and the bed itself, which was covered by a lovely patchwork quilt in bright colors and patterns. Pax's scales allowed him to curl up just about anywhere and be comfortable, but in mortal skin, he did so appreciate soft fabrics.

"It's like I never left," Bertram said to his reflection.

"You didn't. But bear in mind, it's still been ten years in this iteration of the world, so you may be in for some surprises." Pax propped his hands behind his head. He could almost take a nap here, but then, he had slept for centuries. Maybe he'd just close his eyes for a spell and enjoy the quaintness of being mortal.

"You're wearing my crown. You *stole* my crown?"

Pax peeked an eye open at the approaching king. Prince? Pax didn't know any of the current royals in power, so perhaps Bertram had merely been a noble before he was crowned, or not even that. Pax would be rediscovering all these kingdoms too. "Did I not mention it's good manners to offer a boon when gifted a scale?"

"No, you did not." Bertram looked very adorable with hands planted on his hips as he stood at the foot of the bed, glaring. He'd seemed so spooked earlier that Pax had feared he might not see a return of the forceful and fearless king who'd first caught his attention.

Pax could appreciate beauty in any mortal. His favorites, however, often shared similarities—men of strong build but shorter stature than his own, someone he could encompass but whose strength came through in well-defined muscles. He also enjoyed the contrast of darker hair and skin against his own ivory brightness. Compact, dark, and handsome, rather than the idiomatic tall.

Just like... *he* had been.

Gar.

No, Bertram wasn't like Gar. Only in looks perhaps. And his boldness. And maybe his challenging demeanor. And how effortlessly sensual he could be in ways he clearly didn't see in himself.

Maybe he was a little like Gar, but that had nothing to do with why Pax had chosen him.

Nothing.

"If I never became king, then that crown is from the past," Bertram said. "You can't wear it around when it belongs to someone else in this future."

Damn. That was fair. But it was such a perfect choice for commemorating this journey.

"Is all that true about dragons?"

"All what true, Bertie? *All* can mean so many things."

"You keep gold and treasure in your lairs?"

Pax grinned. He hefted himself upright and swung his legs over the side of the bed to stand. "If you mean collections of things that are dear to us in highly coveted hoards, then yes, but it's not always gold. I merely appreciated how your crown sparkled. But we can tuck it away for now since this version does indeed not exist."

After lifting the crown from his head, Pax rolled it down one arm and up the other like a magician trying to catch the eye unaware, spinning it faster and faster around the curves of his arms until, after one swift roll around an elbow, it failed to reappear, safely hidden where Pax kept all his personal treasures.

The scowl on Bertram's face was replaced by amazement. Pax liked that as much as occasional exasperation, for a bit of both was preferred in his companions. Pure reverence or pure irritation were equally tedious.

"This is really happening?" Bertram asked, softer again. "You're really a dragon? You really granted my wish? This is the future of the life I didn't choose?"

"Yes, yes, yes, and yes." Pax swept closer to him, looming over Bertram's more modest height. He saw the bulb in Bertram's throat bob in an anxious swallow. The former king wasn't afraid, merely transfixed. His brown skin was like tanned leather but with the unlined and soft texture of silk. Pax had only touched Bertram's chin so far, but he did so hope to experience more. Only if Bertram asked, of course, but Pax had confidence he wanted to.

Pax had definitely chosen right.

"The only question that remains now, Bertie, is what do you want to do first?"

Several knocks on the door snapped Bertram's gaping mouth shut.

"You in there, steward?" a woman called from the other side. "Our high-horse wizard isn't too pleased you demanded an audience today and then failed to appear on time. You'll recall I'm the one who gets to suffer his bad moods. And deliver his messages like an errand girl, apparently...."

"Shayla," Bertram gasped. "Uh, I'll be right there! Apologies! I lost track of time!"

"There's a new one," she scoffed. "Don't keep him waiting!" Then shuffling was heard as she headed away.

"Friend of yours?" Pax asked.

"She's the wife of the court wizard, Liam, a former thief, and denizen of this once-cursed castle for over eighty-five years. She can be a bit intimidating."

That woman had hardly sounded like she was in her eighties. And Sapphire had been cursed? Fascinating! There was the scent of powerful magic about the place now—wild magic, which easily explained a lack of aging and why Bertram, who was otherwise human, didn't look older either.

Pax needed to learn more about the centuries he'd missed, and now he'd gone and lost another decade by granting this wish. He could sense the chilling pulse from the Sapphire below him in the bowels of the castle, so at least he knew which kingdom he was in.

"*She's* intimidating," Pax repeated, "but a court wizard you ignore?"

"I wouldn't normally," Bertram said, "but I... I don't even know why I'm going to see him. I don't remember the ten years that have passed!"

"Why would you? You didn't live them," Pax said and then waggled an eyebrow with a closer lean toward Bertram. "And it would spoil the fun. Now, come on, let's find out what this wizard wants." He turned for the door. "Is he talented—?"

"Hold on." Bertram grasped Pax's elbow. If Pax hadn't wanted to be stopped, he could have dragged Bertram after him like a youngling, but he was in a generous mood given the excitement ahead. "You can't go around the castle like that!"

"And why not? What's wrong with my appearance?" Pax stared down at his current form. He hadn't forgotten to hide any scales.

"It's... distracting!" A darker hue filled Bertram's cheeks, and his eyes flicked downward.

Pax's thighs did look rather stunning in this tunic. "Is it?" He let his voice drop lower. "I find this favored version of my mortal self to be so much more comfortable and... airy." He shifted his hips to better show off how high the slit in his tunic went.

"Pax...." Bertram chided in easily rekindled discontent. Good. Pax preferred a companion who could hold his own when pushed. "You'll call too much attention. If people realize something is amiss with you or me, what then?"

"I suppose that's true. And this is exactly why my other form exists." Pax snapped his fingers, and before the sound had even stopped reverberating, he was young and smaller again, almost eye to eye with Bertram, with undershirt and trousers returned. "Who shall we say I am? A visiting apprentice from another kingdom, hoping to study with you and learn... what is it you did before being king?"

Bertram blinked, head cocked slightly, as if he needed a moment to comprehend that this changed person, with a higher voice and smaller frame, was still Pax. That was always fun to witness in mortals. "Um... governance. Bureaucracy. I'd taken over being steward here in the castle.

I have many of the same responsibilities as king in a way, but on a smaller, more manageable scale."

He was steward ten years ago too? How....

Stagnant.

"So, all the hard work of managing finances and squabbles and day-to-day monotony, but without the praise or condemnation of being a true leader?"

"I... well, I wouldn't say... a steward's duties are important!"

"Of course." Pax was only teasing, but he wasn't wrong that it seemed Bertram preferred to do his governing where he came under less scrutiny, and whether he could handle when scrutiny was severe was one of the truest tests of being a good king.

Pax had never known a gemstone to choose wrong, and green eyes meant the Emerald had accepted Bertram. But then, mortals were unpredictable, even when guided by the hand of fate.

As much as Pax craved both new and revisited experiences, Bertram needed some of his own. "Shall we?" He gestured to the door.

"You're staying?" Bertram remained spellbound and perplexed-looking. "You're really going to accompany me while I explore the results of my wish?"

"Naturally. What's the fun in granting something if I don't get to see how it turns out?" Pax grabbed Bertram's arm and waggled an eyebrow again, which probably landed a bit differently since he had to look *up*.

Bertram didn't resist and, at last, allowed Pax to drag him from the room.

BERTRAM WAS home, back in the Sapphire castle where he'd grown up.

His room was in one of the old servant's corridors, which had eventually been where new sacrifices were given lodging as they continued to be sent to the Frozen Kingdom, year after year. No one was truly a servant during the time of the curse or now, but everyone had duties and responsibilities, and people were generally expected to take care of themselves—do their own washing, mending, housekeeping. It was a collaborative community but one that fostered self-sufficiency.

There were many other rooms down Bertram's corridor, and many other corridors with similar layouts, connecting to various staircases that snaked throughout the castle. Some of the rooms had been repurposed storage spaces when the population grew into the two-hundreds. They didn't need rooms dedicated solely to one court member's wardrobe when they were down to five cursed inhabitants in the beginning. Even when sacrifices began filling the once-empty halls, the Frozen Kingdom's castle became like a small village, utterly loyal to each other and ready to fight to the death against anyone who challenged their home.

Bertram had known nothing but peace here. Finances, squabbles, and day-to-day monotony was right. No wonder he'd floundered when faced with true unrest. He'd been loathsomely unprepared to become king.

He should have looked at the candle clock more closely and quickly glanced back before the door closed behind them. It was late afternoon, same as when they'd left Emerald. The usual bustle was about the halls, most of the faces familiar, so it might have been a month or two ago rather than ten years into an unknown future. But that was Sapphire, one of the immortal kingdoms, where some things could stay the same for years.

"Hello, steward."

"Good afternoon, steward."

The familiar greetings as Bertram took the lead down the hall further soothed his frazzled nerves, the ends of which had been like raw wounds lately, constantly aching and irritating him. This was what he knew. This was where he excelled.

Maybe this was where he belonged.

A gasp left Pax as the narrower passages of the hallways opened to the expanse of the second-floor landing overlooking the foyer. It was smaller than Emerald's but with higher ceilings, all the way to the third floor before the highest levels of the castle became closed off.

Pax dashed to the railing and Bertram followed. Perhaps it was homesickness, but he thought the stone walls and pillars looked more polished, the paint fresher, and even some of the tapestries had been replaced or mended, making the castle feel brand-new instead of centuries old.

There were hardly any of the original tapestries from before the curse, most having been frozen into chunks of ice, burned up, or otherwise ruined. The tapestries lining the walls now were mostly made by current inhabitants, not all blue and silver as royal representations, but often multicolored and much more symbolic of what the kingdom

had become, just like the quilts on everyone's beds that had been made
by Shayla.

Well, some were made by Shayla. Others were made by her and
Liam's daughter, Raya, who'd picked up the craft. Bertram didn't have
much skill in tailoring, weaving, or the like, though his mother had tried
to instill in him an appreciation of such arts. Josie had also made many
of these tapestries, and hers was always obvious from the shimmer—or
meant she'd lent some of her golden thread to others.

"How lovely! Is that your crown?" Pax asked.

"The same. That's Reardon wearing it, the Emerald King before
me. He and his husband, Jack, made that tapestry themselves."

The one Pax was taken with was at their right, hanging from
where a winding staircase led to the throne room outside the kings'
chambers. Bertram remembered being very young when they'd finished
it, a depiction of their wedding, with both kings facing each other, heads
bowed, brows bearing their crowns, while their joined hands were
wrapped in blue and green ribbon, symbolizing the union of them and
their kingdoms.

The figures were outlined in shimmers of both white- and yellow-
gold thread, provided by Josie, who'd once been cursed to turn everything
she touched into gold, whether she wanted to or not. The remnants of that
power with the curse lifted had become a gift, and she used it to create
and help others create some of the most beautiful pieces in the castle.

"I've never seen thread that glitters." Pax truly sounded like a
young man not yet of age. He acted it, too, with the excitement in his
voice and way he hefted his feet from the ground to further lean over the
railing. Bertram would have reprimanded him if he didn't know that this
particular young man had wings when he wanted to. "Although, um, it
seems a bit uneven in places, if that's not too rude to mention."

Bertram laughed. It was no secret that the tapestry was imperfect.
"A sign of which stitching belonged to Jack, the Sapphire King. He never
had much knack for the craft either."

"Either?"

"Jack's my uncle. I'm afraid I never had the skill for it, despite my
mother's best attempts to teach me. My talents lie elsewhere."

"I can't wait to see them." Pax dropped to his feet again and turned
with the hint of a leer.

He was far too young to stir Bertram's passions, and yet stir they did because he knew the truth, potent enough that he could almost see through the magic that made Pax look this way, knowing what was considered his true mortal form.

But that was magic too, wasn't it? The real Pax would have filled the entire foyer with his scaled body and enormous wings, horns bucking up against the ceiling, with no way back outside except by shrinking himself or destroying the place.

Bertram was in the presence of ancient magic compacted into the form of a boy, who, when Bertram gestured in the direction of the alchemist tower, raced ahead through the corridors like an actual apprentice on holiday or being given his first assignment on his way to mastering a profession.

Perhaps this was a dream, but Bertram didn't think himself clever enough to come up with someone like Pax.

The alchemist tower was in what had been an entirely separate wing of the castle once for the court wizard, Liam, to utilize. Then cursed to be a creature of lightning, he'd been dangerous for others to be around, just like the other cursed court members. Many of the nearby rooms had since been turned into additional living quarters, but Liam still claimed his original chambers and the tower itself.

"No, no, no, it's a sort of motion sickness, not magic aversion."

"We've no proof of that! We need willing test subjects, both people who get nauseated from horse or carriage travel and those who don't, as well as testing that there's even such a thing as 'magic aversion.'"

"I certainly have an aversion to you sometimes, sister, and you have more magic than I."

"You're the one who grew up in the Mystic Valley!"

The parrying female voices ended their banter in a shared laugh.

Bertram smiled upon entering the tower fully, coming around the corner to the main work area. The laboratory was a lower-ceilinged and somewhat smothering space, with close-set shelving covered in books, equipment, and ingredient jars, but Bertram found it comforting. Barclay, his father, had often worked up here in the days of Bertram's youth, being an alchemist himself.

While creating something from nothing or achieving a unique result from a combination of ingredients was fascinating, even as a boy, Bertram had busied himself more with other tasks. He'd catalogued ingredients, restocked the storeroom, or better labeled things that Liam had scrawled illegibly on, all leading to his love of organization and helping the castle run more smoothly.

That everything looked just as coordinated now made Bertram feel like his work had been worth it. The bread and sour fruit smell was also pleasing and familiar since they brewed the castle's ale and wine up here and had begun to export it to other kingdoms in recent years. Some of the inhabitants had gotten rather passionate about the craft and were always trying new flavors and levels of intensity.

"Steward, there you are!" Raya greeted upon noticing him. They'd grown up together, born the same year, and she looked no different than he'd last seen her.

She was a mix of her parents, with half-elven ears, darker skin like Shayla, and Liam's blue eyes. Her hair was a rich chestnut, intricately pinned like her mother's too, with baubles adorning some of the braids in sparkling metal or colorful beads. Her clothing was a combination of alchemist and forager attire, with leather trousers and a fitted tunic covered by a colorful robe she'd likely made herself.

Joslyn, Liam's older daughter from a failed marriage before the curse, was all alchemist and spent just as much time in Diamond as here. Or she had a decade ago. Also a half-elf, she had dark hair and almond eyes. Her skin was fairer, but one could easily see the connecting sisterly threads between the two.

"Hail, Raya, Joslyn. I hope your father isn't too cross with me."

"And here he wanders in." Liam's voice preceded his arrival from the storeroom—with two new apprentices, it seemed, a young man and woman, both laden with twice the number of supplies as Liam. The wizard had blond hair, long elven ears, and wore especially intricate robes like that of a mystic. "Did some disaster strike? For I've known nothing less to disrupt you from your schedule before."

"In a manner of speaking, Master Liam." Bertram bowed his head in apology, and then gestured to Pax beside him, who looked like he was barely containing himself from touching everything in sight. "This is Pax, a visiting apprentice from Diamond."

"I've no time for another apprentice." After setting down a small crate of extra bottles and ingredients, Liam began to unburden the young woman first, carefully setting it all onto shelves, while the young man stood with his arms quivering.

Raya and Joslyn moved to assist him.

"I'm not here for you, sir wizard," Pax said, marveling at a unique glass bottle within purview that may have been a perfume bottle once, given its elegant shape, with a long neck and bulbous bottom, and bearing a ring of silver where the bulb grew and a hanging blue gem like a pendant. The glass itself was rosy pink. "Although I would be honored and amazed to learn anything from watching you. I am here to shadow the steward."

Everyone froze and then slowly turned to look at Bertram.

"Not to be replaced!" he soothed them. "No, no. Like many a loyal citizen of Sapphire, I'm not sure I have the desire to ever leave these lands."

"Oh?" Joslyn said with a stiffer stance. "Forgive me for being so *disloyal* for splitting my time all these years."

"No! I meant—"

"Yes, and how awful of me to want to expand my horizons elsewhere as well," Raya added.

"You're... leaving?" Bertram gaped at her.

Now, a look of confusion crossed the others' faces—all but Liam, who'd returned to filling the countertops and shelves with supplies.

Bertram would need to be careful to not project his ignorance of this world. What would be the consequences? Was this real or purely a mirage, an illusion played for his benefit? He should have asked more of Pax before venturing into the unknown.

Pax—who had inched his way closer to a shelf with various jarred dry ingredients and was reaching toward one labeled "Lilium," and under that was its colloquial name "White Dragon."

Bertram lashed out a quick smack to Pax's back to deter him, which was thankfully hidden by the counter between him and the others.

Pax glanced at him with a smirk.

"Did you bump your head?" Raya asked. "Wasn't that what you wanted to see Father about? Coordinating the shift in responsibilities to his new wards?"

"O-of course!" Bertram amended.

"As if I'm incapable of directing them myself," Liam muttered.

"I... I am so sorry," Bertram continued. "I've been terribly scatterbrained today, showing Pax around. Somehow, I forgot."

"Regardless, we are well prepared." Liam slapped the counter behind him without turning, and there on top was a stack of parchment. "As you can see, everything is accounted for, and once we finish with this unloading from the back, we're on schedule for the next set of foraging, and all responsibilities and quotas will be met." He turned at last to affix Bertram with his cobalt stare. "Satisfied?"

Bertram scrambled to gather up the parchments, pretending to look them over but unable to digest most of it—lists, duties, dates.

"Well?" Liam pressed.

"More than satisfied! This is perfect, Master Liam, thank you, all of you, for the trouble." He rolled up the parchments to tuck into his doublet, while Raya stared at him with a look he could only describe as... unsettled.

"Do you mind now, steward?" With the crates the apprentices had been carrying emptied, Liam whirled about once more. "Aren't you also the one getting all up in arms about the excess of children being liberal with magic? I have a potion to brew that should finally resolve that."

Just like in Emerald....

"Not limiters?" Bertram asked.

The others froze like before and gaped at him.

Pax had gotten hold of the dried White Dragon during Bertram's neglect and nearly dropped the jar, letting out a fumbling exclamation and apology that at least turned accusing eyes onto him.

When they turned back, Raya looked even more unsettled. "You would truly suggest that?"

"Well... Reardon invented them. And, of course, I'd never mean mandated, but they can be useful in preventing unwanted magic, can't they?"

The very limiters being called for as required on children and other magic users in Bertram's time had first been created by Reardon. Since he had no magic, he'd been the perfect test subject for how to nullify magical effects, his goal being to find a way to help those who feared their magic getting out of control—adults and children alike.

He'd had help in the construction of the limiters, usually imbued jewelry, from the Fairy Prince, Nemirac, as well as others. But the invention hadn't seen widespread use even a decade ago, only personal, or on demand.

"Don't judge him too harshly," Liam said. "He's only thinking logically."

"*Only*," Joslyn sneered.

"The potion won't constrain children, you see," the young woman apprentice spoke up, "but should prevent certain magic from harming them or anyone nearby."

"Like a personal bubble of deflation," added the young man.

"Truly?" Pax moved from his perusing of the shelves to a stool in front of the counter. "I'd love to stay and watch you brew it." He had the White Dragon jar still, which Liam swiped from him, and seemed to scrutinize him more carefully.

"Only if you stay out of the way, young man, and stop touching things that don't belong to you." Before Liam had even finished speaking, Pax was reaching for the bottle he'd shown interest in earlier.

Pax grabbed it but handed it to Liam. "It's such a lovely design, I thought you might use it for the final product."

Liam narrowed his eyes further but huffed and took the bottle to prepare the experiment.

"All right, you two." Joslyn gathered the young apprentices to her and kissed both their foreheads. "Be good for your grandfather. Your aunt and I need to get some maintenance done on the pulley system before we depart."

Bertram realized then that he knew these apprentices, though they had been very young children the last time he'd seen them.

With Joslyn and Raya about to leave, he hurried to think of something to keep them and learn more of the changes in the castle. "No one to assist you?" he asked Raya.

"Not since Wynn left for Ruby. Best you get on that, *steward*," she said pointedly, "or the castle will fall apart before you've found his replacement."

Wynn, like another uncle to Bertram growing up, being a good friend of Barclay's, had often talked about moving to Ruby. He'd finally done it? He'd been instrumental in most of the innovations in the castle over the decades, and Ruby was the capital of invention and technology.

Joslyn breezed past Bertram. Her children, Liam's grandchildren and now apprentices, were beginning preparations for the potion, while Pax looked on with excitement, practically bouncing upon his stool. But when Raya made to follow her sister, Bertram stopped her.

"Raya, I'm so sorry for being neglectful of your departure. I'm sure it slipped my mind purposely because I can't imagine the castle without you."

"Right." She bristled.

"I mean it heartfeltly, of course."

"Steward," she said again—always that and not his name, "I honestly can't recall the last time we exchanged full sentences. You won't miss me." She smiled despite the sting of her words and kissed his cheek, before following Joslyn from the tower.

What all had Bertram missed?

CHAPTER 3

"MIGHT I make a suggestion, sir wizard?" Pax's voice brought Bertram's attention back to the laboratory.

There was a table in the open area on the other side of the counter, containing a small cauldron where Liam and his apprentices were mixing the ingredients they'd gathered. A mortar and pestle rested on the table as well for anything needing to be crushed before being added.

The apprentices were doing most of the work, giving Liam leave to whirl on Pax with another scrutinizing glare.

"A pinch of powdered iron?"

"Young man—" Liam began but didn't finish as his face scrunched in contemplation. "That… isn't without merit. A pinch of powdered iron, Allora," he ordered the young woman.

"Yes, master." She snapped to attention and retrieved the ingredient from the shelves.

Bertram moved to Pax's side to watch, needing the distraction from his troubled musings. People grew apart. It happened, and he and Raya had never been *that* close. It was just another thing to get used to, he told himself, nothing terrible. He didn't need everything about this future to be perfect, only a better outlook than his fears.

As the apprentices mixed the ingredients in the cauldron, which was being heated by a metal plate with runes for Fire along its edges, Liam picked up the bottle Pax had requested he use. He drew upon it with a glowing touch that only those with innate magic could manifest, forming the rune for Need like a lopsided X.

While the potion simmered, the apprentices cleared a mostly empty cabinet on the far side of the laboratory and filled its middle shelf with empty bottles that had seen better days.

"Magic is brilliant to witness," Pax whispered to Bertram, as if he wasn't a being of pure magic himself, "but alchemy allows for so many possibilities."

Bertram used to agree. He'd loved observing his father up here, creating potions used by the citizens and as trade, or experimenting on ways to improve them. But once he'd focused on more menial duties, he couldn't remember the last time he'd stayed to watch.

"All right, Allora," Liam said, and she snapped to attention again like an apprentice should, "have at it as the control for our... audience."

Liam began to ladle the completed potion into the bottle, casting a new rune on its side, the simple vertical line for Ice. The rune vanished once the contents had been cooled. Meanwhile, Allora stood facing the shelf with empty bottles. She took a breath, and her right hand erupted in sparks. With a well-aimed thrust of her palm and fingers splayed, she shot a bolt of lightning at one of the center bottles, and it shattered.

She'd inherited her grandfather's magic, whereas with Joslyn and Raya, it had skipped a generation. Her brother, if he was without magic, looked delighted at the display rather than resentful.

"And now...." Liam handed her the bottle.

She took another breath and downed the whole thing.

No obvious effect followed, no glow about her or response in expression, but when she turned back to the shelving and attempted to launch another bolt, it got no farther than a hair's breadth in front of her and fizzed like a failed spark to light a fire.

"It worked!" The young man clapped in celebration.

"Um, may I ask...," Bertram began, expecting the sharp glare that Liam passed him for interrupting. "How is that any different from a limiter?"

The apprentices looked about as disgruntled as their mother and aunt had, but Liam answered, "A fair question. Because nondisruptive magic can still be used." He filled the now empty potion bottle with water from a jug and handed it back to Allora. "Fire, please, to boil it."

She drew the rune, which had connected slanted lines like a sideways mountaintop. The rune pulsed, caused bubbles to form in the bottle as the water boiled, and then faded just like Ice.

"Someone else can also negate the potion." Liam drew a rune on Allora's forehead this time—Need, like the one on the bottle. When the one on her forehead pulsed and faded, so too did the bottle's rune.

She turned to fire another bolt of lightning, and like the first time, one of the distant bottles shattered—her magic restored.

"Unlike a limiter," Liam said, "such a thing could not be forced on anyone so long as a single other person deemed them worthy of being free."

"Some people may need the occasional slap on the wrist or help," the young man offered, "but that shouldn't mean shackles, sir steward."

"Indeed." Bertram nodded. "It's all very clever, Master Liam."

"'Twas Allan's idea," Liam said.

The young man beamed, and his sister looked just as proud.

It was a clever idea, but if this potion existed back in Bertram's time, in Emerald, would it be enough to sway the split opinions of the people? Some might still think it shackles, others not enough. There needed to be something else, some catalyst for them to compromise.

But no, Bertram wasn't here, experiencing the fruits of his wish, to dwell on the same issues as his present.

"My sincerest gratitude, sir wizard! And apprentices, of course." Pax hopped down from his stool.

"Yes, yes." Liam waved him away, but then he eyed Pax curiously. "You have quite a bit of magic about you to want to be a steward."

"Ah, but magic can be useful in many professions." Pax raised a hand with a small wave and... nothing happened, but he did smile quite widely before giving a bow, and then grabbed Bertram to drag him from the laboratory.

"A-a-and thank you for your report!" Bertram called back. He felt practically flown from the tower with how effortlessly Pax moved him, displaying a strength that should have been impossible for such a small-framed man.

But not for a dragon.

With Pax close, and their heights nearly identical, Bertram picked up on a potent and pleasing scent emanating from Pax's skin, or maybe it was his hair, maybe all of him, like bergamot and leather. It was impossible to not take a deep breath of it, and easy to do so without being noticed since Pax leaned closer too.

"If he hadn't added the powdered iron, her magic would have been amplified and blown up half that wall," Pax whispered. "But brilliant otherwise, don't you think?"

He released Bertram as they exited into the hall and was suddenly holding the very bottle he'd been coveting.

"You stole that too?"

"They have plenty of bottles. But none that held the first successful test of a brand-new potion!"

"Pax...." Bertram attempted to swipe it back from him, but Pax whirled it around his elbow like the crown, and it vanished.

"Oops. Wherever could it be?"

He was ridiculous. Childish. Gleeful and enamored by everything he witnessed, which was... refreshing to be around, but not at all how Bertram would have expected an ancient dragon to act.

Then again, he knew very little about dragons, least of all this one.

"Not friends of yours any more than their mother is, I take it." Pax nodded ahead, and Bertram looked to see that down the hall, Joslyn and Raya hadn't gotten far, stopped by Caitlin, the healer. Her husband, Branwen, was master of arms and had been another pseudo-uncle to Bertram growing up.

Raya noticed him and didn't do a very good job hiding what seemed to be scorn mixed with pity.

"She was once," Bertram said. "We were babes together."

"You were close?"

"Not *close*. But companionable at least."

"A lot can change in ten years, Bertie."

Bertram looked at Pax, and despite the dragon's frivolity, he had a sweet nature too. "Yes, and a lot can change in hundreds, yet you take it all in stride."

"Why focus on the negative when there is so much good about and fun to be had?" Pax smacked Bertram on the shoulder hard enough that he stumbled a step and had to laugh.

"Mother! Mother!"

Three children came running into view from down an adjoining staircase, a young teenage girl and a set of twin boys who couldn't have been older than ten, dressed identically save one having a red tunic and one blue. The twins latched on to Caitlin and began trying to pull her away.

Caitlin was Mother? That meant....

Like Liam's grandchildren apprentices, when Bertram last saw these children, they'd been much younger, the twins having only just been born when he left for Emerald.

The teenager, Sarah, looked like a mini version of her mother, with the same fair skin and brown hair and eyes, and the boys were like their father, a bit tanner, with blue eyes, square jaws, and sturdy frames that were destined to grow into powerful men someday. Finnian and... Florian, was it?

"Boys, I am in the middle of something." Caitlin dislodged herself with the firm and practiced tone she'd had since long before she became a mother. "I've no time for child games right now. I'm sure Sarah will play with you."

"But we need at least four for hide-and-go-seek," one of the boys pleaded, latching on to her again. "It's no fun only looking for two people."

"I'm busy, darlings. Perhaps later."

"Raya? Joslyn?" Sarah attempted, more patient than her brothers.

"We're late as it is, sorry," Joslyn said.

"*Tag* it is then," the other twin announced and proceeded to ignite a fireball over his palm—just like his father could.

"Don't you dare!" Caitlin warned. "If I find one more scorch mark where there wasn't one before...."

"I'll have a go!" Pax called, already several paces ahead of Bertram before he noticed the dragon had left him. "At hide-and-go-seek, of course, not target practice. We can save that for when we're out of sight," he mockingly whispered.

The boys giggled, and Sarah looked like she thought the *elf* who didn't appear much older than her was rather fetching.

"A visiting steward apprentice from Diamond," Bertram hurried to explain as he caught up to them. "Pax. Entirely trustworthy."

Was he? Bertram had just admitted to himself that he knew next to nothing about Pax.

"Well, if you're vouching for him, steward," Caitlin said.

Was he?

"That is a lovely ribbon, milady," Pax said of the light blue ribbon tied at the end of the braid over Sarah's shoulder.

"Thank you, young sir." She preened.

"Come on, then!" the twins chorused, grabbing Pax's hands and hauling him up the staircase where they'd come from, at which he laughed and allowed himself to be towed.

"Who's counting first?"

"Sarah!"

"Why always me?"

"Pax!" Bertram realized they'd be apart for the first time since they arrived.

"I'll find you!" Pax called back with a wink. "And how about I find *you* all too, and I do the counting first?"

Raya and Joslyn were giggling as well, and Raya said to Bertram with a touch of softness, "I think that apprentice might be good for you."

"Yes." Bertram sighed. "Perhaps he will."

"Did you need something, steward?" Caitlin asked.

Even she had the habit of calling him that, as if his name was never used.

"No, um… there's just so much to be done today, I can't recall all I had on my schedule."

"Doesn't Branwen owe you some weapons inventory?" she offered. "I'm sure he'll find you once story time is done. If only the boys were young enough to still enjoy it." She gazed after them with fondness, the children already scattering, while Pax's voice could be heard counting to twenty.

"I might go to the library, then. Clear my head. I wish you the best of luck, Raya. Truly." Bertram looked to her with as much heartfelt appeal as he could. "You too, Joslyn."

"Thank you," Raya said, and Joslyn nodded.

It seemed he'd continued to neglect attachments like his mother always warned him about, but that didn't mean this future was a dreary one.

Bertram thought on that, letting his mind wander as he headed toward the library. Everyone he passed greeted him as "steward," like earlier, but they smiled cordially, and the castle was in pristine condition, with everything running efficiently. The report tucked into his doublet from Liam was proof of that—even if he hadn't really read it yet—and now he was off to gather another.

But surely his life wasn't only reports and bureaucracy.

The library had always been one of Bertram's favorite rooms in the castle. It had the highest ceilings and was overflowing with its collection of tomes, which had already been vast before the curse, but had been added to over the decades by the castle's inhabitants, sometimes from personal belongings, sometimes books they wrote. There were no windows here, but the large room with row upon row of tall shelves was brightly lit by torches and runic magic.

There were always a few people milling about, but twice a week in the afternoon was story time for anyone who wished to hear the master of arms' resonant voice read from classic children's tales. Branwen could be heard before Bertram even turned to enter the library, despite being all the way at the back, seated within the hollowed-out groove in the floor.

There were many paths like that in the library, leftover from the days when Jack as the Ice King would leave a trail behind him that melted and could be hazardous to the books. Now, those paths led to reading alcoves with soft cushions, or to the story time chair where Branwen sat, while the path in front of him was lined with children and their parents sitting at rapt attention. Bertram had sat there himself quite often when he was a boy.

Branwen noticed him, a broad and burly man, with mild scruff, a mostly shaven head, and pale blue eyes like those of his twins. Bertram was quick to raise a hand in indication that there was no rush, and Branwen seemed surprised—because of leniency? To see Bertram here at all? He couldn't be sure, but that too troubled him.

Since there was truly no rush, Bertram turned to peruse the nearest shelves. The perimeter of the library was for history books and organized by year. This right side from the entrance started from the earliest accounts of the Gemstone Kingdoms throughout all the known ages.

Including the age of dragons when wild magic first formed the gemstones. Bertram touched a leather spine that was wide enough to bear the imprint of a dragon's silhouette and pulled it out.

Perhaps it was time he educated himself on his new friend.

CHILDREN KNEW how to approach life right. No reservations, no existential dread of potential death, illness, or disappointment in how one's life might go, just pure zest for anything and everything they could experience.

Being an immortal creature, Pax had long since decided to live with a child's abandon.

"Found you!" He whipped aside the tapestry with the very obvious ten-year-old-sized lump behind it. The last of the twins had been caught.

Finnian sagged but quickly brightened again. "Who was first?" He bounded away from the wall.

"That would be your brother in blue, which means… your turn to count, Florian!"

Florian and Sarah had been tailing Pax since he discovered them, sometimes offering hints and suggestions—not that Pax needed it. He probably could have found them all ten times quicker, given he could sniff them out with superior senses, but he figured he owed them a few constraints on his talents.

They'd limited themselves to only this floor, and no private rooms, but anything else was fair game. Now, Pax could really shine since it was his turn to hide. He couldn't make himself invisible but near enough, and he could change his size to almost anything. He wouldn't do either of those options, though. He needed to give these budding youths a sporting chance!

Sarah was perhaps a bit too infatuated with him, poor dear. Not his fault his human form was so charming, even the more diminutive one. So, he was quick to dash out of sight when Florian began counting so she wouldn't try hiding with him.

Pax passed several promising rooms as he scurried away, but all were filled with too many people, and bystanders were likely to give away his location. He hadn't been inside the Sapphire castle since it was, well, a very different castle than it was now, perhaps even with fewer wings, but he thought he remembered there being....

Aha!

Having passed his hand along the corridor wall, he came upon a stone that was smoother than the others. A firm press caused part of the wall to move inward and then slide to the side, revealing a secret passageway. Pax ducked into it and quickly found the corresponding stone within to close the wall behind him. Braziers lit the corridor, though Pax would have had no trouble seeing in pitch blackness. He chose a direction at random and went... right. Technically, the children hadn't said they couldn't use passageways—assuming they knew about them.

After a few curves in the corridor, Pax came upon a set of steps. They had said nowhere other than this floor, so he readied to turn back, only to feel the steady and familiar thrum of the Sapphire nearby. It was quite close, not far from where those steps led.

He couldn't say why exactly, but he found himself heading down the steps after all. He'd said a brief hello to the Ruby. He supposed one was due for the Sapphire too.

The steps descended more than a single floor, and at the bottom, after a few turns led to another smooth stone in the wall, it opened Pax into a corridor. Different steps led up at his right, a room for laundering was at his left, and a solid wall blocked him from where he heard the Sapphire's song.

He snuck past the washing room without anyone noticing him and summoned a part of his magic that attuned with the shadows. While it didn't make him fully invisible, it did turn him transparent, allowing him to phase through the wall to where the Sapphire called to him.

There was a different way to reach this part of the castle, because through the wall was what appeared to be a storeroom. It was empty but with lit torches, and what would have been another secret passage in the wall had been left open, as if inviting anyone to pass through.

Pax did so, and here again was another stairwell leading down. This path he remembered, though he had not walked it since well before the days leading to his long sleep.

Braziers were lit here as well, the stairwell winding like a spiral, deeper and deeper, until it ended at a humble-sized room with the Sapphire at its center. No one was here, but it was obvious the denizens of the castle came often, for there were pedestals and offerings of flowers and smaller crystals, almost like an altar to a deity. The room was bitterly cold since this was the land of ice.

Strange, then, how Pax's eyes prickled with heat.

"It's been an age," he greeted the Sapphire. Like the Ruby, it seemed to pulse brighter in answer, its magic communing with his. "Why, we haven't been in the same room since… Mother passed through you."

She'd always liked the cold, so when she abandoned the Gemstone Kingdoms at the end of the age of dragons, she'd chosen the Sapphire to lead her from this world to another. She'd liked these lands best, he remembered, because of the surrounding forest and the castle up on its hill looking down on the valley of Diamond.

"*I hope you know what you're doing,*" she'd said, "*choosing to remain behind for these barbaric mortals. They're on the brink of destroying themselves.*"

"*Perhaps they will,*" he'd answered, "*but the good, the glory, and the passion I see in them is worth sticking around for.*"

"*Perhaps,*" she'd echoed him, "*but there may come a day when you no longer believe that.*"

He hadn't met Gar yet, but his mother was right. There had come a day when none of it felt worth it.

His eyes burned, and he thought he might touch the Sapphire before leaving if only for a cooling balm, but then he heard approaching feet and flattened himself to the wall beside the door. A young couple entered, approaching the Sapphire while chatting amiably, and Pax turned and fled up the stairs before they noticed him.

Once at the top, he shook his head, banishing the foolish wetness from his eyes, and plastered on a smile like the wiliest of rowdy children. *Be like them*, he reminded himself, *without attachment or a care in the world*.

Cheerful mask renewed, Pax hurried back to where he'd come from to rejoin the game of hide-and-go-seek so his young friends could find him.

CHAPTER 4

"Ya know, the good ones are in the other section."

Bertram gasped as he looked up from his book to see Branwen standing over him. There weren't chairs in the first section of the history shelves, so he'd ended up hunkered on the floor with a small pile encircling him. He was onto the fourth or fifth book about dragons, looking for as much as he could on the platinum variety in particular.

Part of him wondered if Pax had lied about his type because he was nothing like anything Bertram had read so far.

"I'm sorry, Bran." He scrambled to his feet and then reached down to collect the tomes he'd finished. While reshelving them, he glanced at the section Branwen had indicated, which was fantastical more than historical accounts, and likely contained some of the bawdier dragon tales.

About them... with *mortals*.

He cleared his throat when Branwen stared at him in apparent amusement.

"Not looking for that type of story today," Bertram said. "Only curious about the facts." He finished replacing the last of the books, which had confirmed what he knew and clarified what he didn't.

Some believed that the color of a dragon was a direct correlation to their temperament, but while that assumption could prove true, it was no more factual than all elves having magic or all dwarves being good at blacksmithing. The color of a dragon's scales did say something about their birthplace and abilities, however, as well as the size they could reach as an adult.

Platinum dragons were the largest.

They were also seen as the wisest and most benevolent, and therefore, the most disheartened by mortal failings. They were the last to leave these lands, to slumber, or to pass on to other worlds. When the Gemstone Kingdoms fell to war and prejudice in ages past, they'd eventually seen no reason to stay.

As for their birthing, a red dragon was likely to be born near Ruby, in the mountains, especially if there was volcanic activity. They were born of other dragons, not out of the earth itself, but the surroundings of where their parents called home infused some of its magic into them and manifested in their color and power.

That two red dragons could give birth to a blue if they chose to live closer to Sapphire was fascinating to Bertram. Each color spewed a different element too, but since red dragons, who breathed fire, had once been the most plentiful, many attributed fire-breathing to all dragons.

Other colors correlated to kingdoms the same way, but since platinum dragons were all colors and none of them at once, they could be born anywhere, belonged everywhere and nowhere, often signs of powerful magic being passed on from dragons with great wanderlust. That, at least, felt like Pax, who never seemed to sit still.

Even a platinum's lair was different from other dragons, for as transient beings, they brought their lairs with them, pocket dimensions in the very cracks of the veil between worlds that they could enter whenever they pleased.

That must be where Pax kept his spoils. What a dragon collected and held most dear was the true sign of their personality. But what did Pax collect? The few items Bertram had seen him carry off had no connecting thread. Did it have no rhyme or reason, just like how the magic at his disposal was beyond Bertram's comprehension?

"In your own little world there, Bertie?"

"Hm?" Bertram realized his thoughts had strayed after reshelving the books, brought back to attention by that familiar nickname. Branwen was one of the few people who used it other than Bertram's mother—and Pax.

It felt different when Pax said it.

"Apologies again. I'm not myself today."

"Don't know about that," Branwen said, crossing his arms with a look down at Bertram as if sizing him up for a sparring match.

He was never as fancily or colorfully dressed as the other court members, in mostly brown for his attire, focusing on utility over fashion. Anyone meeting him for the first time, between his gruff appearance and gruffer voice, might expect a firm and unfriendly man. Until they witnessed story time.

"Been up in your head for years now," he went on. "And you were rarely interested in *those* types of tales." Branwen nodded back at the bawdier books. He'd written some of them, quite talented with racier writing under a not-so-private pseudonym, further rounding out the weapons master who could spout fairy tales and hold the attention of babes for hours. "'Bout the only one left from that first batch without a partner on your arm."

Was that true? Once the curse had been broken, not everyone had children right away. Not everyone wanted to, but several, like Bertram's parents, hadn't wasted any time, since the immortality of the cursed magic had meant children couldn't be born at all before it was broken.

About the only one? Did that mean—

"There you are Bran. Oh! And steward, I see. I didn't notice you."

Ambrose.

As if summoned by Bertram thinking of him, another of the "first batch" as Branwen had put it, who grew up with Bertram and Raya, appeared from the library entrance and spotted them among the stacks of the first row. If ever Bertram had been enamored of one of his childhood friends, it was Ambrose, and the ten years that had passed had done nothing to dim the brilliance of his appearance.

Son of Oliver, the fletcher, first sacrifice to the Ice King in the days of the curse, and Oliver's love, Amelia, Ambrose was a flaxen-haired and blue-eyed beauty like his parents. He had the height and muscled form of his father, but a fairness in his cheeks like Amelia. He didn't require the spectacles Amelia wore but had the accurate eyesight of a sharpshooter and had nearly outdone his father with a bow. He wore his hair long, past his shoulders, with the mildest wave and fullness to it that Bertram had so enjoyed running his hands through those nights when they'd indulged in exploration with each other as youths.

They'd done so quite often in those formative years. Ambrose hadn't been the only one Bertram dallied with, and Bertram was hardly the only one for Ambrose, but if ever Bertram was tempted to choose one partner to keep close, it had been him.

Ambrose wore a mix of blue and green that made his eyes gleam with both colors. It reminded Bertram of his royal doublet that he no longer had. Ambrose was just so majestically handsome that he practically glowed.

"Steward?"

"Hm?" Bertram startled again. This future had him second-guessing himself at every turn, constantly distracted, but he realized it had been a long time since he'd really looked at Ambrose. "Sorry. Did you say something?"

"I asked if I was interrupting," Ambrose said, bearing a subtle smile that was patience and charm in one brief twitch of his lips. "I respect that the steward's relationship with the master of arms is just as important as the fletcher's."

The fletcher? He'd succeeded his father. Bertram had always expected it, but it saddened him that he'd missed the celebration of the passing of the quiver.

"So...?" Ambrose tried again.

"Nothing that can't wait!" Bertram sputtered.

"Really?" Branwen offered a perusing eyebrow raise. "You're rather lenient today. I expected a worse tongue lashing than your uncle used to spew at me for not having those weapons reports ready. Twin boys and a teenage daughter do not make for many quiet or productive nights. And when they do, I'd rather not spend it doing inventory."

Ambrose snorted, a puff of air that disrupted a few strands of golden hair that he then had to toss back with a glorious shake of his head. "Well then, perhaps I can lend some good news, as I've just finished an inventory of arrows, bolts, and ranged weaponry. Consider a portion of your work complete, Master Branwen."

Branwen laughed heartily and grabbed Ambrose around the shoulders to reel him in for a half embrace. "Now that's why I prefer you to your father, Rosie! Thorough and with a better temperament to boot."

Ambrose laughed along with him, the pair equal in height as they leaned congenially closer, which made Bertram feel suddenly small and separate. "I'll be sure to tell him that when we join him and mother in Amethyst."

"You're leaving?" Bertram couldn't hold his tongue. Oliver and Amelia were gone? And now Ambrose would be joining them?

"Only for the festival," Ambrose assured him.

"Oh! Of course."

Festival Day in Amethyst was when they celebrated their own curse that had lasted for a thousand years. They'd considered the magic that changed them into monsters and creatures of myth to be a blessing in disguise, and many still chose to remain in those forms despite the curse having been lifted like the one in Sapphire. Newcomers could even discover their own "cursed" selves upon crossing the border through the Shadow Lands Forest or entering through the Veil Curtain.

"I put the report in your chambers," Ambrose said to Branwen, "but I figured I'd tell you in person as I passed the library. As for you, steward"—he returned to Bertram—"while I hate to remind you of a slight when you're being so forgiving, I am behind on recruiting those new archers. There just aren't as many citizens keen on learning the skill, but I promise an update within the fortnight if you'll offer me an extension."

"Always! I trust you to make the right call, Ambrose. Quality is more important than urgency."

"Well... I believe I've said those exact words to you before and been ignored or told that both should be possible with enough effort. Glad to hear you're having a change of heart." Ambrose smiled, dazzling as ever, and all the reasons Bertram had chosen to be stoic and focused on duty rather than indulgence lately seemed of little importance.

"Master Branwen?" A woman came forward, holding the hand of a bouncing young boy no older than four or five. "Could you point us again in the direction of that same author from today's story?"

Branwen bowed his head at Bertram and Ambrose and ushered the woman and child to the next row.

Here was Bertram's chance to prove he was more than his title, that he could find the balance he'd apparently been neglecting even worse in the future than he had in years past. He'd ask Ambrose for a drink or to join him tonight for dinner.

Then Ambrose was bowing his head and turning to leave too!

"Wait!" Bertram clutched his wrist before he could escape.

"Yes, steward?" Ambrose turned with a note of surprise, like it had been ages since they'd touched informally.

Even Ambrose wouldn't say his name?

"It's just that I... I was wondering if...." Bertram's eyes, not quite able to find Ambrose's when he felt so alien in this time, so uncertain, remained on the hand he had hold of at the wrist, and there he noticed something new.

A band of gold around the ring finger of Ambrose's left hand, where a bridegroom would wear it.

Only one indeed.

"Something else?"

There was plenty of time, Bertram had told himself, *to wait on frivolities*, but how much of that time was he destined to waste?

"No." Bertram looked up with a rallied smile, withdrawing his grasp. "I've just begun to realize how duty driven I've been, and I am sorry if it's made me insufferable lately."

Ambrose shifted to face Bertram fully, and the kindness in him, the stalwart strength of a good man was there to offer pity, after he'd likely been more patient over the years than Bertram deserved. "It's quite all right, Bertram."

The sound of his name on Ambrose's lips helped, but still, he said, "I don't think it is. But thank you. And please, I hope you have a marvelous time in Amethyst." With whoever was on the other end of that "we" Ambrose had mentioned that Bertram only now realized didn't only mean his parents.

Ambrose bowed like before to take his leave. "Careful!" he cried as soon as he turned, shifting aside to permit the racing twins who barreled past him.

Branwen's twins, which meant—

"A library! Brilliant!" Pax entered just as Ambrose left, trailed closely by Sarah. Her hair was loose of its braid, and the blue ribbon she'd been wearing was now tied into a smaller braid framing the side of Pax's face.

Bertram scowled.

"A gift, I assure you!" Pax said when he noticed him.

Sarah was called away by Branwen, who thankfully recognized the disruptiveness his twins brought and needed her assistance in wrangling them.

"I do believe that poor girl may be in love." Pax joined Bertram. "But like you, Bertie, I only dally with those of age and experience."

As quickly as Bertram had felt annoyed, he remembered who he was dealing with—not a young man, smaller than he was, not even the adult form he sometimes took, but the most powerful creature in all the kingdoms. Pax was every element, had access to nearly every known magical ability. He could warp reality and bend time, like he'd done when bringing them here to a future not yet written.

And he'd been off playing hide-and-go-seek with children.

"I think there was barely a reading nook in here the last time I walked these halls."

"You've been to the castle before?"

"Many ages ago. Something troubling you, Bertie? Not enjoying your wish?" Even as Pax asked that, he turned to scan the nearby spines.

Wish. That was something else Bertram had sought in the tomes. It seemed not all dragons had the ability to grant wishes with a scale, which might have been why Bertram found only one book that mentioned it. A rare gift, possible from any of the colors but only from the oldest and most powerful. Those other than platinum had far more limitations in what they could grant too.

There were also accounts of dragons giving scales as courting gifts, but he'd swiftly paged past that.

"Cara Zhan!" Pax grabbed one of the books Bertram hadn't gotten to yet. "I remember when she penned this tome. Hideous cover. I hope it wasn't meant to be a likeness to me...."

Dragons in Ritual by Cara Zhan was one of the oldest tomes in this section, its pages brittle and cover only well-kept due to being made of leather and tucked away from harsh rays of sunlight. On it was painted a faded illustration of a silvery dragon opening its maw toward the viewer as if to spew forth its deadly breath attack.

Which Pax could do too, and it could be whatever element he wished.

"History section? Ha! Only because she curbed her language. Purely an excuse to attend as many orgies as one could fit in an elven lifespan. See here where she says, 'Bore my soul to receive their gifts'? What she actually meant—"

"*Pax*," Bertram hissed, given no amount of whispering was enough to spare young ears when another pair of children ran past.

"Oops. Wrong time."

This was a dragon?

The *last* dragon?

"No, you don't!" Bertram snatched the book from Pax when he made to tuck it under his arm. "This tome is one of a kind!"

"See, that only makes me want it more."

"Pax—" A ruckus in the hall drew Bertram's eyes up, a combination of familiar cadences erupting in laughter and loud greetings that brought him instantly back to childhood. "Zephyr and Nigel...."

"Who?"

Bertram hurried out of the library, not thinking to put back the book he'd rescued. "My predecessor and his husband. They're back."

A few castle denizens Bertram didn't know had run into the former
steward and his longtime companion, who last Bertram knew had been
traveling like Reardon and Jack. Maybe they still had been, all these years
later, for it seemed a merry reunion to everyone who spotted them.

Nigel, a lively half-elf with mismatched and multicolored clothing,
and Zephyr, a human, more subdued and primly dressed, with dark hair,
blue eyes, and a fair face. Neither were large men but filled whatever
space they shared as if they were giants.

"A whole slew of gods, for every tiny little thing!" Nigel exclaimed
to the growing welcomers. "Worshipped as if the cause of unexplained
events and alchemy be wild magic folk reaching through the veil. So
curious! As if every rainstorm or life event was part of some god's plan."
He laughed.

"Could be true," Zephyr argued. "Us surviving over two hundred
years together would almost have to be some grand design at our
expense."

Nigel turned to kiss his cheek at the jab, a normal sign of their
playful banter. "Good thing ol' Zeph here can whisk us away on the wind
when under threat. A few of those locals weren't too welcoming where
pointed ears and magic were concerned."

"*Old* Zeph?"

"And not a sign of age on that fair face to show it!" Nigel appeased
with nary a beat. They kissed upon the lips this time.

"Any riveting bard tales to share with those lucky enough to greet
you first?" Bertram approached.

"Bertie!" Nigel exclaimed, and a little of Bertram's wounded heart
lifted to once again hear his name, his nickname even, rather than his
title. Nigel broke from the group to hug him heartily. "You look well!
And yes, I do have a tale or two! Shall we hear the one of the lover fair,
whom the gods all want to bed?"

Already his voice took on a rhythm to speak his tale in verse. He
stomped and stomped, addressing all around him then with a sweeping
of his arm, and pulled more in to listen from the farther rooms and halls.
No singing, only verse, but from Bertram's knowledge, that was best,
and he found himself stomping with the others gathered close.

> *Born of beauty uncompared,*
> *his matchless charm ensnared*

that every bawdy lush would have to
fight to have their share."

"*Hail lovers,*" Zephyr droned, in time but drearily spoken, as if having helped his partner say this tale many times.

"*Bring your best,*
rival well,
only men of worth and virile strength
will catch me in their spell."

Nigel elbowed Zephyr companionably, and while he feigned reluctance, he started stomping with the crowd.

"*Courtesan of love and splendor,*
even he would soon surrender
when laid claim."

Nigel whirled about to raise his voice, clapping now and kicking with the crowd's stomps as he flew into verse two.

Stumbling against Pax from the jostle of onlookers, Bertram remembered *his* companion—the dragon, who observed Nigel's performance with stomps and claps of his own, like nothing he'd seen in his countless years could compare with each new thing he witnessed.

"*On the day his manhood won,*
his body meant for one,
the gods decided for themselves
to share till they were done."

"*Hail lovers!*" Zephyr shouted with appropriate zeal this time.

"*Challenge met,*
men of all,
I will bring you to your knees
until the last of gods does fall.

"*Courtesan of sex and splendor,*

gods will also soon surrender
when laid claim."

Another jostle forced Bertram to cling to Pax's arm or be pushed back a row. Pax glanced up at him with bright, vivid eyes that sparkled with all the colors Bertram knew to be in his scales. Then those eyes flicked over Bertram's body, as if inspired by Nigel's tale.

"Every bed of theirs he tilled
and sought their needs fulfilled,
ascended as a god himself
for all the passion spilled."

"*Hail lovers!*" Zephyr seized Nigel and spun him about in a joined dance.

"Bring your best,
share me well,
only gods of worth and virile strength
deserve to see me swell.

"Courtesan of love and splendor,
all who taste him will surrender
when laid claim."

Nigel twirled Zephyr into the crowd, right to a ready Branwen, who crushed him in a hug, and Zephyr laughed.

"Courtesan of sex and splendor,
you as well would soon surrender
if laid claim."

Three successive stomps signaled the end, and Nigel swept his arms back to drop into a low bow, and then swept them upward again just as dramatically to emphasize the need for more and more applause.

"Thank you! Thank you! Tips are always welcome, and occasionally claimed on their own if forgotten." He produced a coin from seemingly nowhere and tossed it toward one of the watchers, who scowled at his open purse that was likely lighter than it had been a moment ago.

"Masterful as always, bard!" Branwen announced, dragging Zephyr along with a beefy arm around his neck, much like he'd been with Ambrose. Zephyr, maybe with no one other than another court member or his beloved, allowed it with the most miniscule of scowls. "Maybe not one for the dining hall until after the babes are gone," he finished, since his children, among others, were peeking out the library doors.

"Says the man who tells thrice as randy a tale with the written word!" Nigel launched himself at Branwen for his own vigorous hug.

"So, about those dragon orgies…," Pax whispered, lips practically on Bertram's ear, and Bertram flinched. Then flinched again to remove his arm from Pax. It wouldn't have felt so wrong if Pax had been in his adult form. Maybe Bertram should have let him walk around in that loincloth.

No, that would have been bad for different reasons. Pax's preferred mortal body was just so supple, strong, and brilliantly gleaming.

Like Ambrose.

Ambrose, who caught Bertram's eyes from across the crowd, having stayed nearby or at least returned at the sound of Nigel's tale.

"Who's this, then?"

While the crowd was vying for Nigel's attention, he and Zephyr had returned to Bertram, with Branwen back with his children.

"Pax, sir bard." Pax greeted, saving Bertram the trouble. "The good steward's ward, you might say. Are you a thief as well as a poet with that coin trick?"

"Trick? 'Tis a skill, lad! In fact, I noticed someone had a book they pinched that isn't allowed to leave the library."

Bertram remembered the book he'd been holding and realized he had no idea what had become of it.

"One does need to keep their most coveted skills up to par." Nigel reached behind him—only for his face to go blank. He groped at his belt but came back with nothing. "Where did—?"

"Looking for this?" Pax produced the book as much from nothing as Nigel had the coin.

When had Nigel taken it? During the bard tale? Their hug? Regardless, Pax had it now, and Nigel looked positively captivated. It wasn't often that he was out-pickpocketed.

"Ward of yours, Bertie, or Shayla's spy network!" he praised. "Well done!"

Shayla's spy network? Zephyr had been Spymaster once, not a part of the steward's duties that Bertram had wanted to take on. Had he even known who took it over? He hadn't wanted to take on much of anything other than what was familiar. Easy.

Monotonous.

Of course he wasn't meant to be king if this was what he did with his future. He wasn't even sure what he did want, but he knew it wasn't this.

"One can always get better at honed skills," Pax said with a wink at Bertram, "even the ones we're best at."

Bertram was certain he wasn't talking about pickpocketing now. But Bertram couldn't think, not even to let his mind stray to the tempting thoughts of Pax's other form, because it was just another reminder of everything he hadn't indulged in. Ambrose was wed, people were leaving, had left already, and so much else had changed.

But he hadn't. He'd stayed exactly the same and missed a decade whether he'd lived those years or not.

"Don't encourage him," Zephyr said to Pax, hanging on Nigel's arm. "Interested in stewardship, then?"

"And history and revelry and bard tales too!" Pax declared, twirling the book about his elbow to make it disappear, gone to his hoard now, no doubt, though anyone watching likely assumed it was sleight of hand more than magic. When he turned to look at Bertram again with another all too leering grin, the expression dropped just as quickly. "Bertie?"

Bertram must look affright, but it was too much—the past and present mixing with things he'd squandered. He thought he might scream if he didn't take a breath, but he couldn't, couldn't breathe or even see clearly and—

"What troublemakers do we have here?"

That longed-for breath came in a gasp, as first a voice and then the sight of the two most calming people to Bertram finally appeared in this future that he was struggling to face.

His parents.

CHAPTER 5

SEEING BERTRAM'S parents made it clear to Pax where the young king had gotten his good looks and lithe but sturdy build.

Bertram's mother, Queen Josephine, or Josie, was fair and trim, with beautifully braided and adorned brown hair that glittered in places where her clips and combs must have been woven with golden thread. His father, Prince Consort Barclay, was a touch shorter than his wife. Bertram had inherited Barclay's darker complexion and hair, though Barclay wore his long and tied back, with his face bearing a well-kept goatee.

Following the family reunion, Bertram promptly forgot all about Pax, reduced to a relieved child at the sight of his parents as if being comforted after a nightmare. Pax had hoped to shake Bertram of his doldrums by granting this wish, but he seemed strangely broken, when all Pax had seen so far of this place was an intriguing experiment by alchemist wizards and Bertram holed up in a library.

In a section on dragons.

Certainly nothing he could have read there would trouble him. If anything, those books painted Pax's people in too good a light.

As dinnertime was upon the castle, and Bertram had seemingly abandoned Pax to be whisked off by a curious father and doting mother, Pax was adopted by the bard Nigel and his husband, Zephyr. It seemed Nigel appreciated anyone who could best him and was desperate to know how Pax had swiped that book. Pax wasn't about to tell him that he could slow time enough to do nearly anything faster than a mortal could.

"How about 'The Thief and the Erl King'?" Nigel asked, trading bard tales and songs with Pax now, as they tried to stump each other with ones they didn't know.

On the bottom floor of the castle, back from the foyer, was a set of double doors that opened into a grand hall where they sat for dinner. Rows upon rows of tables could accommodate nearly everyone coming and going during mealtimes. At the very back was a raised platform with a head table set apart for royals and court members, which currently included Josie, Barclay, and Bertram, as well as Liam, and a lovely dark-skinned woman who Pax took for his wife—the very much not eighty-five-year-old-looking woman who'd knocked on Bertram's door.

This left an empty chair beside Bertram, for all other options for court members were also couples or had babes, like the weapons master, father to the children Pax had played with. Although it wasn't Branwen or his family who Bertram kept gazing at among the tables.

It wasn't Pax either, though Bertram had remembered him long enough to meet eyes once they sat and gestured at the empty chair next to him. *Eventually*, Pax indicated with a shrug, because he could immerse himself so much better in a crowd, and it seemed Bertram needed his time with family.

This angle also afforded Pax a better look at the figure who held so much of Bertram's attention. The man was handsome, human, and almost golden in coloring, with a warm smile and powerful build. Too powerful for Pax's tastes, but clearly not for the equally handsome elf attached to him, a half-elf maybe, who leaned against him, cuddling and stealing occasional kisses, while they ate and traded drinks from one's wine goblet for the other's ale.

When Bertram gazed on the pair, the gold one in particular, there was longing in his eyes. Not love, Pax didn't think, but missed opportunity. Josie seemed to notice as well and nudged her son to attention.

"Well?" Nigel pressed Pax.

"One of my favorites when sung," Pax answered, not moving his eyes from Bertram. "Very driving. But Soren wasn't really a thief, you know. Just hungry."

"You know his *name?*"

Pax tried to field Nigel's curiosity, while simultaneously craning his exceptional ears at the head table.

"Is that regret I see on my son's face?" Josie asked. "It's been years, Bertram. Surely you aren't now seeing what you lost?"

"I might be," Bertram said. "It just… wasn't important to me then."

"And that's perfectly all right, dear, if romantic attachment isn't something you seek. But friends, making other connections with people, at least some of the time, is important too."

"I know. I hadn't realized how much I was missing that, even though you often reminded me. And I never said I didn't want romantic attachment, Mother. I just… got caught up in other things."

Things Pax could free him of, if he wished it, which Pax believed he did.

"Be careful you aren't caught up forever," Josie said, "or something you want might get farther and farther away until you've missed your chance entirely."

The golden man. Not a lost love, Pax was certain now, but an almost. An almost lost was better than a *had* and lost, Pax knew.

"Hang on." Bertram turned accusingly. "You waited 200 years for Father!"

"By being discerning!" Josie argued. "Not for lack of trying with others. I didn't say that." She cringed and glanced at her husband, who thankfully was engaged in conversation with Liam.

Bertram cringed as well but laughed.

Then he caught Pax watching him, not knowing Pax had been eavesdropping—hopefully—and smiled wider.

"And that is the true story of how a hungry young man, not truly a thief, began the golden age between dragons, wild magic folk, and mortal-kind," Pax concluded, having eloquently told the tale while listening to Bertram and Josie without missing a beat in either activity. "However!" he announced louder, standing, and noticing how Nigel continued to gaze on him in awe, while Zephyr seemed less impressed. "I also enjoy the tale in verse. Might we perform it together, sir bard? I've no talent for song myself, but I can keep a beat like you do."

"Let's hear it, then!" Nigel encouraged.

"*Some brigands steal*—" Pax leapt onto his seat, clapping and stomping loudly to command the room—"*For more than just a meal, while others are just praying not to starve.*"

Nigel joined him in harmonizing timbre, leaping up as well, and Pax reconnected gazes with Bertram, who finally looked resolved enough to start embracing more of life's pleasures.

> " *'Twas the way of once a thief,*
> *Who hung on the gallows high,*
> *In a town immune to cries.*
>
> "*Down came the hunt....*"

"BRILLIANT! ABSOLUTELY thrilling! I haven't performed a bard tale in—"

"Ages?" Bertram interrupted.

"Literally." Pax laughed and spun about to land on Bertram's bed, becoming his larger form as he hit the soft cushioning of the quilt.

Bertram's eyes widened, and then he glanced away as though fearing he'd catch too good a peek up Pax's tunic. Pax did wear a form of undergarment in this form! Though it mostly only covered him snug between the legs, while leaving his hips and buttocks free.

"Still troubled, Bertie? Not the future you hoped for?"

"Not to be celibate and alone my entire life," Bertram grumbled. His eyes widened again at the admission, and he quickly moved to sit in the desk chair where his view of Pax was less direct.

It seemed he needed a break from celibacy more than he could admit, being thirty and blushing that hard—well, forty, technically, and not a day over twenty-two in appearance.

"I pushed things off for an entire decade," Bertram said thoughtfully, reflective as he slouched in his chair, "pushed people away, lost touch. But that's just me, isn't it? I mean, I can change my outlook. I can change me. So long as everything else is better, maybe it still could be the right decision to not remain king."

"No need to rush things," Pax said. "This is your wish. When you're ready to return to the real world, I can bring us back to the moment we left."

"No cost of another scale?" Bertram eyed him skeptically.

"Not at all! You wished to see all this, not to remain here. You needn't waste any magic on getting home." Pax hefted himself upright to sit cross-legged, which made Bertram's eyes dart away again, probably because the loincloth rucked up to his waist. "But if you want to change your outlook, Bertie, and enjoy more of life, you're in good company. While we're here, what indulgences might you like to try?" He was tempted to take on a more provocative pose, but this one seemed to be working well enough.

"I… want to see the other kingdoms," Bertram said. "I want to… eat, drink, and be merry for once in my life."

"That's the spirit. And for tonight?"

Bertram's eyes snapped back to Pax like a whip crack. "I-I… I should sleep."

"Mmhm. And would you like company for that, Bertie?" Pax let his thighs part just the tiniest bit more.

"I, um…."

Not yet, Pax read, but he doubted he'd have to wait much longer.

"In that case, if you don't mind, since I have slept plenty recently...." Pax rolled to his feet and dropped off the bed to land soundlessly on the floor. "I'm going to stretch my wings again."

"But—" Bertram leapt after him.

"*Carefully.* I'll start off so small, no one will even notice me, and I'll only grow to my true, glorious girth when I am too high in the clouds for anyone to see."

Pax threw open a curtained window, revealing the landscape he only briefly allowed himself to remember was his mother's favorite.

Rolling hills. Copses of trees growing denser and darker into the forest that led to Amethyst. Diamond's valley far off but discernible as a dotting of lights in the other direction. He could see it all despite the dark of night that had fallen. If he truly wanted, he could have zeroed his gaze all the way to Emerald through the brighter and less dense forest ahead.

Pax jumped onto the windowsill into a low crouch and heard Bertram gasp. He must have been eager to see Pax's dragon form again. Hardly one to deny anything desired of him from someone worthy, Pax glanced over his shoulder with a grin.

Bertram's eyes were nowhere near his face.

Even better.

"Good night, Bertie," Pax said in a singsong voice and waited for Bertram to eventually, slowly, drag his eyes upward. Then Pax leapt out the window.

The wind caught his wings in the same instant he unfurled them, and he became the size of a bat cutting through the night. He would never dull the look of his scales, however. Stray onlookers wouldn't notice, but he wanted Bertram to witness every flap and claw at the air with his talons, marveling until he saw Pax fly out of sight.

Marvel he did, for Pax felt Bertram's eyes on him the entire time, as he grew larger with every surge of his ascent and finally disappeared into the clouds.

"THAT SOUNDS like a wonderful idea!" Josie exclaimed.

"Very refreshing of you," Barclay agreed. "You need some time away, without responsibilities weighing you down. I know it's been harrying lately, and I don't remember the last time you took a holiday."

"Of course, we're incredibly offended you chose to do so upon our arrival," Zephyr said—mostly joking. Probably.

They were down in the foyer at the bottom of the winding steps that led to the throne room and what had once been Reardon and Jack's bedchambers. It still was their bedchambers, for whenever the former kings came home. Bertram wondered where they were now, but he figured he'd worried enough people yesterday with odd questions.

And an odder apprentice, who was back to his younger form after being buff and beautiful and shudder-inducing on Bertram's bed last night. And having leapt from the window, one moment with his tunic hitched so high in his squat that it was indecent, and the next a creature of legend winging into the night.

Pax really had the most delectable thighs in that loincloth, among other telling curves and... bulges when he crouched or had his legs spread.

Bertram honestly didn't know which form was more impressive, that or when he morphed into an actual dragon and flew away. Again, he hadn't gotten a good look at Pax's dragon self, because he was always headed away from him. What he had seen was stunning, awe-inspiring, and gleaming with reflective light and colors like a multitude of stars had descended to form his scales. Bertram also longed to see Pax's combined version again, elven and dragon mixed, and wondered if he'd get to soon.

"Sorry, Zeph, but I'm... I need the break," Bertram said. "And you're right, Mother, Father. I have been squandering too much time on duty and forgetting the other aspects of life. I think I'm going to take my new apprentice up on his offer to explore the other kingdoms. For *education* and... fun."

Pax was a few paces away with Nigel, exchanging thieving attempts on each other that Nigel kept losing.

"I'll keep things running in your absence," Zephyr said, having agreed to reclaim his old role as steward for the time being. A mischievousness claimed his expression as he rubbed his palms together. "Been a while since I got to order people around."

"Oh?" Josie challenged. "And here I thought you did that naturally."

"If you'd prefer to handle all your queenly duties without me—"

"Not a chance." She then returned her attention to Bertram and gathered him close for a firm hug. "Be well, dear. Enjoy yourself. There will be plenty of time for duty later, and if you're needed, we'll call you home."

"Thank you, Mother."

A passing denizen hailed Josie and Zephyr, stealing them away, but Bertram still needed to say goodbye to his father. Barclay gathered him just as close for just as firm a hug.

Then gasped.

"It's happening now, is it?" He pulled away to hold Bertram in front of him.

"You *know*?" Bertram realized. Or knew, maybe even years before now. His father was a seer, after all, gifted with visions at a touch. "Can you tell me—"

"There's nothing to say. You need to experience this yourself. But I do believe, I *know*, that you will find the answers you're looking for. Eventually."

Eventually. That should have comforted Bertram but left him more uncertain of what he might decide at the end of this... holiday.

He took a few breaths after Barclay departed, leaving him to retrieve Pax from his thief-off with Nigel.

"How—" Nigel looked positively flabbergasted as he stared at Pax's most recent acquisition. "I didn't even know I was wearing those socks!"

"*Pax*," Bertram chided.

"Time we were off, sir bard!" Pax conceded. "Been a pleasure sparring with you." He handed the socks to Nigel, who looked absolutely tickled.

Then Nigel winked at Bertram. "He's not as young or at all what he appears to be, is he?"

Damn Pax for showing off so much!

"Um, what makes you say that?" Bertram asked.

"Bertie, I am over two hundred years old." Nigel slung his socks over his shoulder with a discerning look. "I know an old soul in a young body when I see one."

Pax failed to look innocent, but Nigel didn't ask more questions. He laughed and slapped them each on the shoulder—the socks being what slapped Bertram.

"Go have an adventure worth telling a bard tale or two about, eh?"

"You know, I think I just might. Ready?" Bertram gestured Pax up the stairs.

"Where are we going if not into the open world?" Pax asked, even as he followed him.

"A shortcut for getting to the other kingdoms. The Veil Curtain is a device first created by one of the wild magic folk, who still rules over Diamond. The Fairy Queen, Mavis."

"If you're wondering if I know her, Bertie, I'm afraid not. All the wild magic folk had left before I went to sleep, so if some returned, I won't necessarily know them."

Bertram *had* wondered, but it was probably better if no one recognized a dragon in their midst. "And what and who do you know, Pax?"

"Shall we find out?" Pax grinned and darted up to the landing. "Diamond, is it?"

At a slower pace, Bertram joined him and led the rest of the way into the throne room. It hadn't always been the throne room. The grand hall downstairs was used for that originally, back before the days of the curse. But when Jack was Ice King, his presence had stung those around him with bitter cold, and he'd used the room outside his bedchambers for audiences instead.

He and Reardon kept it that way. The grand hall was for dining, for community, and up here, the more often used throne room now also housed the Veil Curtain.

Pax stared at it in awe.

About halfway down the long room and to the left beside the floor-to-ceiling windows was the same device with alternating rings on a platform as the one in Emerald, combining magic and alchemy to transport those who used it to connected kingdoms. The tapestries adorning the walls here hadn't changed, nor had the matching twin thrones at the far end, one silver and the other gold.

Bertram had planned an early departure to ensure no one else would be here, for this Veil Curtain saw just as much traffic, he imagined, as Emerald's did in his time.

He walked up to the device with Pax bouncing giddily beside him. "Diamond it is."

CHAPTER 6

As SOON as the alternating rings on the curious device stopped spinning, the storm magic around them burst with a final flash of light, and they were on the platform of an entirely different device, its rings starting at a rapid spin and slowing with their arrival in Diamond.

Pax shivered from the excess of magic. The Mystic Valley felt even more potent than he remembered, both from the many elves who inhabited it, more inclined toward powerful magic than most humans or dwarves, and from something… else. Sapphire had buzzed from remnants of its curse and the immortality infused into the castle grounds. But here, Pax felt the same power as if from its source.

The Fairy Queen, Bertram had called the ruler of this kingdom—one of the wild magic folk returned.

Fascinating.

"*Pax*," Bertram hissed at him. Probably because he'd been getting tired of his diminutive form and was back to being half a foot taller, broadly built, and trouser-less.

"We're among elves!" Pax gestured around them as they stepped from the platform into a grand study. Everything was colored as if made from silver and gold, gorgeously ornate, the ceilings high, the windows gilded, and the walls all lined with bookshelves and curious devices that people were perusing.

Others had formed a queue, waiting to use the Veil Curtain next, and nearly everyone in the room was an elf. Some were discreetly dressed, certainly, but plenty were in skimpier tunics like Pax. Elves had always been a bit freer with showing off their bodies.

"See?" Pax pointed out a particularly fetching elf in the exiting queue they were following, whose top barely covered the entirety of her breasts with thin wraps of fabric that crossed each other and tied around her neck. Her skirt was little more than a belt with fluttery pieces of cloth hanging both in front and back to showcase her long slender legs.

Pax needed an outfit like that.

Or to get Bertram into one.

Bertram was as modestly attired as ever, in an orange doublet, with shades of marigold and brown for his undershirt and trousers. He'd packed only his coin purse and a small rucksack; the latter Pax had offered to keep tucked away in his hoard during the day so Bertram needn't carry a thing.

"I… suppose it's fine," he conceded, though his cheeks had darkened again. "The Fairy Queen might recognize me if we cross paths, but no one else should know us here. It hardly seemed like I left Sapphire at all these past ten years, and even in my time, I'd visited Diamond the least."

Whether jewel tones of blue and green or something closer to a sunset like today, Bertram was a striking figure, and unlike how he darted his eyes from Pax, as if not trusting himself when looking at him, Pax made it very clear when he was taking in Bertram.

"No one should know us," Pax repeated. "Which means you can be and do as you wish, with no thought of consequence."

"I wouldn't say no consequence—"

"None at all." Pax stopped them upon exiting the study. Where others coming and going either joined the line that led to the Veil Curtain or dispersed throughout the castle, Pax pulled Bertram aside. Like when they met, he tilted Bertram's chin up with a crooked finger and unleashed its talon that he knew no one else could see, only enough for the coolness of it to make Bertram's breath catch. "None at all, because you're with me."

Bertram shuddered, nodding as the bulb in his throat bobbed the way it had when they first met too.

"And I for one want to see if the gardens, shops, and taverns here are as impressive and raucous as I remember." He released Bertram's chin to twine their arms together for the stroll ahead. "Follow my lead?"

What had shaken Bertram back in Sapphire seemed to be driving him forward now toward the exact type of adventure Pax craved. "By all means, lead."

Pax started them down the hall he knew led out of the castle. He could feel the call of the Diamond in the distance, not inside any stately building but beneath the open sky in a lush park, surrounded by the ethereal plant life of the valley, an echo from nearby Aurora Wood. It wasn't the earth's magic that this gemstone communed with, however, but the skies—the storm—itself.

"Who needs another castle anyway?" Pax said. "Let's get out into the sunshine!"

The Diamond castle glowed like it was lit with its own internal sun, between the silver and gold and white stone and marble surfaces. But a castle was a castle, and Pax wanted a city's streets to walk through with the bustle of community and commerce.

Since the valley was in the hollow of what was almost a canyon—if that canyon's landscape was made of the same shimmer of colors as the sky on a cold night—exiting the castle was like finding oneself at the base of a great dome. Everywhere one looked was color and glowing lights like a fairyland, spanning leagues and up the sides of the canyon itself.

Pax had flown over the Aurora Wood when he left Ruby, and the plant life here was the same, with some of the colors in the foliage found nowhere else in all the lands. Distant waterfalls framed the valley as well, and sparkling streams were arched over by bridges made from the same pearlescent materials as the castle. Other buildings were also white, silver, or gold, so that the sun hitting the valley made it positively glisten.

"I've only been here a few times, when I was younger," Bertram said in quiet reverence. "I forgot how... magical it all looks."

And Pax could show him so much more.

Starting with breakfast.

"Follow me, Bertie, and the magic will never dim."

Colored lanterns lit the pathways that would have been in darkness before the sun rose, now snuffing out with the receding dawn. Homes, like the castle, were more often along the outskirts of the valley and built up along the canyon walls, but closer to the center were buildings taller than any in Emerald, all surrounding what Pax knew, but couldn't see from this low vantage point, was the Diamond gemstone in the center of its magnificent park. That was the city center, more nature than municipal, with trees and gardens and a lake that all the streams poured into.

Some shops were new along the marketplace that circled the city center, some remodeled, some had clearly changed hands from one family to another, and some no longer existed, but with the immortality of this kingdom like in Sapphire, there was a pause, an agelessness on part of it that hadn't changed since Pax's time.

Like sweet dough fried to perfection with a crispy bite and soft insides, dusted over its surface with sugar. Pax could have eaten a platterful. Or licked the remnants of sugar from Bertram's lips when his eyes glittered upon finishing his first taste.

Pax settled for running the pad of a thumb across Bertram's plump lips. Quite plump actually, pouty even, with a faint quiver from Pax's attentions, so effortlessly sensual in that way Bertram had no idea he exuded.

Slowly, Pax sucked his thumb into his mouth to lick the sugar clean. "Delicious. Satisfied? Or would you like more?"

Just as it seemed Bertram might crumble and dart his eyes away with another blush, he steeled himself and said, "More. If you will." He opened his mouth with a tilt of his head in wanting, waiting to be gifted his request.

Sensual indeed and full of surprises.

Pax plucked one of the pillowy pastries from the bag they shared, each the tiniest bit too large for a single bite. At least for most, but Bertram opened wider as Pax fed it to him, like he meant to take it all in one go. He didn't quite succeed, for the mouthful would have been difficult to chew, but near enough that when he flitted his tongue out to pull in the last of his bite and swiped over his lips to collect the lost sugar, even the bulging of his cheeks never lost their allure. Quite the contrary.

"Shopping next?" Bertram asked with a deceptively devious innocence after the display he'd just made. "But shopping means *paying*, Pax. Not theft."

"And trade! Or have the Gemstone Kingdoms forgotten the art of bartering?"

"You can barter. But with... what?" Bertram asked, as they continued down the street.

He eyed Pax's minimalist clothing that left no possibility for hidden pockets.

At least not in this dimension.

Pax popped the final pastry into his mouth, taking it all in one grand gobble where Bertram had failed—perhaps a little aided by how his jaw could unhinge, being a dragon, but only slightly.

"Even one as brilliant as I am does occasionally acquire a duplicate of something on accident—or on purpose." Pax held up the now empty pastry bag, and with a flourish of his hands, it was gone, replaced by a medium-sized white leather pouch that glimmered in the light like a rainbow in an oily puddle. "I had two of these dragon-hide purses made once, one hundred years apart, but by the same leatherworking family. Their craft had been passed down so identically, you can't tell them apart. This is the newer of the two. I think...."

Bertram stared at it with a look akin to horror. "You... you had a purse made from the skin of one of your own people?"

"Of course not! This was made from me."

The shock on Bertram's face only grew.

"When we shed scales, sometimes the skin sloughs off with them, making room for new skin to grow in its place, and it's still very versatile and strong. Why, you couldn't pierce this with a blade if you tried, unless it be magical." He handed the bag to Bertram, who took it with a renewal of the amazement Pax preferred. It was no more painful or disgusting for a dragon to shed its skin than a sheep to be sheared.

"I don't know how I'd feel about having some part of me worked into a coin purse, but it is beautiful, Pax. I'm sure you could trade it for just about anything."

"Then let's find us a few somethings." Pax indicated a shop that had caught his attention as soon as they turned down the street—a silk merchant, with just the sort of garments in the window displays that he was looking for.

It was a general clothing and accessories shop, so while it specialized in silk, there was leather and jewelry and designs of all kinds. The owner, an elven woman who radiated magic and experience and was likely hundreds of years old, was skeptical of the purse when Pax presented it. But as soon as she began inspecting its quality and properties, she could find no blemish, no sign that it was fake, and its near indestructibleness and dazzling appearance made her eyes glitter from the thought of what she could get for it.

She announced they could choose whatever items they wished for from the store—within reason.

Bertram took that to heart. He wasn't a man who fussed over adornments, other than the crown he'd worn for duty, and Pax had to coax him, reminding him that indulgence didn't have to serve a purpose other than desire.

"I suppose this short cloak is quite lovely," Bertram said.

It was a mix of thicker brocade fabric and silk paneling, all in shades of bronze and gold that matched his current attire and would have complemented his blue and green pieces as well. It was more shawl or scarf than cloak, draping across the shoulders without much length in back, and pinned beneath the left shoulder with a simple but elegant brooch.

Pax noticed a different brooch in a display among others, a normal circular pin, but its structure was a coiled dragon, its wings small but present at its sides, in a color not quite silver or gold but he dared say could have been a mix of both, almost like it was platinum.

"This one." He claimed it, removed the one attached to the cloak Bertram held, and handed him the new one. "Try it on. I'm sure a dragon will look splendid on you."

Bertram did blush this time but smiled and headed to a long mirror on the wall to fit the cloak upon his shoulders. This gave Pax the opportunity to claim the outfits he'd been eyeing, not identical to the fetching elven woman's but with the right sheerness and lack of covering to satisfy him.

Not to steal, of course—the owner had said they could take what they wished—but after showing her the items he'd chosen, he hid them away in his hoard. He wanted their existence to be a surprise.

"Dazzling," Pax said as he rejoined Bertram, meeting his eyes in the reflection. Nearly the entirety of Pax's face could be seen over Bertram's head. The image of their difference in size seemed to stir another wave of passion for Bertram, and his throat bobbed in that tempting way that Pax was beginning to adore.

"Yes," Bertram said, though he wasn't looking at himself. "N-nothing for you?"

"I took what I wanted. No need to carry when I can collect." He wiggled his fingers.

Bertram's brow creased, but he nodded.

He had a soft-spoken way about him, closer to his true self, Pax supposed, than the bold king who'd calmed the masses after a dragon sighting and confronted would-be thieves. Oh, Bertram could rise to the occasion, but part of him longed to shed the structure and obligations he'd shackled himself with and fade into the background where he could quietly exist and simply be as he pleased.

That was nothing like Gar.

At least... not like he'd become.

"Shall we?" Pax suggested.

They spent the rest of the morning perusing the market, ate lunch at an outdoor café, and barely took a break before they were off again, since there was much of this kingdom to see. It seemed, whether Pax intended it or not, their course was leading them in an ever-shrinking spiral toward the Diamond. All paths eventually led to the gemstone, and Pax didn't fight its pull.

"Aurora Wood starts right behind the Emerald castle," Bertram said as he admired the foliage lining the walkways of the park, "and I think I've been in it... once? Look how beautiful the colors are from these plants. Iridescent blues and shades of pink, found only in the wood and here. How did I ignore it all for so long?"

"It's astonishing how much time one wastes when they think they have plenty of it."

"Says the thousands of years old *immortal*."

"I didn't finish." The gemstone was ahead of them now, with a few onlookers pausing to pay respects or touch it in quiet communion, though most acknowledged it no more than the average tree that had been standing in the same spot for generations.

Their path arched around the Diamond, or one could step onto the lowcut grass to approach it directly. Pax started by circling it.

"'Twas mortals who taught me to appreciate every beat of our hearts and first breath to the last, because I saw so many of them living every moment of their short lives with fervor. Especially children. They have no concept of time, so they embrace everything without fear.

"It's not how much time is left, Bertie, but that time exists at all that disrupts our enjoyment of life. Whether a decades long friendship or a passion that burns over only a few nights, I seek to remember every experience like a treasure to be kept close."

"That's... beautiful," Bertram said as they paused along the path.

"Don't sound so surprised." Pax smirked. "Ah, but it seems someone forgot one of their own treasures. There's a cap left behind." On the base of the dais where the gemstone sat was a lone floppy cap, black with gold trim and a white feather.

"Not forgotten," Bertram said. "A reminder. That's Janskoller's cap, left there when he and the Fairy Prince crossed over to the wild magic lands."

"Janskoller returned and then went back to his people again?"

"You knew the ancient bard?"

"Him, I did. The most talented of them all back then."

"This was a different Janskoller than the original," Bertram explained, "the name passed down through bard apprentices. He was human, but his beloved, Prince Nemirac of Diamond, was half wild magic from his mother and very much immortal. They traveled for years together, but Nemirac grew concerned with the gray in Janskoller's hair and his limited time. He knew Janskoller would never be content to simply live on immortal lands forever, so they compromised. A new adventure in immortal lands where no mortal had ever traveled before.

"If the hat remains, they must still be gone. Do you think them... safe over there?"

"The wild magic realm is unpredictable," Pax admitted, not that he had ever been there himself. He knew only stories, for he'd been born in the Gemstone Kingdoms when the gemstones were as much babes as he was. "Dangerous, to be sure, but not evil. More... neutral. If this Fairy Prince is part wild magic himself, he's surely keeping them safe. And if that bard is anything like the original, I bet he prefers a little danger."

Bertram laughed and nodded his agreement, having known the pair, it seemed, at least a little. "*Don't* take the cap," he said with a sudden snap of his head. "You'll cause a stir, and it's rude."

"I'll resist," Pax promised with a raise of nimble fingers. He breathed in the heady presence of magic all around them and felt more content than he had since waking—at least enough to leave that spoil where it was. He gestured Bertram onward. "Not too shabby a future so far, yes?"

"Here," Bertram agreed, "but Diamond has no direct connection to me. I haven't even let myself wonder how Emerald is faring...." He cringed as he said it, marred by a wave of visible guilt.

All Pax need do was crane his ears for any talk of the Emerald Kingdom, and he could put Bertram's fears to rest. Sapphire was in good standing, clearly, and Diamond too. So, surely—

"*—Emerald's unrest spills any further from their borders, there'll be war—*"

"*—deplorable conditions, every mage in Emerald chained with limiters—*"

"*—think a good ruler could have been found before Emerald got this bad, but even Sapphire is building up weapons stores—*"

Oh.

Well fuck.

"Pax? Something wrong?"

"Nothing! Why wonder about Emerald when there is beauty all around us?" Pax spun about to walk backward, spreading his arms to encompass their surroundings. The trees, flowers, even the walkways with colored lights lining them, and certainly the people of Diamond were beautiful to behold. Beyond the park was even more of the surrounding market district with shops and taverns they had yet to explore, all equally appealing.

No need to spoil their fun just yet.

"Take this poor fellow." Pax plucked a lily from a cluster planted around one of the lights—a white lily, possibly even one of those White Dragons that the court wizard in Emerald kept dried in a jar. It was wilted, the edges of its petals browning. "Why, he's still beautiful, just a bit bruised and in need of a little life infused back into him."

The lily glowed, and then the spots that had been browned turned verdant again and stunning ivory, the petals straightening to seek the sun and opening wider with an expulsion of its sweet scent.

At this, too, Bertram marveled, though other magic users of an earthly leaning could have done the same. Pax was simply all kinds of magic and could command every element, no matter which kingdom it tied to.

He shortened the stem with a slice of his nail and fitted the flower into the brooch of Bertram's new cloak, so that the fabric the dragon wrapped around with its pin snug and secure now sprouted a radiant blossom.

"Is that what you're doing with me?" Bertram asked, with a bashful smile upon his lips.

"You are beautiful," Pax said, tilting Bertram's chin up. He did so enjoy the brush of soft skin mixed with the prickle of stubble, "and a bit bruised, I think, and in need of more life in you, without a doubt. I'm sure we can get your bud to blossom."

Bertram shuddered, anticipation shining in his eyes like he expected a stolen kiss. But life wasn't infused without effort, and the blossom in question needed to really, really want it.

Pax pulled away to retrieve another lily. After he coaxed it back to health like the first, he said, "This one I'll keep," and passed a hand over it, causing it to vanish.

"Where do you keep sending things?" Bertram asked as they continued down the path. "A separate dimension of sorts, I read?"

"Bertie, it is far better to experience something than read about it. Take, for example, those dragon orgies—"

"*Pax.*" Bertram glanced around as if to be sure no one else could hear them. "You're the only dragon here."

"Then I guess I'll have to be enough."

Bertram laughed.

"If you're so curious, how about a question answered for an exchange in experience?" Pax took hold of Bertram's arm, keeping their stroll close and intimate.

"You mean you'll answer a question if I agree to… do something?"

Pax grinned.

Any reservations Bertram had over what Pax might request were clearly less important than his curiosity. "Where is your hoard?"

"Specifically? In, yes, a pocket dimension between worlds, but technically at the nexus between Emerald, Ruby, and Diamond, in a lovely spot in Aurora Wood."

"And no one else can see it or stumble upon it by accident?"

"That's a different question."

"But—"

"Ah, ah, ah! My turn." The sounds of a flute, lute, and percussion were on the air now as they drew closer to more buildings, and Pax was able to pinpoint exactly which establishment they originated from—putting the whispers of the Emerald Kingdom far from his mind. "Right now, we are going to enjoy that song."

LISTENING TO musicians in a tavern wasn't the worst first request Pax could have made of Bertram. The day was spilling into the afternoon, and plenty of people were enjoying late lunches, early drinks, and tapping their tables and feet to the songs being played or even dancing out in the open area of the tavern proper.

Pax dragged Bertram right into the middle of it.

A familiar song was being played that Bertram had learned as a boy, "The Ride-Along Bard," one of the oldest still told and perfectly paced for a group dance. Participants traded partners, arms locked to twirl about, and continued along the formed circle until they returned to their original partner.

> *"For no bard is humble,*
> *And no hero's flawless.*
> *All that matters is the stories we tell."*

When Bertram hooked arms with Pax once more after an initial round, Pax twirled him faster and faster, refusing to pass him back down the circle, but swung him in close until he launched him outward, leaving him laughing and nearly losing his balance—right in front of an empty harpsichord.

Knowing the song was about to finish, Bertram claimed the stool in front of it and waited.

> *"But all the heroes were lies or had died on their feet,*
> *So she drank and lied her way too.*
>
> *"For no bard is humble...."*

Cheers rang out upon Bertram's first accompanying chords.

> *"And no hero's flawless.*
> *All that matters is the stories we tell.*
>
> *"When the dark falls,*
> *And swords clash in the night,*
> *Strong ale is better than a fight."*

The final notes were loud and resonant, which Bertram let linger the way his father and Wynn used to, alternating swiftly between two dissonate chords and then finishing with a final sharp and fortissimo major chord to close it out.

The tavern—bard and musicians all—erupted in applause and louder cheers than before.

Bertram was hardly a master, but it was one of few artistic pursuits he'd excelled at.

"Full of surprises, eh, Bertie?" Pax plunked down beside him facing the room. "I have a request I bet this fine crew knows, if you'll play along?" He leapt up just as swiftly and went to the lead bard to whisper in his ear.

The bard laughed, nodded, and passed it on to his musicians.

Bertram didn't know the tune they began, at least not at first, but it was easy enough that he felt confident joining in after only a few bars.

Pax plopped back down beside him, facing the harpsichord this time. "You're going to love this one, Bertie."

> *"When magic ruled the gemstone realms,*
> *And dragons filled the skies and seas,*
> *'Twas not man nor woman born*
> *Who would not get on their knees*
> *For a lick of magic's tease."*

Bertram fumbled a few notes before finding his rhythm again. *This* song. He should have guessed.

> *"We have all been called to a bawdy, lusty life.*
> *Those who came before paved the way as husband-wife,*
> *And we'll keep it on*
> *Till the wyrms return."*

He could feel Pax's eyes burning into the side of his face, as the *dragon* next to him sang along in a low, husky voice.

> *"Some say the lords of kingdoms all*
> *Have dragon blood inside them still,*
> *And no man nor woman born*
> *Would refuse to have their fill*
> *If a dragon were to spill.*

> *"We have all been called to a bawdy, lusty life,*
> *Those who came before paved the way as husband-wife,*
> *And we'll keep it on*
> *Till the wyrms return."*

Bertram fumbled again, not from the words he started to remember but the slide of a hand on his thigh that he would swear bore talons.

"The dragons may be gone for good,
But something could arouse them yet,
For some men and women born
They haven't quite yet met
Would beg to be made wet.

"We have all been called to a bawdy, lusty life,
Those who came before paved the way as husband-wife,
And we'll keep it on
Till the wyrms return.

"Oh, please wyrms return!"

Despite the squeeze on his knee, Bertram finished strong, and again, the tavern and musicians applauded him.

Pax seized him from the stool to make him stand and face the room, leading him into a bow before his audience. Then he tugged Bertram against him and whispered, "You know what else you simply must try in this kingdom...."

Don't think dragon dick.
Don't think dragon dick....

"The hot springs."

CHAPTER 7

THE SCALE from Pax wasn't the same as it'd been before Bertram made his wish. He hadn't noticed when he found it in his pocket yesterday or transferred it to the pocket of his trousers that morning. But as he stared at it now, having unloaded his things in the room they'd purchased for the evening in one of the most lavish inns in the city, Bertram saw how some of the scale's glimmer had dimmed.

Its magic was used up, he supposed. But even without that ethereal shimmer, the platinum color that could look like a rainbow existed within it in the right light was still beautiful.

"Your turn to change, Bertie."

Bertram closed his fist around the scale as if to hide it, which was silly, but he didn't want Pax thinking he was so enamored with him that he couldn't even think... clearly....

"Oh...," he moaned with the most blatant of besotted exhales upon seeing what Pax was wearing. Clearly, having most of his chest and legs showing with a short tunic and no trousers was not the most erotic he could look.

This was.

He may as well have been in the nude save a loincloth, but the embellishments of this new skirt-like garment were as majestically detailed as that of a courtesan to a king.

Bertram snapped his slack mouth shut at the thought but couldn't avert his eyes. The belt holding the garment on Pax's waist was naught but a thin gold cord, with teal and white silken fabric hanging from it, gaping at the sides from his hips to reveal skin all the way to midthigh. The front was thankfully higher set, more appropriately secured beneath the navel, where a golden ornament like metal-worked flames drew the eye to Pax's finely muscled stomach.

Parallel slits in the front revealed so high up his legs when he walked that too strong a breeze might expose everything beneath. He wore nothing else but gold bangles on his upper arms and wrists, a circlet over his brow, and a matching necklace that was akin to a collar.

"This one's yours." Pax grinned, preening from the attention, as he tossed onto the bed what could hardly be considered clothing.

There was jewelry that had clanged together, more bangles and whatnot but in darker bronze. The main articles were two leather-like belts, possibly made of cork, one shorter in radius to be worn midwaist, the other meant for the hips, which draped far less fabric than Pax was wearing.

"*Just* this?" Bertram barely dared touch it.

"And the sandals." Pax dropped a pair onto the floor in front of him.

"B-but... I'm not built like you are! I'll look—"

"Ravishing. Trust me." Like many times before, Pax loomed over him and took hold of his chin, tilting it upward for their eyes to meet. Bertram's gaze still flicked downward at the expanse of exposed skin before him, breathing in Pax's unique smell—bergamot and leather, somehow citrus and floral both with a hint of musk. "You said you would follow my lead, didn't you?"

"Yes." And Bertram did want to see where that path ended. "But doesn't our new arrangement earn me an answered question?"

"Clever boy." Pax chuckled. "It does. Go on, then. Still want to know about my hoard?"

"Yes, but... specifically...." Bertram considered how to ask a question and get more than one answer. "How did your hoard—and you—remain undetected all this time?"

Pax's mouth twitched, like perhaps that wasn't worded in a way he wanted to answer, but he said, "My hoard only allows people to find it if I wish for them to. It's invisible otherwise, completely imperceptible, and someone could pass right by it, even through it, without knowing it was there. And I... was deeper in the mountains than the dwarves dared go. Until recently, it seems."

"They've been mining more. But why—"

"That's another question, Bertie." Pax moved the finger beneath Bertram's chin to press against his lips. "Now, let's see that hot springs attire so we can enjoy our dinner and a soak in the style of the locals."

"Right. Of course."

It took a bit for Bertram to get it all on correctly, given several of the pieces were so small, it was difficult to tell just how and where they were meant to cover him. In the end, gazing at himself in the full-length mirror of the privy, he looked closer to a courtesan than even Pax. His amount of cloth hung only between his legs to above the knees, and definitely didn't cover all of his buttocks from behind. At least it came with a snug undergarment, or Bertram would have felt completely exposed.

He thought himself a bit thicker in places than Pax, but his muscles were toned, accentuated by the higher waist belt especially. His chest hair was an even dusting, not too pronounced, and he felt like a dancer in a secret dungeon of depravity. He knew they wouldn't be the only ones dressed this way, though. After all, Bertram had seen these garments in that merchant shop too.

Each room had its own private pool downstairs that was theirs alone. Eventually, they'd return to this room, which, just like Bertram's room in Sapphire that Pax hadn't truly shared with him….

Only had one bed.

"Well?" Bertram presented himself to Pax, who lounged on the bed so luxuriously, he didn't seem real. Especially when he sat up and dragged his eyes over Bertram with a heat and intensity that made Bertram's barely covered loins ache.

"Worthy of the most talented sculptor to capture your image. Truly! But you need to relax, Bertie." He got up with the same grace as always, almost floating forward, even with his feet treading instead of wings slicing the air. "A nighttime stroll through the grounds, hot water enveloping your skin and weary muscles, and all your worries will melt away and leave you open for even more new experiences."

Bertram expected another grasp of his chin, but Pax seized him by the waist instead, his soft hand and forearm tickling the skin of Bertram's lower back. A kiss? Now? But again, Pax denied him, as if knowing exactly where his desires wandered. If Bertram slouched and snuggled close, he could have rested his head beneath Pax's chin and been entirely encased.

"Best stay close," Pax whispered, his breath fluttering the short strands of Bertram's hair. "You're going to stir so many onlookers to passion that they might try to steal you away from me."

"You're flattering me." Bertram darted his eyes downward and saw how close they were in their scant attire, hips nearly pressed together, but just far enough that only the fabric brushed.

"Yes. And entirely earned. Come." Pax swept him outward to walk side by side, still holding him about the waist. The effortlessness of it reminded Bertram yet again that he was a mere mortal at the whims of a god. It felt both thrilling and terrifying to know how powerless he was in this creature's presence, but though he couldn't have resisted Pax if he'd tried, he didn't *want* to try and leaned comfortably against Pax as they left the room.

It had still been light out when they went to their suite. All looked different now, and Pax didn't bring them back down to the lobby but down a different set of steps that wound into the glorious back gardens where the hot springs resided. With the sun setting, the way the colored lights and lanterns lit this place was even more magical than their first views of the valley that morning.

This was a fairyland. The pathways led through archways of lush trees, hiding the various hidden pools that could be spied on with only a careful peer through branches and thick foliage, revealing flashes of different shades of bare skin. Small brooks and waterfalls were down one path or another, their sounds extra soothing as they flowed near the springs. Steam filled the air with the sweet scent of oils mixing with the multicolored flowers like those in the Diamond gemstone's park.

Some of the lights and lanterns seemed to float, assisted by magic. Others literally flew for there were sprites about like otherwise only seen in Aurora Wood.

"Well trained and domesticated compared to the pests of the wood, I assure you," Pax said as a sprite flew near them. The firefly-like creature resembled a tiny naked elf with butterfly wings and glowed a cool mint-like green. Others were in every shade that existed, dancing about as if enjoying the surroundings as much as the patrons.

A few swiped food, without being as intrusive as a buzzing bee. Bertram saw now how there wasn't any formal dining here, but buffets set out with the most scrumptious of fare and scantily clad servers going around with more food and drink on platters.

Bertram and Pax didn't stand out at all, though Pax did command attention and received many a perusing eye from other passing patrons and servers alike. Bertram did, too, a little, and let himself enjoy it, whether it was only curiosity at how he'd claimed such a partner or actual praise of him.

"Here we are." Pax plucked two goblets from the next passing platter and handed one to Bertram. It was filled with a strong and sweet-smelling mead that left Bertram's insides warm. They ate as they walked. Drank. Took in the sights of both beautiful landscaping and people. The occasional view of a naked body through the lights and trees at one of the pools warmed Bertram's cheeks as much as the liquor filling him, and he found himself buzzed with anticipation to take his own soak.

The entrances to the pools were the loveliest displays. Branches wove into circular archways, covered in colored flowers and tiny sparkling lights, which also hung like a curtain over the opening behind sheer colored cloth, inviting one to peek inside.

At long last, when Bertram was full from food and relaxed from mead, they reached one such archway, bookended by small tables that had two fresh goblets on one and the number of Bertram and Pax's room on the other. They traded their now empty goblets for full ones.

"You needn't undress for the hot springs if you don't wish to," Pax said, even while running the backs of his fingers down the front of Bertram's loincloth. "The cork and fabric choices were made to get wet."

Bertram hadn't realized it between the sights and fine cuisine, but now that they had paused in their perusal of the grounds, he felt the telling discomfort of how relaxation and excess had turned to arousal. The promise of what was to come, even if not blatantly stated, their attire, the mead, and Pax's constant touches up and down his back and occasionally lower to feather down his thigh, had all left him throbbing.

Pax sniffed near him and glanced down his body with a grin. He must be able to smell it. He knew. And he licked his lips before ushering Bertram behind the curtain and dangling lights.

The private pool area was even more beautiful than the rest. Thicker trees surrounded it, with lights winding around every branch. Smooth stones lined the edges and bottom of the pool to keep the water clean as it filtered in from the natural springs. The steam here was more enclosed and made Bertram relax further with a deep sigh.

"I'd remove your sandals, but otherwise, go on. Enjoy it. I'd guess you've never been here before?"

"No." Bertram laughed. He'd never lounged in a body of water larger than the tub in his room.

Keeping his goblet close, he went to the edge of the pool where one side had built-in steps to make submerging easier. The fragrance from the bath oils was like an extra dose of Pax's scent, and Bertram wondered if Pax knew and had somehow requested it. He slipped from his sandals at the side of the pool, and the first step into the water coaxed a moan from his lips.

"That's lovely...."

He descended slowly, not dizzy or too inebriated yet, but in a haze close enough that he didn't want to trip. His loincloth floated upward when he sunk deep enough to sit on an outcropping of stone like a bench, and the heat encasing his clothed cock made it pulse.

"Move around the edge, Bertie. You'll be able to feel where the water comes in from the springs."

Bertram could hear Pax but couldn't see where he was. He scooted along the bench, seeking what Pax had indicated, while also looking for his companion. Pax seemed to be following him around the pool just behind his back. Bertram started to look over his shoulder, but just then felt a jet of especially hot water strike the base of his spine.

He moaned again.

"You'll make me never want to leave this place." He dropped his head back on the upper stones and closed his eyes in bliss. He didn't even want another sip of mead but fumbled to set it on the ledge.

"You'll want to leave. There are just as many unexperienced pleasures in other kingdoms that I wish to show you."

"Yes...." Bertram didn't mind that thought at all.

He heard the drop of what sounded like heavy cloth and a tinkle of metal, and when he looked behind him to see what Pax was up to, he found the skirt-like garment in a crumpled heap.

But no Pax.

Bertram whipped his head forward, facing the stone steps, and somehow—though not surprisingly—Pax had beaten his ability to follow him with his eyes. He was halfway into the pool, the top of his thighs just having submerged along with other now naked aspects of him that a strong and telling V pointed toward beneath the water.

How might the lights dance over Pax's scales if they were present?

And where might other scales appear that Bertram hadn't seen when Pax was clothed?

"I hope you don't mind?" Pax swam toward him. He still wore the circlet, necklace, and bangles, and the knowledge that he wore *only* them made Bertram's cock jump.

"N-no...."

"What are you thinking, Bertie?"

"You... keep taunting me."

"Taunting? Why, if you want something, you need only ask for it." He floated closer, a devious light in his silvery eyes, as his hands touched Bertram's knees beneath the water and spread them apart to drift between them. "Or… take what you want."

This was marble perfection before Bertram, glittering and gorgeous and nearly all-powerful. Pax's hair didn't even wilt from the steam but floated atop the water like moonlight dancing. His pale pert nipples were just above the water's surface as he slid his hands farther up Bertram's thighs, daring him to touch back.

Did Bertram dare touch a dragon?

He was glad his hands started under the water because he was certain they shook as he pressed his palms against Pax's stomach. He ran them slowly up Pax's chest, over the buds of his nipples, and up his shoulders to his neck, where he clung suddenly and lurched forward at the feeling of Pax's thumbs teasing the edges of his undergarment.

He crashed a kiss to Pax's lips that was hungry and impatient, not willing to wait any longer for all Pax had implied he'd offer. Pax squeezed the crease where Bertram's thighs met his hips, and then slid up his waist to tug him closer. With Pax between Betram's legs, it was easy to float higher into Pax's lap.

A bobbing cock brushed up against him, and Bertram moaned. He could feel it touching his thighs and teasing his cheeks, where he was barely covered.

Was Pax… ridged?

Scaled?

"You can have as much of me as you want, Bertie." Pax mouthed from Bertram's lips to the curve of his jaw and held him tighter.

"Will it… cost me another wish?"

"This is a boon I offer freely. It's been centuries, after all. Millennia. And you do wish to indulge, don't you?" Pax set him back on the stone bench, dislodging them with the same ease and strength he always exuded, and grinned as deviously as ever.

"H-here?"

"To start."

But there were people around! Bertram could hear them in other similar grottos, and a passing group laughed loudly as they walked the main pathways. Wandering eyes could catch glimpses through the trees just like Bertram had. He even thought he felt eyes on him then, amused by the intimate pair so closely met in the water.

It made his gut ache and cock swell to bursting.

"Well?"

"Y-yes."

Pax ducked beneath the surface.

Bertram tensed, hands groping for the wall to brace himself. He felt Pax back at the crease of his undergarment, only now, Pax was slipping his thumbs fully beneath the fabric to drag them down Bertram's legs. They floated to the top of the water's surface like a white flag being waved in surrender.

Nothing else happened at first, just Pax's hands back at Bertram's thighs, massaging and parting them like before. His hands were so soft, even underwater, and yet Bertram would swear he felt the graze of talons.

Cock free-floating in the hot pool, knowing a dragon was between his thighs, apparently scrutinizing it from every angle, made Bertram's breath catch, and he clawed at the rock wall behind him until—

"*Ohhhh….*" He slapped a hand over his mouth to hush how loudly he erupted. A tongue, and oh, what a tongue, had flicked over his slit and even inside it, thin enough somehow, almost like it was….

Forked.

"Oh skies… oh fuck…." Bertram dropped his head back again, trying to give over to what he couldn't, wouldn't want to stop, as Pax didn't even mouth him yet, but slid a thin dragon's tongue into his slit like a miming of fucking him. It thrust in and out, building a tingling heat at the bulb of Bertram's head. He was going to burst, embarrassingly right that moment.

Pax swallowed him down the next instant, as equally impossible as his forked tongue, all the way to the base and nearly taking Bertram's sac in too.

Bertram sank so suddenly, his chin dropped beneath the water. The helpful consistency of bodily fluids was usually dulled in water, but in Pax's mouth, he stayed slick. And as Pax sucked Bertram, his tongue kept snaking around his head, the forked end plunging in and out of him.

Surely, he would come any second now. Yet somehow the combination of a hot suctioned mouth, tight throat, and intruding tongue made him cross right over the brink into madness, and he couldn't. Those were definitely talons on Pax's hands, as he gripped Bertram's thighs. The forked tongue was no illusion either. And with Pax's head in Bertram's groin, he could feel the zinging scrape of scales from Pax's cheekbones brushing his inner thighs.

Bertram wanted to see him, this dragonkind version of Pax. He could only catch glimpses of platinum swaths beneath the water, but as he looked down, daring to reach from bracing himself on the wall to grip Pax's shoulders, he felt scales too.

A tail slapped out of the water as Pax began to suck him harder, slithering his tongue even deeper into Bertram's slit and forcing it wider. The next awestricken glance downward brought Bertram's attention to horns. As Pax bobbed and bobbed, the sharp points of his vertical horns peeked upward to break the surface with tiny little splashes.

"Ah, ahhhhhh...!" Bertram's voice broke in a cracked cry that thankfully lost its volume, and he became boneless. His hips stuttered a sharp, releasing rhythm, forcing Pax's face closer, but he... he didn't come. He couldn't, not with that forked tongue penetrating his slit. He *could*, but he couldn't, his mind too utterly bewildered. But he needed to.

He needed to!

"Please... *please*...." Bertram squeezed plaintively at Pax's shoulders.

The tongue wound its way out of him and curled around his cock beneath the base of his head, giving several rhythmic twists.

"Ah!" Bertram spilled, so blinded by the pleasure of it, he gasped like he was drowning. Pax's mouth never left him, hollowed cheeks, throat, and tongue equally working together, and drank Bertram down with a rumble vibrating through his spent cock like a growl.

Bertram's hands fell limp from Pax's shoulders. He could barely keep upright, chin in the water again and mouth nearly sinking below too. When was the last time he'd experienced anything remotely close to that, and why had he denied himself for so long?

Pax surfaced with a backward splash of water being flung from his long hair, and any draconic aspects he'd released were gone. Taunting Bertram again, even if he'd deny it. He licked his lips as if Bertram was the best thing he'd tasted all day.

"We can soak again later. Shall we head back to our room?"

Bertram panted, flush and exhausted, but also more keyed up than he'd been in years. He doubted he'd have much trouble reigniting for another round.

Allowing himself to catch his breath while Pax floated smugly in front of him, Bertram eventually sat up. He reached for Pax's shoulders, yanked him closer, and kissed him deeply, as plunging and lewdly exploring as a human tongue could.

When he pulled away, Pax's smile was almost comical, and Bertram wasted no time in answering.

"Yes."

CHAPTER 8

PAX NEARLY took Bertram in the grass when he retrieved his wet undergarments from the pool and flung them at Pax to catch.

"For your collection."

That Bertram walked back to their room with a breeze between his thighs made Pax even more eager to return between them.

"—*more extreme by the day*—"

"—*worse than the time of the curses*—"

"—*golden age? More like tarnished*—"

Further discussion about Emerald's unrest reached Pax's ears without him trying to listen for it. Later. *Later.* The singular mission Bertram was on now was as good for his education as seeing direct repercussions from his wish—and very good for Pax.

"Are you falling behind?" Bertram called over his shoulder, since Pax had indeed faltered while catching those snippets of concerned discussion from other patrons.

"Merely enjoying the view," Pax answered, which wasn't a true lie. The way Bertram's undergarment had contained him covered little more than Pax's own—when he wore any, which he wasn't now—and so, the fine curves of Bertram's cheeks had peeked out from the thin drop of cloth over his backside earlier too. Only now Pax knew, with each tempting sway of those rounded hips, what naked treasures lay beneath.

In their room, there was no noise, no conversation to be overheard that might sully their evening, other than the ambient sounds of crickets and the gentle buzzing of sprites outside their window. The view wasn't as spectacular as from the castle, mostly flowers and trees and more of those sparkling lights, adding atmosphere without giving any wandering eyes a view into their chambers.

Fresh goblets of mead were in reach, added to their room while they'd roamed. They wouldn't be disturbed again.

Bertram draped himself across the bed with the same wantonness Pax usually displayed, a flattering mimicry, as he then reached to take a sip from one of the goblets. Content, relaxed, but not yet inebriated, he painted the very picture of decadence with so much bronze skin revealed, adorned in bronze jewelry, and with the cloth covering him falling just enough to the side for his half-returned hardness to show approval.

Pax hadn't let Bertram get a good look at him naked, redressed in moments when they'd exited the pool. Bertram looked on him hungrily now, expecting that to change.

"All right, Bertie...." Pax strolled seductively toward the bed. "Considering I did so much of the work up till now, surely I deserve to be unwrapped like an exquisite gift."

Bertram laughed. He was a different person like this, carefree and captivating. "How right you are. Then please, bring my gift within reach." He set the goblet down to shift to the side of the bed, leaving room for Pax to splay himself beside him.

Pax did so without removing a single trinket. That was for Bertram to decide what would stay or be carefully discarded.

Tensions eased, Bertram was clearly ready to rekindle the unshakable leader Pax knew him to be. He shifted his stretched-out body closer, rolled onto his side, while Pax remained flat, and caressed a warm hand over Pax's chest.

"Is this form real?"

"As real as any other a person might touch."

"You're just so... beautiful." He pressed divots into Pax's skin, especially around each pec, caging Pax's nipples in the center of his palm. "Every version I've seen of you is, but this, compared to any human, elf, or others I've seen, is... incomparable. And I met the Fairy Prince. Slighter than you, more my size, but at the time, a man with the most beautiful face, hair, and more grace to his movements than any I'd known. You are somehow all that and yet with the masculine height and breadth to your body that makes me tremble."

Pax couldn't think of a response. He'd been praised many times. Courted. Adored. Even supposedly loved. But he didn't think anyone had waxed with such poetry as Bertram was now.

Not even....

No. If Emerald wasn't going to spoil tonight, then neither was Gar.

"I still expect this to be a dream, but no nightly youthful emissions could compare with what you did to me in that pool."

Pax laughed, thankfully broken from his stupor. Bertram's touch, his beautiful brown skin, felt as silken as the fabrics between them. "What we're about to do might surpass that. At your pace, of course."

The not quite request made Bertram's face alight with a wider smile. He continued his caresses but began straying lower. *Lower*. Passing the golden cord to get at the skin where the fabric dropped from the sides of Pax's hips. He drew his hand more center, seeking one of the slits, and caressed there too, up Pax's inner thigh and finding the velvety skin of his sac. Pax hummed at the gentle massage Bertram offered but watched Bertram's eyes for the moment when he drifted higher and discovered—

Bertram's eyes widened, and he glanced down, shifting the fabric aside to let him see what he'd felt.

"You are scaled there."

"The one part of me that always stays its true form. Well, proportionately of course."

A smile cracked through Bertram's awe, but he still stared as he slowly began to stroke Pax. Pax had discovered the thick but trimmed and concentrated tuft of hair around Bertram's shaft. In contrast, Pax had none, and Bertram seemed entranced by the smoothness offset by scaled texture. "Can you feel my touch through them?"

"Very much so. When our thinner scales are... caressed... it sends tiny vibrations through the skin beneath. Ah!" Pax arched upward as Bertram stroked more firmly. "Even more sensitive than the uncovered bits. *Ohhh....*" He arched again when Bertram circled his tip. "Well... other than that part maybe."

Bertram chuckled. He found the clasp that kept the garment closed behind the flame-like ornament, undid it, and let the two halves fall open to leave Pax bare. He tugged the article from beneath Pax to drop it from the bed and got between his legs with rapt attention on his body, taking in every swath of pale skin, though only Pax's cock bore scales at the moment.

And one other place, but Bertram would have to discover that himself.

He did when he rocked Pax backward. Bertram couldn't have known what he would find, hands running up the back of Pax's thighs, as he pitched him forward. He gasped, eyes on the path to Pax's opening, which displayed a ring of those same thinner scales around the prize.

"How does it feel... here?" Bertram circled the ring with the tip of a finger.

Pax moaned. No point in holding back when Bertram was doing so wonderfully. Though Pax still had to tease, even while his voice caught and his breath was near panting. "Barely feel a thing."

Bertram chuckled again and rocked forward to swirl his tongue where that finger had orbited.

"Ohhh... Bertie. You were absolutely the right mortal to grant my scales to."

"I am grateful for it. So much I've missed. So much I'd forgotten. So much I long to know again." Bertram licked with bold abandon, first around the ring of scales, once, twice, and then, with a swift swirl within the ring, closer, tighter, until the final flick was a swipe over Pax's bud, with a gentle press inside.

Pax shuddered. He hadn't expected to be so much the recipient, despite having asked for attention. Bertram kept worshipping Pax's hole like he was even more articulate when using his tongue for this. "You... are very much welcome to sheathe yourself there, you know."

The offer caused Bertram to flounder for words.

"Or do you have your heart set on riding your first dragon?"

Bertram laughed, loud and lovely. "Yes. But given it's been quite some time and I am but a mere mortal, you will have to ease the way for me. If you will?" He lowered Pax's legs, brown eyes intense and pupils large, and began to crawl up him.

Pax nodded his approval of whatever Bertram meant by that. Then Bertram pivoted. He was still dressed—technically—but his undergarment was safe in Pax's hoard.

Meaning, as he backed his finely sculpted bottom toward Pax's face, he presented a ripe and willing opening of his own, beneath which a heavy sac hung, leading to that dark tuft of hair and luscious shaft.

Pax licked him gladly, getting him wet to make way for stretching fingers, and growled in pleasure when he felt Bertram swallow him moments later with an underside lick along his scales. The rhythmic suction Bertram began, with tender accompanying strokes and occasional fondling of Pax's sac further encouraged his own licks and eventual intruding stretches of both thumbs working to part Bertram for a deeper plunge.

As if taking the pleasure he was being granted as a challenge, Bertram tongued Pax's scales with bolder licks, sucked his cock harder, faster, and squeezed Pax's base almost too tightly. If Pax wasn't adept at holding his elven form, he might have sprouted more scales and dragonkind parts. But not yet. Not yet. The first time with someone new, he wanted them constantly thinking about how much they wished he'd transform.

Pax pushed in his thumbs, spread them, plunged his tongue, and then worked two fingers in as deeply as he could thrust them. He repeated the cycle. Thumbs. Spread. Tongue. *Fingers.* Three times. Four—

"Fuck!" Bertram pulled away and spun about with impressive speed, cheeks gorgeously flushed and lips shiny and plump with arousal. He was still covered by the loincloth and both belts secure, but his cock bobbed upward from concealment.

He lowered himself slowly, sitting on Pax, while his eyes never left Pax's face. There was awe in the expression, for as much as Pax felt pleasure from his tender scales being encased, he knew the pleasure they gave another was even greater.

Rocking on Pax's tip, Bertram pumped his way down a few inches at a time. Then lower. *Lower.* Until his head dropped back like it had in the pool, and he moaned.

"Do you like the feel of my scales, Bertie?"

"And the sight of them."

"Not tonight. Wouldn't want my novelty to wear thin."

"Y-you… are no novelty." With his head tipped backward and Pax fully sheathed inside him, Bertram began to move faster. Faster. His mouth dropped open every time he brought his hips down, and the way he writhed was more elegant than his motion on the dance floor or his hands playing across the harpsichord.

Pax gripped harder at Bertram's hips and stopped their motion entirely. "Not so fast." Bertram squirmed to get back to their rhythm. "Be still. We should enjoy this, given it's been so long for both of us. Mm…." He closed his eyes as if perfectly content. "I could fall asleep like this, just buried inside you."

"Do so and my next wish will see you bald."

"Villain!" Pax bucked up sharply, but only once, before holding Bertram still again.

"*Pax.*"

"Yes, Bertie?"

"Please...."

He peeked an eye open to see Bertram biting his lip and looking especially enticing.

Pax rolled upward to drive even deeper into Bertram than before.

"Ah!"

He rolled again, his hold on Bertram firm, impaling him with every thrust. Accented in glittering bronze jewelry and the loincloth doing nothing to cover him anymore with how hard and bouncing his cock had become, Bertram was a vision. When he gazed on Pax with adoration, he only looked more beautiful himself. And hopeful, glancing over the edges of Pax's skin, still seeking more scales. Pax wouldn't give in. Not tonight.

But he did offer reprieve to Bertram's squirming and started to pump faster. Bertram had been leading, rocking upon Pax, but the control belonged to Pax now, and Bertram was relaxed and wanton atop him, totally given over. He thought this was as good as it got.

Silly mortal.

Pax did what only a reptilian spine could and rolled upward into a tight curve, swallowing Bertram's cock, as he continued to fuck him.

"Skies! Oh, Pax...."

Shaky hands cradled Pax's head, stroking his hair. The tenderness made Pax buck harder and suck harder too, until Bertram erupted with a second hot flood down Pax's throat, and Pax drank it down like the sweetness of the mead.

He hadn't come himself yet, and after licking Bertram clean, he flipped him onto his back. Bertram stared in blinking bewilderment at the sudden change but had little time to react before Pax slammed back into him. Wilted and spent and clearly overstimulated, Bertram's moans and gasps became whiny, almost pained.

"Pax...."

Pax didn't let up, fucking harder—*harder*.

"Ah! Ohhhh, Pax... please, it's... it's...."

"Too much?"

Seeming to sense the challenge, Bertram peered at him through slits of squinting eyes. He was biting his lip again and started to nod, only to shake his head. What he was feeling was beautiful agony, and he wanted more.

Pax obliged.

He hoisted Bertram's legs higher beneath the knees, folding him in half as he fucked him. Bertram was at his mercy, but not lifeless. The way he arched and writhed and moaned was more stunning to witness than....

Than....

Anyone Pax could remember.

He spilled inside Bertram with several sharper thrusts and finally pulled free to let the come dribble out of Bertram onto the sheets. Bertram laid beneath him as limply content as when he'd nearly sunk below the water in the hot spring.

Pax kissed him, offering one final boon by allowing Bertram to feel the prick of his fangs. He kept them visible when he pulled up and reveled in how Bertram admired them.

"You are so... beautiful," Bertram said.

"As are you."

"No."

"You are."

"Mildly handsome, maybe. But you, Pax, are more radiant and deserving of a lover's devotion than any before you, for anyone, in any place or time."

Bertram left him unable to find words yet again. No one else had ever said anything quite like that to Pax before.

And meant it.

"You could write sonnets with that tongue," he eventually praised, but he had to collect himself.

Only dalliance, he thought. Just for fun. No attachments.

Not again.

He kissed Bertram to prevent further poetry, fading his fangs to dull teeth, and then handed Bertram one of the goblets to sip from, while he wiped his lover clean. They lounged, side by side upon the bed with their drinks, leaning against the headboard, with Pax nude save his adornments and Bertram close enough to the same.

"Where to tomorrow?" Pax asked. "Stay here? Or shall we move on?"

"Ruby?"

"Ruby's no fun." Pax hid the flinch the name stirred in him but didn't want Bertram suggesting Emerald yet either. "How about Amethyst?"

"Actually, that would be perfect! I nearly forgot." Bertram gazed at Pax with building excitement, a new man having some indulgences fulfilled. "Tomorrow is Amethyst's Festival Day."

BERTRAM HAD been in Amethyst more than Diamond, though it still astonished him every time he arrived to see the strangeness of the kingdom, not only from oddly angled buildings and gnarled black trees that glittered as if dusted with stars, but from the people.

Every storybook creature from myth or legend could be seen in flesh and blood in this land, from those with snakelike bodies, to people with wings, to those born of two different myth-like people, combining their traits. Nowhere one turned led to ordinary, the sights of Amethyst being the only things capable right now of pulling Bertram's stare from Pax.

He was really very sweet and attentive. *Talented.* Bertram never imagined that the grooves of scales on a partner's length could feel so stimulating. He'd thought about scales and horns and clawed hands and that tail all the way to their bedchamber from the pool, where those aspects had teased him with their barely seen presence—but then hadn't reappeared.

Another time, Pax had promised, and even if Bertram hadn't planned to take the dragon back to bed, he would have jumped at the chance to see that promise fulfilled.

"Welcome, all, to Festival Day!" an orange-colored creature greeted them as they exited the Veil Curtain. They'd used Diamond's amongst several other visitors this time, for many were headed to Festival Day.

Their greeter was made up almost entirely of tentacles aside from his otherwise normal torso. Tentacles moved him across the ground beneath a long robe, and his arms were tentacles too, three each that worked together at their ends like large fingers, waving them forward. He had tentacle hair that coiled upward and a long tentacle beard, covering any sign of a mouth.

Klarent, Bertram recalled, a sort of chronicler of Amethyst's history who he'd met a time or two, so he ducked his head as they passed to avoid unwanted questions or recognition. He wanted to be just like anyone else enjoying this day.

"Be sure to visit the tower for a history tour! I and my lovely spouse, Daedlys, alternate tours at the top of each hour until sunset. There are tours of the castle as well—" Klarent continued as they hurried away amongst the queue, and Bertram grabbed Pax's arm to better duck his face between them.

He felt scales.

Looking up with a start, Bertram took in the changed form of his companion. All the aspects he'd longed to see again were plain before him. Certain accentuating edges along Pax's skin were dusted with scales like an artist's use of shadow. The fangs on his eyeteeth that Bertram had felt in last night's final kiss glimmered within Pax's broad smile. He walked a bit taller on clawed feet like a gargoyle, his hands the same, as one delicately curled around Bertram's arm while he clung to him.

The horns were back, the tail swooshing behind him, and—wings! Diminutive compared to his true dragon form, but Pax had wings, twitching as if in want to spread wide but keeping tight against his back. He was wearing his normal vest-like tunic, not the even skimpier attire from Diamond, just like Bertram was back in normal clothes, but he wondered what this dragonkind version of Pax would look like in silk….

"Now this is a spectacle!" Pax announced, seemingly unaware of Bertram's gawking. "To think I missed a curse that could cause such wonder. And they all like it! They all embrace it! And, oh my…." He glanced down at himself. "It seems I'm showing the creature in me as well. It just felt so natural to let loose, and no one is looking as if I stand out at all!" He turned to Bertram with a grin. Then grinned wider. "Save you, of course."

"I… forgot. One can call upon their own cursed—or in your case, true—form when in Amethyst."

"Truly? And what would you look like, Bertie, if you gave in to the beast?"

"I don't know. I've never tried to change while here."

"Mm…." Pax hummed curiously and tilted closer for the base of his central horns to brush Bertram's forehead. "My mind runs wild."

Bertram was certain all of Pax ran wild, but he was being granted what he'd longed for, to see this version of him again, in all its splendor, and no one indeed, whether local, visiting, or someone keeping their base form like Bertram, thought to stare.

Amethyst's Veil Curtain emptied into the market, very near the Amethyst gemstone. It caught Pax's attention next, for he swung them around to pass closer beside it and bowed as though greeting an old friend.

"You feel different, don't you?" Pax spoke to it. "Like corruption once held you captive but has since been banished. Well done!"

"Can you hear the gemstones?" Bertram asked. "Do they speak?"

"Not in words. They hum. Sing. Call to magic and echo all the magic that has touched them." He returned to his jubilant self with a hug of Bertram against him. "But not so alive as the celebration happening around us! Food? Games? Dancing? Let's experience it all."

It was morning, and unlike any Festival Day during the thousand years of the curse, it was daylight. The curse had been a time of eternal night, and after so long trying to make their world seem brighter, day made Amethyst absolutely blinding now with jewel-toned colors and brightly lit crystals. There were far more people here than in those days, too, since visitors were greatly encouraged. The prominent color amongst stalls for festival shops and signs leading patrons to games and food was the same royal amethyst as the gemstone itself.

"There's a shop that has fortune-telling for Festival Day, and many trinkets for sale outside," Bertram explained as he led Pax through the market. *He* led, because unlike in Diamond, he knew the ways of this strange kingdom better. "Klarent, who greeted us at the Curtain, and his husband passed the shop to their daughter. She's married to a local watchman and carpenter's son. You can see them, there, both second-generation Shadow Lands folk with third-generation children."

The shop stood along a line of others near the main tavern. Kenner, like a lizard combined with a bull, for his parents were one of each, was a decade older than Bertram but also looked eternally twenty. A few teenage children were beside him, helping him man tables of extra silk displays and jewelry. Each child was a mix of scales and fur and, somehow, shadow. One even had a head of tendrils.

Pax seemed curious about them but then noticed Kenner's wife, Gorganna, taking a break from fortune-telling. She paused to kiss her husband's cheek and patted the heads of her children, gliding amidst a sea of tentacles for her lower half, though differently from Klarent. She hovered above the ground, for her whole body was shadow, see-through like a wraith and floating, and her hair was another set of tentacles like a mane of writhing snakes.

"To think, here I'm the boring one," Pax snorted.

Hardly, Bertram thought. Especially if anyone knew what he truly was.

While Bertram didn't know anyone well in Amethyst, he recognized more faces, given their uniqueness in these lands. For the most part, little had changed, and yet... enough had. Children were grown. People were wed. New buildings had been erected. Even with a thousand years of being cursed, this kingdom, so unchanged in other ways for centuries, had managed to never grow stagnant.

"Bard songs in the tavern! Only a small fee to enter." A man with a face like a fish thrust a pamphlet at them, which Pax naturally took, and it turned out to be a voucher—two for one ales.

"We'll have to make good use of this!" Pax nudged him.

"—burned to the ground! They claim accident, but I hear the monarchs aren't buying it, least of all Ash—"

"Now there's a game!" Pax lurched Bertram away from whatever strangeness he'd overheard. "What's this, then? Prisoner's... Folly? No! Prisoner's Base!"

Indeed it was, for their strolling had led them to the base of the market steps, where a large open area was set aside for the game, in which two teams attempted to steal the other's flag.

"Is this a line for next game? Shall we join, Bertie?" Pax was already dragging him into the queue for future players, and he was hard-pressed to refuse—

Until he spotted some of the players out there now.

A tall, well-built, beautiful man with long golden hair had just captured the flag and was racing across the field to solidify his claim, while a slightly older man, who looked suspiciously like him but with shorter hair, gave chase.

Ambrose. And Oliver, his father. Amelia, Ambrose's mother, was on the field too. His husband, whose name Bertram didn't even know, was at the far end toward where Ambrose raced, guarding their team's base and jumping with unfettered joy as his love outran his father to win the game. The crowd cheered. Oliver looked especially proud despite being beaten and winded.

Ambrose's husband met him with a kiss.

"Isn't that—?"

Bertram yanked Pax's arm to drag him in the other direction, up the market steps and into the next area of the festival before they could be spotted. He'd forgotten Ambrose would be here. Taunting him. Reminding him....

Of all he'd let himself neglect.

"Sorry, Bertie," Pax whispered, upon the conclusion of their ascent, where there was a space for dancing and lively music keeping those twirling in motion. It almost stung more that Pax understood why Bertram had run.

"It's fine," he lied. It *was* fine. But that didn't mean he wanted to see Ambrose in the life he'd made for himself so clearly happy.

"Strapping man," Pax said, with such an obvious leading tone that Bertram shot him a glare. "Oh, stop. It's obvious you were an item. And more obvious that you don't mourn him but merely what he represents. Otherwise, I'd be jealous."

"You are unfairly observant."

"If I wasn't, I wouldn't have known to claim you as my own."

The music and moving bodies were distracting and yet not enough to deter Bertram from how much Pax captivated him any time their eyes met. He didn't think Pax had meant to say that, because he looked startled and then tried to cover it with a wider smile.

All the lights and different hues nearby brought out the colors in Pax's eyes like his scales.

"It was no grand love," Bertram admitted. "I've never known love like that. Certainly not the sort to mourn over or that inspires epics to be written."

A noticeable cringe marred Pax's features that he, again, failed to hide.

"Pax? Have you—?"

A whoosh like a pop of air or the sound of a weapon slicing brought both their attentions to the edge of the path. The congestion of festivities ended there, leading to the trail that went to the tower, once for alchemy and now a library and place to learn history. Shadows were cast by a tall lamplight beside them in the perfect shade of violet.

And from that darkness stepped the Shadow King.

"Who are you?" he asked Pax, his white-on-black eyes glimmering as if they were made of shadows themselves.

His skin was just as white, hair long, straight, and deep black in contrast. His nails were claws, thinner and sharper than Pax's talons, and instead of only his eyeteeth being pointed, all his teeth were razor-sharp, like the sharpness of his long, pointed ears.

"What are you?" he demanded with a voice that echoed beneath the thrum of the music and noises of the crowd. "You... you feel like you're a—"

"Local?" Pax grinned with a guilty shrug.

"Ash?" Another stepped from the shadows, as if not having realized where he'd exited. Prince Consort to these lands, Levi, was a beautiful young half-elf with blue skin, red hair, violet eyes, and a tattoo of stitches across his neck.

The king, Ashmedai, who Bertram had met before but was always intimidated by, descended upon them like a wave, sweeping Levi in beside him, and Bertram felt himself instantly transported.

CHAPTER 9

TRAVEL BY shadow.

How fascinating!

Pax emerged from the darkness in the Amethyst castle. He'd never experienced a drop in his stomach before, being a creature who *flew*. After glancing around to be sure Bertram was with him, if a little startled-looking, Pax took in their surroundings with greater awe. This castle, this kingdom, was not like the version he'd known at all.

What once had been polished stone and marble in bright and gleaming hues was now black, with red and gold accents that matched the regal brocade of the man who'd whisked them away. He wore a circlet like the ones Pax and Bertram had donned in Diamond, gold with a ruby at its center that matched a silver circlet with an amethyst stone on his companion.

The kingdom's current royals, it would seem, and this *Ash*, as the slighter one had called him, was no mere elf-made monster by a long since banished curse. He pulsed the very magic Pax could feel from the earth, from the Amethyst itself, which could only emanate from a person if they'd been born from that magic. Shadows flocked to him, moved with him as if commanded, compelled, and their presence made him appear larger, as if he might erupt into a towering and more menacing form at any moment.

Part of Pax hoped he would.

"Magnificent!" He walked right up to Ash and smacked his chest with the back of his hand. "Love the décor. Who'd have thought one of the wild magic folk could have an eye for design."

They were in a study, the furniture arranged around crystal sconces that created a constant area of shadow where they'd arrived. This was one of the castle towers, Pax noted, as he glanced out a nearby window overlooking the city. All the castles in the Gemstone Kingdoms were built upon elevation, save Emerald, and this one was as impressive as Diamond with how it gave view to the entire kingdom. Amethyst might be smallest, but it was still striking, nestled within a shelter of forest trees and the high rock walls of a basined lake.

Inside the room, a massive candle clock was fixed to the wall, a large black bookshelf sat opposite it, covered in tomes, and, of course, there was the furiously fuming wild magic monarch.

"I am Ashmedai, Shadow King and ruler of these lands, and I would have you explain yourself."

"Bit stiff, isn't he?" Pax turned to Bertram, whose eyes had gone considerably wide. Just because Pax couldn't use what was usually his substantial height to his advantage, given he and Ashmedai were nearly eye to eye, didn't mean he was one to bow.

"I remember you," the blue one said, peering at Bertram. He was fair and youthful, with a whiff of unique magic about him that Pax couldn't place, alchemy maybe, like his pieces didn't quite fit his body, despite being proportionate. Unlike Ashmedai in black, gold, and red, he was mostly in violet to match his eyes, with details in silver. "You're from Sapphire. Barclay and Josie's son."

"Do you know the truth of your companion?" Ashmedai asked Bertram.

"I, um… know what he is, Your Majesty." Bertram stepped forward with obvious reticence. "Pax never hid it from me. You can tell?"

"Here I thought only clever bards would notice my scales when not visible." Pax glanced down at his current dragonkind form. "Although I realize they are visible at the moment…."

"There is a *dragon* on my lands," Ashmedai bellowed, "and I would know why."

"A… dragon?" His consort shifted closer to him but also reached for a pair of twin daggers on his belt. Pretty, curious, and ready to defend. Pax was impressed all around.

"This is but a small approximation of what I look like." Pax grinned at the blue-skinned man. "Would you like to see more?"

"*Pax.*" Bertram dashed in front of him, shooting him a glare that turned diplomatic before he spun forward to address the pair who'd kidnapped them. "I asked to come to Amethyst, Majesties. For the festival! Pax awoke only recently from within the Ruby Mountains, took interest in me, and suggested adventure. We don't mean any fuss, only to enjoy the celebration like anyone visiting. I swear it."

"You slept?" Ashmedai asked Pax. "But chose to return?"

"As did you. I never expected any wild magic folk would."

"And I never expected to meet another dragon. There is one other like me who returned to this world."

"The Fairy Queen of Diamond," Pax recited. "So I heard. Haven't met her. I really mean no harm…. Ash, was it? I can see you too, by the way," he whispered and let his eyes flash with more platinum glow, not that he needed to show off to see through Ashmedai's guise.

Like a gargoyle made of shadow, his real form had many similar aspects to Pax—wings, claws, a tail, jagged horns that spiraled upward from his head. But instead of pale skin and shimmering scales, Ashmedai's coloring, like any shadow, couldn't be defined. Sometimes he seemed black or the deepest shades of purple, other times, he caught the light and other colors, indefinable and constantly undulating between each possibility.

"Emboldened by the Amethyst itself…. Beautiful."

"Forgive me," Ashmedai said with a lack of patience that opposed his words, "but I am wary of someone so powerful, whose intentions I do not know, being near my people and my beloved Levi."

"Nor do I know the intentions of you." Pax held his stare. "This is a cursed land, isn't it?"

"*Was* cursed."

"And how did that happen?"

"Pax!" Bertram scolded him again, pleading over his shoulder.

Static was brewing, like the precursor to a storm.

So be it. Pax hadn't had a worthy brawl in ages.

"Don't—"

Pax stepped out of time, effectively moving so swiftly that everyone else looked frozen, and took in Ashmedai's true form more carefully. It overlapped the form he displayed, and overlapped another too, just like Pax had several. It seemed Ash had his own mortal appearance, that of an elf without razor teeth or inverted eyes.

Pax moved, sidestepping Bertram, whose head was tilted upward where Pax had been, and turned his attention to the half-elf-looking man with blue skin—Levi. He made no sense. He was an overlap of dozens of faint figures, but they all seemed empty. Only him, this version that looked most like him, was truly present, as if countless people had been shoved into a single body, but only one survived.

It disturbed and captivated Pax, who reached to touch an especially bright afterimage of magic or alchemy or something that outlined the tattoo across Levi's neck like a mimic of stitches.

A hand seized Pax's wrist with such force that a mortal's bones would have been crushed. He looked to the side and somehow, though not truly moving as fast as Pax, Ashmedai's head and eyes were turning to meet his, and he looked like the very raging demon all the wild magic folk had been accused of being in ancient days.

The seeming pause in time shattered as Pax was flung backward, leaving a dent in the stone wall beside the bookcase. That almost hurt. How fun.

Pax leapt from the wall with a push of his clawed feet, leaving two more dents, and slammed into Ashmedai with his wings propelling him forward. Ashmedai caught him in a powerful grapple, purposely rolling them onto the permanent shadows cast by the crystal lights, and when they rolled again, they were in another room.

"Pax!" Bertram shouted, sounding several rooms away now, and Pax and Ashmedai were in a bedroom.

Pax knocked into the edge of the bedframe with a hiss. He splayed his hands over Ashmedai's chest and thrust himself backward out of the shadow creature's hold with a catch of wind summoned from his body.

"I am all the elements, Your Majesty," Pax said with a glow encompassing him like a prismatic shimmer, calling a little fire and ice and earth and, yes, even shadow to join some of the windswept storm beneath his wings. "How many are you?"

Roaring monstrously, Ashmedai sprang at him with all those razor-sharp teeth in the same shadow non-color as the rest of him.

Vines sprang from Pax like his own tendrils, wrapping around Ashmedai's incorporeal form. The gargoyle was all Pax could see now, but he was caught, stretched midair like a fly in a spider's web. One pulse of prismatic power through those vines and Ashmedai would be *ashes*.

"Ash!"

Levi and Bertram appeared in the bedchamber doorway, panting and panicked. Fools. Pax wasn't actually going to hurt him.

A snap was heard as Ashmedai swept a rotation of his arms to cut the vines holding his wrists. His claws sliced through the rest, and he dropped to the floor with an audible crunch into the stone. His taloned feet were larger than Pax's. So were his wings. So was most of him. But

Pax didn't bother growing or shedding this form for the truth. He was far too impressed.

"You are *something*, aren't you?"

Arms spreading wide by his own power this time, Ashmedai summoned every shadow in the room like a maelstrom suctioning everything to its center.

No—to *Pax* until he was smothered and felt himself drop right through the floor.

He landed in what looked like the castle foyer and immediately looked around for where the shadows were darkest. He felt the descent before it happened, stepping out of time once more, and turned to see the frozen figure of Ashmedai where he'd appeared from the shadows behind Pax, an ominous looming beast about to unleash something stronger than the wave that had brought them here or the shadows that swept him downstairs.

Ashmedai was still, or near enough, but his eyes found Pax again and some of his shadows moved too. He should have been immobilized completely, but part of him was strong enough to cut right through the veil.

Pax swatted the shadows away, only for them to adhere to him and wrap around his forearm with a wrench. The sting surprised him where the shadows touched, a burn, like Pax's own ability to erase if he be cruel. He phased out of its hold the same way he could phase through walls, and with that thought, he spun and flapped his wings to thrust himself toward the nearest wall and do just that. He was halfway through it, seeing a quick view of the next room, a dining room perhaps, with a curiously out-of-place red ball on the floor, before he felt himself tugged out again.

Pax scooped the ball into his hand just as he was yanked into the foyer and time returned to normal. He hurled the ball past Ashmedai's head, and the king turned just as he'd hoped. A quick, but not too strong pulse burned the shadows keeping hold of Pax, and now free, he readied to spring at Ashmedai again.

"Prrp!"

The ball rolled back between them along the floor, and after it came a bounding cat. But no ordinary cat. It romped through the air, not over stone, its own form more translucent than Ashmedai the gargoyle.

Appearing fluffy despite not having normal fur, the gray, ghostly figure retrieved the rolling ball with a swoop down and launched right up again. It carried the ball in its mouth to Pax as if awaiting an outstretched palm.

What could he do but provide?

The cat dropped the ball into his hand.

"Ash!"

"Pax!"

"Both of you, stop!"

The voices of Bertram and Levi preceded them vaulting down a nearby staircase. Levi skidded to a stop at the bottom when he saw the cat, who was chirping and rolling through the air, encouraging Pax to throw the ball again. Bertram made it a little farther before he, too, stopped, and furrowed his brow.

"*Aurora…?*" Ashmedai's voice echoed, but his monstrous aspects began to fade like so many wisps of shadow, leaving him as his razor-toothed hybrid of truth and elven guise.

"Like Aurora Wood?" Pax tossed the ball up and caught it again.

Aurora chirped and hopped in anticipation.

"You do shimmer, milady. A pleasure to meet you." Pax bowed to her. Then, placing a little magic into the toy, he threw it through the stone into the neighboring room, pleased he was right that she could dash right through the wall after it. "Are we done, then?" He turned jovially to Ashmedai. "That was loads of fun, but I am a bit hungry. I've been thinking about that festival food since we arrived."

Aurora returned before the king could answer, and Pax gladly tossed the ball toward a different corner of the castle for her to give chase.

"You speak the truth. You don't mean any harm," Ashmedai said, all tension gone. Levi joined him, and they shared a curious stare. Then a small humored smile. When Ashmedai turned back to Pax, he bowed. "My apologies. I see now that I hastily judged you. I am afraid I can be rather protective of my love and my people."

"The mark of a good king," Pax said. He didn't mean those words as a reminder for Bertram, but in his periphery, he saw Bertram's posture hunch. "All this from a cat's opinion over Bertie's?"

Aurora returned once more, only this time, she brought the ball to Levi. He chuckled and threw it for her.

"We call her a cathom," Ashmedai said, "and Rora has never steered me wrong before. But my apologies to you as well, steward." He nodded to Bertram. "I do remember you."

"Bertram, please, Your Majesty."

"Bertram. I'll admit, I did have something to do with how the curse here was cast," he said to Pax, "but not on purpose, and I played my role in ending it."

"And this kingdom is better for it, I dare say. It's wonderful!" Pax gushed, meaning it heartily. "The people here seem truly happy."

"You're really a dragon?" Levi asked with new wonder in his expression. "This is just a half form like Ash's?"

"Indeed, it is. If you'd like to give that festival a real show, I could prove—"

"Best you not," Ashmedai said. "Although if you're here, awake, all will know of you eventually, I imagine."

"Oh no. I wasn't planning on sticking around for long once Bertie and my fun is done."

Another hunch was seen. A wince? But why? Was Bertram surprised? Disappointed? What did he expect once his wishes were gone?

The tingle of warmth in Pax's chest that blossomed from the thought of Bertram wanting him to stay was more dangerous than an elemental brawl. He needed to be careful. He needed to be sure that the right boundaries weren't crossed, or he'd be headed down the same perilous path as last time.

"Please accept my apologies." Ashmedai bowed again. "And enjoy our Festival Day."

"Anything you recommend?" Pax skipped to Bertram's side and tugged him close, shaking him a little to dislodge some of that sourness from his expression. How else would he shake it from himself? This was meant to be fun! Just fun. "Best food on a stick maybe?"

Levi chuckled once more—also possibly because Aurora was not done playing fetch.

Then Ashmedai said with confidence, "Fire Chicken. Assuming you don't mind eating something with scales."

Pax wasn't sure how to respond to that.

"I can bring you back to the festival. Travel the shadows again."

"Oh no!" Pax squeezed Bertram closer. "If you don't mind, I'd prefer we walked. The view from up here is quite spectacular. You up for that, Bertie?"

"U-um… yes! A walk might calm my pulse. I am so very sorry, Your Majesties." He pulled away to approach Ashmedai, while Levi was quietly explaining to Aurora that this was the last throw.

"I hope your parents are well," Ashmedai said to Bertram. "I didn't realize you'd be coming today. And please, if I can call you by name, call me Ash as others do."

"Of course."

Pax hurried around them to the front doors, throwing them open to see the waiting sights of the distant village, all alight with color and people in the warm sunlit glow of morning. Levi came up beside him with that newfound wonder, and since it seemed Bertram and Ashmedai were ready to follow, Pax started forward, with Levi keeping pace beside him.

"That's an interesting tattoo you have there." Pax indicated the inked stitches he'd nearly touched.

"Symbolic."

"To never lose your head?"

"At least not a second time."

Oh, Pax liked this place. But as he opened his mouth to ask for that story, he noticed Levi's curious stare was looking a bit smug. "What?"

"Nothing! It's just… a familiar mask."

"Mask? I assure you, my blue friend, this is closer to my true form than most."

"Physically perhaps, but I think I may have seen someone smile like that to hide their loneliness before." He glanced at their companions amiably chatting behind them.

"Loneliness? How could I be lonely amidst a festival?" Pax spread his arms wide to encompass the nearby celebration.

"Easily," Levi said, still smug. "Believe me."

What does he know? Pax thought bitterly and refused to meet his gaze again.

They parted ways with the king and prince consort in the festival throng, and Pax was glad for it. He wasn't *lonely*. He was never lonely! Even when he'd slept, he'd had the memories of all the people he'd known to keep him company in his dreams. And when he didn't, he would have his hoard to return to, filled with memories he might otherwise forget.

"You stole that from the cat?"

Pax startled from his musing over the little red ball clutched in his talons. Another memory to be added to his collection. "She brought a different one back each time. She has plenty."

Bertram chuckled, and Pax palmed the ball, only to flare his fingers outward to show that it was now gone. His focus should be on Bertram and all they could share and enjoy before Pax left him behind as just another memory too.

Which was *better*. It was better....

"I realized something, Pax. Does no one remember you flying from Ruby and over Emerald a decade ago?"

"Oh, that didn't happen in this world. Why complicate the wish? This is about you, Bertie." And how much fun Pax could have in his company. "Now let's go find out why a chicken has scales."

They experienced all the things Pax had intended for them to— shops, games, dancing, food. If that big beautiful blond man, Ambrose, ever came within view, Bertram would carefully steer them a different direction. Sometimes, Pax wished Ambrose would see them. Maybe fuss a little and look put out, jealous to see someone else with the prize Bertram made. The difficult ones to win over and keep were always more worthwhile. Ambrose hadn't been able to do it, but Pax had Bertram positively charmed.

Not that he planned to *keep* him. A brief romance was better. A worthy companion. An exciting adventure. Then Pax would be on to the next one. And the next. That's how it had always been.

Once.

"Pax? Are you having fun? You've seemed a bit... distracted since the castle."

He looked to see Bertram tearing off a bite from his Fire Chicken. At least the cooked version didn't include scales, but the live ones certainly did in this kingdom. He'd even had to step out of the way a few times from some strange creatures rolling through the streets that looked like a cross between a dog and an armadillo.

The sun was getting low, and Pax had maybe been trying a little too hard to enjoy himself. Fun wasn't supposed to be work! He enjoyed Bertram's company more than he'd expected, but he wasn't lonely or wishing for something more than dalliance. Eventually, he'd deposit

Bertram back to his life, wishes fulfilled, and move on to a new conquest without regrets.

"Just enamored, Bertie, by a kingdom so unlike the one I knew—and what those plump lips of yours look like smeared in red."

Bertram laughed, licking his lips of the spicy sauce left from the chicken. "I was thinking we might head to Ruby next, get a room there, so we can wake—"

"And leave before the nighttime merriment!" Pax hurried to squash that idea. Always Ruby on Bertram's mind, where Pax had no intention of returning to. "No, no. We should get a room here."

"All right. Anything else you'd like to try before we do?"

"I was going to say a bite."

"Oh! I already finished—"

Pax kissed the taste from Bertram's mouth, letting his tongue swirl deeply between sauced lips. "Mm... the king made the right recommendation."

Even if his consort was faulty.

Pax plucked the empty stick from Bertram's hand while he was still blinking mutely and tossed it into a nearby rubbish bin. He swept Bertram right off the edge of the path, between two busy stalls, and continued to the empty space behind. Pinning Bertram up against one of the sturdy wooden walls was a far better distraction than fruitless thoughts.

The next kiss still tasted of spicy sweetness, but the base of Bertram beneath was its own kind of spice that spurred Pax to kiss him harder. He could feel the brocade and silk of Bertram's short cloak beneath his hands, with its dragon broach that still held the white flower, since the life Pax had infused in it wouldn't wilt for weeks.

Bertram clung to him in reply, fingers gripping the edges of his vest so that the backs of them brushed Pax's nipples. The tingle the act sent through Pax made him nip with his fangs at Bertram's bottom lip.

"Ah!" Bertram moaned, finding the scales that lined Pax's ribs and trailing his fingers all the way along them. "You said... when your thinner scales are caressed, you feel vibrations through them. Do you feel that here?" He brushed the scales a second time while tonguing Pax's fangs, and then kissed up the side of his mouth to his cheek and the scales lining there.

"Those aren't the thinnest... but I can lead you to all the especially sensitive ones." Pax made good on that by snatching one of Bertram's hands out of his vest and dragging it down his side and hips to his thigh at the edge of his tunic. He brought Bertram's hand beneath the fabric, first to the scales on his outer thigh.

"Pax… I want to ask you something."

"Answers for an experience, right?" He started to lead Bertram's hand around to a few of the scales on the in—

"—in shambles really breaks the heart for Emerald."

Bertram's head snapped to the side at the eruption of voices.

"Come." Pax pulled him from the stall. "We can—"

"Thirty years of unwavering peace. I can still hardly believe how much went wrong in a decade. That they even blocked Veil Curtain travel! I can't fathom it!"

"What…?" Bertram resisted Pax's pull, trying to get around the stall to the path.

"Bertie—"

"I know!" the first continued, even as the passing pair headed away. "Would they storm our borders next? I hear Ash might storm over there after the festival, but he doesn't want to worry anyone. Bloody purists thinking magic and elves are akin to monsters. We could show them!"

Bertram didn't try to follow the conversation but went slack in Pax's hold, staring between the stalls where new passersby were chatting loud enough to cover the rest. "It's gotten worse. I thought I heard something earlier, but… you dragged me away." He whirled on Pax. "You didn't want me to hear it."

"Because it doesn't matter." Pax curled his talons over Bertram's shoulders. "This is just one possible future, Bertie, and we were enjoying ourselves. You can see what's become of Emerald later, tomorrow even—"

"No." Bertram shrugged off his hold, all teasing and flirtation gone, with a sharpness in his eyes that Pax liked, that he'd wanted to see more of, but not when he'd been hoping for a second romp in the bed of an inn. "I need to see it now."

"Now? You heard them. That device, the Veil Curtain, isn't even accessible in Emerald."

"Then you take me. You can fly us there in no time, can't you?"

"Bertie—"

"Now, Pax."

There was clearly no deviating him, much as it irked Pax to have their evening ruined.

"*Pax.*"

"All right! But we better find a clearing in the wood, or we'll give everyone a fright."

CHAPTER 10

WIND SWEPT over Bertram in such great gusts, he clung to the soft strands between Pax's scales in fear of being blown off into the twilight sky. The strands were like fur or the softest hair he'd ever run his fingers through, so fine that the silken tufts weren't visible until someone was close enough to dig their fingers in and touch them.

Bertram couldn't have been closer now, given he was riding Pax's head.

"Enjoying the view up there, Bertie?" Pax called, his voice the same and yet ten times more resonant supported by the diaphragm of a creature of myth.

Bertram's stomach was meanwhile left in the clouds when Pax swooped unexpectedly downward in a dip that made him cling tighter.

They'd found an enormous clearing, and yet Pax had voiced it might not be enough to house his gargantuan girth—his words exactly. That had proven true, though, and Bertram had been caught dumbstruck experiencing Pax's true form within touching distance rather than soaring by in the sky.

He'd blinked and the trees were bowing outward from the force of Pax's unfurled wings and sheer size erupting a gust of wind from his epicenter. Bertram had been blown back too, braced against one such tree, left gaping in amazement. He'd ventured forth slowly to place a hand on the nearest scale, which was on one of Pax's back feet.

"Tickles." He'd stomped the ground, making Bertram snatch his hand back and laugh.

Pax's long neck had coiled around to bring his eyes nearer to Bertram's level. Bertram didn't even clear from the bottom of Pax's jaw to the top of his snout and felt so miniscule and meaningless in his presence.

But he was still angry. Still anxious. Still completely justified in planting his hands on his hips and demanding, "Now tell me how to climb aboard and take me straight to Emerald."

Pax had, though more so nudged his snout between Bertram's legs until he grabbed on for dear life and was deposited onto the back of Pax's neck. Bertram found it easy to climb the scales, using the tufts of fur between them, and eventually found himself right at the top where Pax's horns sprouted from his head like great curved pillars.

He'd nearly fallen right off again when Pax first flapped his wings to take flight.

Pax was just so beautiful. So magical. Magnificent! But he'd kept the truth from Bertram, and all to... what? Eat, drink, and make merry for just a little longer, even brawling pointlessly with Ashmedai, rather than face the truths Bertram had wanted from this wish?

Not that Bertram had thought to ask about Emerald. He'd avoided learning anything just as much as Pax had avoided telling him. The shame in having to admit that made Bertram cling for different reasons, clenching his fists and gazing upon the faint reflection of himself in the nearest scale.

Pax's platinum scales sparkled more than the trees of Amethyst, so shiny and clear in their metallic sheen that he could see himself almost as distinctly as if gazing in water. The feel of the scales was softer than armor. It was armor, but also pliable and so different from the tiny scale still tucked into Bertram's trousers pocket.

He unwound one of his hands from the fur, tightening the straddle of his hips to make up for it, and ran the flat of his palm over the scale, large enough that he could have spread out both hands and not touched its edges. Near him, around where one of the vertical horns grew, were a few smaller, thinner scales outlining it. He reached to touch those too.

"Careful. You'll get me excited," Pax rumbled.

Bertram scowled and dug his free hand back into the fur. "I'm still upset with you."

"Fine. But I'm sure I can win back your favor. I am quite charming, I've heard."

Bertram hated how true that was. Hated how amazed and enamored with Pax he was, because it made it very difficult to move from awe to accusation. He still sometimes couldn't believe this creature's mouth had been on him. He'd had his mouth on Pax. He'd ridden a scaled cock and spilled down Pax's throat—*twice*. The grandeur of that did make scolding Pax seem tiny in comparison.

A slice through the air near Bertram made his breath catch, and he sat up sharply from how he'd been hunkered on Pax's head. "What—"

Again the air was cut, and this time Bertram saw why.

A javelin had soared past them with the speed only a ballista could provide.

"Hang on!" Pax dipped more suddenly and at a sharper angle than before.

Bertram managed to not tumble to his death, still trying to stay upright and see where they were and where the javelins were coming from.

They were almost to Emerald. He could see the kingdom now—and how the walls of the city had been built taller, with ballistae lining every tower, all currently pointed at them!

"Pax!"

"More prepared than last time, eh?" He laughed. *Laughed*, while Bertram's people were trying to shoot them out of the sky!

Pax lurched to the right to escape the next barrage, javelins whizzing past—one, two, three—and one nicked a swath of scales with a metallic shriek. The ricochet made Pax recoil, and he rolled to escape another onslaught, flipping them upside down.

Bertram clung so tightly from the feeling of freefall, he feared he might rip the fur out of Pax's skin and fall to his demise after all.

"Persistent, aren't they?" Pax laughed again. "We'll land, take refuge in the trees, and sneak in another way. I've got you."

Did he? *Did he* have him? Did he even care, with the way he laughed and tumbled through the sky with the same bold abandon as twirling Bertram in a dance?

Bertram missed most of their whirlwind descent, eyes too tightly closed and body plastered against Pax as he clung. Only when he felt the thud of them hit the ground did he realize Pax was shrinking. What was the top of Pax's head was soon his whole neck, then shoulders, and finally, Pax bucked Bertram off to land on his back in a patch of grass and rolled on top of him in elven form, giggling.

"Are you *mad*?" Bertram shouted.

"What? They barely grazed me! I must commend them for that, though. I don't remember the last time I got dinged."

"And I never wanted the experience! Now, off!" Bertram pushed him with all his fury behind the shove, and though the resistance he met made his arms ache, Pax scrambled away.

The sun was setting, the forest they'd landed in growing darker by the moment. Surely, if the people of Emerald were ready to shoot down a dragon before knowing anything about it, getting inside the city wouldn't be easy even at nightfall.

"Hide your ears," Bertram hissed. "If they're this against magic and elves, you can't look like one."

"Not even but a young adolescent." Pax attempted innocence and shrank to his teenage self.

"No!" Bertram leapt to his feet with a stomp. "Don't you understand? If things are as bad as I fear, then there is no mercy for anyone!"

That, at least, wiped the smile from Pax's face. He stood as well, remaining his younger form, but not hiding his ears. "They won't see anything if I don't wish them to. And we could simply leave, you know. End your wish."

"Before I know what's happened? I can't. I need to see what went wrong. I need to know who's responsible." *Besides me*, Bertram thought, pushing past Pax to head toward the sound of panicked voices and what must be Emerald's city wall. "If you want to be useful, figure out how we get into the city without being seen or having to use the gate."

"I *can* do that." Pax followed him.

"Good."

"Bertie—"

"What?" Bertram whirled around. Pax did look so very innocent and meek in that form, smaller than Bertram, with his eyes seeming genuinely startled and maybe a little ashamed.

"Don't get ahead of me, or you might be spotted. I can handle the hard part." Pax grasped his wrist and took the lead, guiding them through the trees.

They weren't near the path Bertram was familiar with, coming upon Emerald's wall from a side far from the gate. Pax didn't seem to care when they reached the edge of the trees and saw nothing but unyielding stone. He took a breath and the world stilled before he made his first step into the open.

There were guards up on the ramparts, but they weren't moving. They seemed to be scanning the trees but had been frozen, as if time itself had stopped.

And Pax was translucent! So was Bertram! More so than Ashmedai could be or even the cat Aurora.

"You can halt time and make yourself invisible?"

"*Nearly* invisible. And step out of time. It's more so that we're moving so fast, they wouldn't notice us even if we weren't virtually impossible to see."

"But what about—" Bertram stopped before finishing the thought, because Pax wasn't slowing down, but led them straight through the stone, as if it, or they, weren't any more solid than they looked. They resurfaced inside, where more guards could be seen, also seemingly frozen. "You can walk through walls?"

"I can do many things you haven't yet seen. Now, where do you wish to go because I can't keep us like this forever. Well, I can, but it's a bit itchy."

"This way." Bertram pulled ahead, careful not to yank from Pax's hold or lose his protection and magic, much as he might wish to. He was still upset! And would not be as easily charmed as Pax hoped.

It was strange walking past people who clearly couldn't see them, who seemed more like statues than flesh and blood, but Bertram focused on getting them somewhere hidden and close enough to the castle that, once they learned something from the streets, they could reach it quickly.

The side of the city they'd entered from meant Jafari's was close, and it seemed both fitting and an added blow that the alley beside it was the best place Bertram could think of for them to go—right where he'd first met Pax.

"Now what?" Pax whispered once they reached it, keeping close beside him.

Noise from the city erupted into real time with them safely out of view, and given leave to pull from Pax's hold, Bertram did so. "Don't use any magic unless you have to. We need—"

The side door into Jafari's opened, and Pax's hand was back on Bertram in moments, making them nearly invisible again. With night falling, they blended into the shadows seamlessly.

"Hurry. We can't let them catch us leaving, or the Jafaris might be implicated in our escape. They've been through enough."

Escape?

Bertram watched a human woman exit, carrying a child of no more than two, with the slightest of pointed ears, like a quarter-elf, and two older children followed, their ears the same. Then the man who'd spoken appeared, shutting the door behind them, a half-elf with red hair.

Bertram knew him. He was ten years older than he last remembered, but that was Levi's brother, Leslie, who'd apprenticed at Jafari's and now had his own shop down the street.

Or *had*.

"This is foolish," the woman hissed. "There are guards everywhere."

"Chasing a dragon," Leslie countered. "There will be fewer guards than ever while they hunt that thing. Now is the best time to try to reach my brother's kingdom."

"Without magic?" She touched his wrist, and on it was a limiter that glowed red, something they must not be able to remove themselves. The children wore them too, even the smallest one, dozing on his mother's shoulder. "Levi said they'd come for us if he didn't hear anything by the end of Festival Day. If we just wait until morning—"

"They intercepted one of Levi's letters. That's why they were ready for the dragon. They think the dragon is Levi, or the Shadow King, or some other monster."

"Maybe it is, come to save us."

"Then we need to take the opening they've given us and go."

She held Leslie's stare, clearly not convinced, afraid, and rightly so with three children. That they feared this greatly at all formed the heaviest of weights in Bertram's stomach. All because some of them were elven? Because they had magic?

"If only that awful Penelope had never become queen," the woman said and leaned forward to rest her forehead against Leslie's chest.

Penelope? Then she'd roused her followers and took over just like she wanted.

But what of Dain?

"Mama—" the middle child, a girl, began to tug at her mother's skirts, only for torchlight to suddenly shine down the alley.

"Halt! We seek the kin of the Shadow Prince!"

"No...," Leslie murmured. He gathered his family behind him, and Bertram felt Pax's grip on his wrist tighten.

"How unsurprising," one of the guards said, followed by three others, "to find the stitched monster's brother in the streets at near curfew, skulking behind an old haunt, at the same time a dragon descends from over the Shadow Lands forest."

"It's Amethyst now." Leslie stood tall. He looked taller than Levi, broader too, despite being the younger brother. Living in Emerald but being a half-elf, he was a man of almost fifty, who looked about thirty. "We were headed home before curfew and sought shelter after the chaos erupted."

"Did you?" the guard scoffed. "We'll let the council decide if that's true. Tomorrow. You're spending tonight in a cell until we catch that beast."

"No!" the wife cried, backing closer to where Bertram and Pax stood and pulling her children with her—only to trip and begin to fall backward.

Pax caught her, whole and very visible suddenly, and no longer keeping himself or Bertram veiled. "Not to worry, milady. No family should get put in a cell for existing."

She shrieked and jerked from Pax's hold, her children clinging to her closer at the sudden appearance of two strangers from out of nothing.

"Mages!" the head guard howled and seized a stunned Leslie. "Capture them, now!"

"Please, do try," Pax said, as they charged.

His next step changed a diminutive teenager into a grown and towering elf, extra clothing shed, and scales beginning to speckle him, morphing right to his dragonkind form.

"D-dragon!" one realized as they skidded to a halt.

"And what do dragons do?" Pax hunkered like he meant to vault forward, only to roar, and an ice-like mist poured from his mouth.

The wife screamed once more, her children turning in toward her in fear for their lives, as the three guards who'd charged became frozen where they stood, covered in ice like the statues of the once Frozen Kingdom.

"No need to fear," Pax said with a bow when the wife and babes realized they hadn't been hit. "This dragon is on your side. And they'll melt free eventually."

"Dragon!" the head guard yelled and fled out of the alley, leaving Leslie behind.

"*Don't!*" Bertram grabbed the back of Pax's tunic to keep him from following. "You'll only cause more chaos. We have to help them and get to the castle."

"And here I thought I had helped," Pax said with a twinge.

"You did. Thank you."

"Thank you," Leslie echoed, going to his family and hugging them close. The children were staring at Pax in wonder now, and the babe on the mother's shoulder was awake, squirming and fussing to get out of her grasp and touch Pax.

He took hold of the tiny hand reaching for him and shook it carefully like greeting a gentleman, even with what looked like frightening talons. "Seems you need an escape route, hm? I'll make you as invisible as I can, but I suggest you make haste, keep quiet, and head straight for the gate."

The limiter upon the young boy shattered into a harmless rain of sparkles, as did the ones on his siblings, and Leslie too. Mist seeped from Pax then, as if created from his very being, rolling outward from the alley and into the streets.

Bertram imagined the thick fog filling every corner of the city, but even with that as cover, Pax's hold on the small babe's hand became the starting point of a covering of shadow that faded the family into the mist like they weren't there at all.

The babe pulled away to stare in wonder at how his hand was vanishing but clearly not hurting or scaring him. He was soon impossible to see, as the shadows crept higher.

Leslie was last to be covered, and he squinted at Bertram as he was engulfed. "The steward from Sapphire? You came to help us?"

"Yes. And I am going to do more, I promise."

As soon as they were lost in shadows and mist, Bertram heard the sound of their footfalls leaving the alley. They could make it. And once Bertram learned more, once he saw his castle and truly faced what the future might hold, he could go home and erase this future from ever happening.

That's what he had to do... wasn't it?

"Here! Down here!" the guard who'd fled announced, and a dozen more stormed down the alley, leaving no way for Bertram and Pax to escape.

"So much for the subtle approach!"

Bertram's feet left the ground as Pax grabbed him beneath his arms and took flight. His smaller, dragonkind wings spread wide enough that Bertram could see their shadow on the ground, making him look winged too.

A guard with a crossbow fired, and Bertram tensed, awaiting its puncture through his chest, only for Pax to flap upward out of its path and swerve swiftly over the top of the nearby buildings. He dropped them into the next alley with a clear line on the castle gate.

"We can end this now and return—"

"Not yet." Bertram raced ahead.

"Bertie!" Pax caught him and veiled them like before, a trick of shadow magic he knew now, having seen it on Leslie's family.

They continued forward, and Bertram's questions about Dain were answered in gruesome detail upon the gate. He wouldn't have recognized the bones that adorned the metal spokes like the masthead of a ship if not for the tattered remains of Dain's familiar robe.

His stomach dropped at the sight, but he refused to be deterred from getting inside the castle.

Pax walked them into the courtyard as easily as they'd breached the city wall, then again, straight through the castle doors. Inside, the castle seemed frightfully still, and Pax brought them out of concealment, likely thinking they were alone.

Voices soon proved they weren't, in heated debate coming from the second floor, and Pax yanked Bertram toward a room at their right. He used the door this time and shut them inside, but they could hear the discussion coming down the stairs.

"—emergency gathering of the council to determine the scope of the dragon threat, who is responsible, and whether we march on the Shadow Lands before dawn."

"Are we informing the queen?"

"What for? The council's decision is the only one that matters now."

They were mad. They were all mad!

"Learned enough yet?" Pax whispered.

Bertram reeled on him with a snarl. He was his adult form but without scales. He changed forms and wielded magic like it was all some game, but this wasn't a game to Bertram. It wasn't some lark, just some possible future. It was real—as real as that fleeing family.

"What are you doing in here?"

Bertram turned with a gasp to find that the room wasn't empty.

Worse, he knew their companion.

Penelope.

PAX READIED to knock the woman prone or flee with Bertram in tow, but the moment he thought to act, he saw how resigned and unlikely to act she was in contrast—even after she'd looked upon Pax and noticed his elven ears that were apparently an affront in this kingdom now.

She looked vaguely familiar to him, if a decade older than the young woman in Emerald's castle courtyard where he'd first spotted Bertram. She was dressed more nobly now, in a brocade dress with cape and crown. A recognizable crown, given a version of it was in Pax's hoard.

"Storming the castle? Escaping the dungeons? Or just looking for a room to hide in for a breath like I was?" She hadn't even stood from where she sat upon the base of this kingdom's Veil Curtain. It had a glowing red band around its rings like what Pax had destroyed on the family he'd saved.

"Penelope." Bertram went to her, stern with head held high and every bit the bold king Pax first encountered. "What have you done? What have you allowed to take root here? I know what happened to your brother was a tragedy, but to fester your anger into this? Into bones dangling from the castle gates?"

She winced, but though she scowled up at Bertram, she made no move to rise or call for the guards. "And who are you to condemn me? No citizen of this kingdom, at least not one I know. Do you think this is what I wanted when I took the throne? The council was supposed to give voice to the people, but when no one agreed, I simply replaced those in contention with my views with those who weren't. Eventually, there was one unified voice, and only then did I realize how shrill it had become."

"Then stop this. Disband the council. Start over—"

"I don't have that power anymore. And what's it matter? They can't defeat the other kingdoms, all with ancient magic. You've even brought some with you. A rather formidable-looking elf. Do you command the dragon, sir?"

"In a manner of speaking." Pax moved to Bertram's side.

"I just wanted to stop feeling afraid." She rose at last, not in challenge but like she would accept any fate thrown at her. "Now my streets are filled with more fear than sense. Maybe a dragon will finally make a difference."

Pax sneered, though he couldn't say why her words stung so much.

"Are you going to call the guards?" Bertram asked, as she walked around them.

"I don't even know who you are."

"I... I'm just trying to get home. I didn't realize how bad things could become here until I saw it."

"Then go." She gestured to the Veil Curtain. "I can remove its limiters—"

Pax waved a hand, and they burst into sparks like the ones on the family's wrists.

She hardly seemed fazed by the display, merely nodded and continued out of the room.

"We're going to Ruby."

"What?" Pax spun to see Bertram getting onto the platform. "Why? We needn't go there at all. This is over—"

"Did you know I was making a fool's wish?" Bertram asked. "That the answer would be this obvious?"

"I can't see the future without experiencing it, Bertie, but I had an inkling this would be a 'careful what you wish for' sort of ending. The important thing was that you needed to unwind before getting struck by reality."

"You mean distracted." His fists were clenched and practically shaking. "How could you let me revel and make merry knowing this might be the fate of my kingdom?"

"Don't pretend like you didn't enjoy every moment and *asked me* to help you make merry. Besides, I didn't think this was your kingdom anymore, given how quick you were to abandon it."

Bertram's cringe made him instantly regret those words.

He'd only wanted—

"Like you've never abandoned something? You fled Ruby the moment you woke up and keep avoiding going back. Every time I suggest it, you suggest something else. Why?"

"I... don't feel like discussing that. Now, isn't it time this wish ended—"

"Tell me. I think we've shared enough *experience* for me to earn that."

"It isn't your business," Pax said firmly. "Now, are we through—"

"No. Because I can't go back to a world where you still call the shots, when I don't know if I can trust you." He activated the controls on the Veil Curtain, causing its rings to begin rotating.

"Bertie...."

Lightning erupted along its rings, spinning faster and faster. "If you won't come with me to Ruby, then I'll find out the truth without you."

"Bertram!"

A flash burst brightly from where the lightning collided. Then it was gone, and so was Bertram, leaving the rings to slowly halt.

And leaving Pax alone.

CHAPTER 11

RUBY'S VEIL Curtain was in its castle like in Emerald and Sapphire, and Bertram stepped from the platform to find the very normal and comforting sight of the throne room—and Ruby's King and Prince Consort, who immediately spotted him.

"Bertram?"

Travel was slowing for the day, with few people in line to leave Ruby now that night had fallen. Not that visitors could tell time of day easily in the Ruby Kingdom, tucked into a series of connected cavernous mountains where sunlight only reached due to an intricate system of mirrors.

The throne room of the castle was in a grand hall, with the Veil Curtain to the side of the Ruby throne, a seat carved from stone that reached as tall as the ceiling. It had once been inlaid with rubies, lavish in its show of wealth, but the gems had been replaced with colored stones as a sign of the monarch's commitment to ending class division.

This was the kingdom that Bertram had most wanted to emulate, and right there halfway down the hall was Enzario "Enzo" Dragonbane, the Ruby King, his husband, Cullen, and a pair of council members.

One council member, a farell—half elf and half dwarf—named Vanek, who'd also been a former activist when the class divide was at its greatest. He stood beside a familiar face from Sapphire, the elf Raphael. Bertram had nearly forgotten that the pair hit it off when Raphael was visiting the Ruby Kingdom and decided to stay.

It seemed they had somewhere to be, for they nodded their farewells, leaving Enzo and Cullen to greet Bertram.

"We haven't seen you in ages!" Enzo embraced him, also a farell and bastard son to the late Ruby King before him. "But getting in a little late for a diplomatic call, aren't you?" He was the only leader shorter than Bertram and a brilliant inventor before he'd become king. He and Bertram had always gotten along well, and Bertram had served a few years' apprenticeship under him before returning to Sapphire to solidify his role as steward.

Cullen had often said the two could have been long-lost family, given their similarly dark skin and overall bronze coloring, but Enzo's hair and eyes were a shade or two lighter than Bertram's—and of course, Enzo's eyes held a ruby sheen just like how Bertram's had been emerald.

And needed to be again.

"Has something happened?" Cullen asked after embracing Bertram in kind, which made Bertram worry he'd given away his discontent with a telling scowl.

Former Amethyst Prince before Ashmedai took the throne, Cullen could have been a twin or brother to Levi, even more so than Levi's actual brother, with the same build, violet eyes, and similar features, but with brown hair instead of crimson. He was a being as magical and unique as any wild magic folk, maybe even more so than a dragon.

The curse that had taken hold of Amethyst and made it the Shadow Lands had partially been caused because Cullen discovered Ashmedai's hidden identity and was afraid. In his attempt to banish what he feared was a monster trying to trick him, he'd ended up imprisoned in the Amethyst for a thousand years, and all his people had become monsters instead. Freed when the Fairy Prince, Nemirac, drained the Amethyst as part of a futile attempt to ascend as a demon, Cullen had become a dancer of the void, a creature of shadow capable of traveling through the veil between worlds even more effortlessly than how Ashmedai traveled through shadows. Maybe closer to what Pax could do really, like stepping out of time.

"Yes and no," Bertram admitted. "It's not really diplomacy that brings me here."

"It certainly never needs to be, but you look unwell." Enzo squeezed his arm like a worried godfather. He wasn't wearing his crown, since like Bertram, he rarely chose to. "I assume news from Emerald hasn't been good?"

"No. But the reason I came was… I was hoping to hear the story of Dragonbane and the platinum dragon he drove from the city. There's a tapestry depiction of it, isn't there?"

"And many written accounts," Cullen said, as much an expert on Ruby and its history these days as any native. "You came for that?"

"I know it might seem silly, and if you're busy, I can find the hangings myself—"

"Nonsense!" Enzo kept hold of him, taking Bertram's arm to guide him from the throne room. "We'll take you. It's my family's history, after all. And we've missed you. I can't remember the last time you came for a visit."

Cullen took Bertram's other side, and he saw how citizens in line or leaving the throne room eyed their royals curiously, bookending someone who must have been a stranger to them. At least Bertram's relationship with the rulers of Ruby hadn't diminished too much despite his seclusion in Sapphire.

Outside the throne room was yet another grand hall that made up the castle foyer. Twin staircases branched down from the entrance on either side, and Enzo took the rightward one. Ahead of them, in the center of the foyer, with ceilings even taller than the throne room, was a statue of the dragon.

A fourth the scale of the real thing, Bertram had been told. That was the best guess the stories had. Now, having seen a dragon in person, Bertram knew they could probably double that to reach the truth.

If this was meant to be Pax. It didn't look like him, other than being scaled and winged, with clawed hands and feet. The snout wasn't right, and it only had two horns instead of four. Its body coiled up around a central pillar like a menace about to breathe fire.

Or ice.

Or any number of other elements.

Although, it didn't look platinum either, since it was made from the reddish stone of the mountains and looked more reddish still from the ruby-like crystals in sconces around the hall, reflected by torches.

The castle was built into the mountain itself, but the floors had been sculpted smooth, and many pillars were carved into the likeness of former warriors and kings, like the Dragonbane progenitor, on one of the pillars nearest the dragon. He was merely an armored dwarf to Bertram, not even with a discernible face, since he wore a helm with wings up either side—feathered, not dragon-like. He had a long single-braided beard and thick mustache, with a squat but powerful body, and held a large maul. Never a king himself, but he'd been such a well-known and celebrated hero that his descendant, Enzo's grandfather, had used his glory as reason for the family to take the throne.

A sniff near Bertram drew his eyes up to find Cullen leaning close with a crinkle in his nose. "Were you at Festival Day?"

"How did you know?"

"A certain shadowy signature is a little too familiar for me to not know it." Cullen grinned. "You're not still intimidated by Ash, are you? He's really very kind and gentle."

And capable of descending upon an attacking dragon like a wave of angry shadows. "Only a little. Are you not going to the festival this year?" Bertram hadn't even considered that Cullen and Enzo might already be in Amethyst, and not in the Ruby castle to aid him. After all their tangled and tragic history, Cullen and Ashmedai were good friends again.

"We are," Enzo answered. "We had some business to finish, is all."

"And the festival is best at night," Cullen said. "We always have time for you, though. We just won't want to keep Ash and Levi waiting too long. I think Levi's been anxious, worried about his brother still living in Emerald."

"Yes. Of course." Bertram hid his grimace. Half of him thought of this world like a dream, which he knew was Pax's problem too, but the other half of him couldn't let anyone who was in danger go without help.

Then again, Pax hadn't either. He'd stepped in to help Leslie's family, who were on their way to Amethyst right that moment.

Bertram should tell Cullen and Enzo, tell someone, anyone, but what stopped him was knowing he could do better and make it so they never had to escape Emerald at all.

If he could trust Pax.

"What do you know of the story?" Enzo asked, after they'd wound him through several corridors to reach one with the tapestries Bertram remembered lining the length of a wall.

Like most of the decorations in the castle, they were stitched with varied shades of red, accented in browns and goldenrod yellow—except for the dragon, who in these depictions was as close to platinum as thread could make him, in silvery white.

They came upon the six-paneled story backward, so Bertram saw the ending first. Dragonbane, like how he was depicted on his pillar, held his hammer high in seeming victory in front of a caved-in rock wall, to the right of the Ruby gemstone.

Next was the cave-in itself, showing the dragon's neck hunched as it shied from the falling rocks.

Before that was the pair to the left of the Ruby, as Dragonbane fended the dragon off.

Before that was Dragonbane riding it. The picture didn't look like a midair fight, and all Bertram could think of was the feeling of riding Pax, how small he'd felt, how helpless, and yet also protected. He'd been angry with Pax for not taking the attacks from Emerald seriously, but Pax had kept him safe, flipped and pivoted to ensure that the one javelin that did hit them hit *him*, sparing Bertram from even a scratch.

Next was Dragonbane and the dragon facing each other again, but there was a crowd around them, not the close walls of deep caves. It could have been a sparring match or a play for how it looked like the dragon was enjoying itself.

The first banner was the dragon alone, curled around the Ruby gemstone as if in slumber and surrounded by riches, like that cavern held its hoard. There weren't any riches there now, and Pax's hoard was somewhere else.

Was Bertram wrong? Was this not Pax at all?

"I've seen this before, but I'd like to know what really happened," Bertram said.

"I don't know if I can say what *really* happened." Enzo chuckled. "But I can recite the story as it was told to me." He stepped forward to start from the beginning. "It starts with the beginning of Gemstone's history. The first dwarves always lived in the mountains, slowly excavating for riches and digging deeper to make their homes. Many dragons lived here too, flocking to the concentration of magic that had formed the Ruby gemstone.

"The dwarves knew the greatest of riches must lie in the heart of the mountains even before they'd seen it, because dragons were often exiting and returning through an opening in the mountain peak. So, they excavated further, dug deeper, and when they finally found the gemstone, they were greeted by the dragons as friends, impressed by dwarven ingenuity, and they shared their riches with them.

"They helped the dwarves build this kingdom, but slightly away from where the Ruby rested so it could be enjoyed by all. The Ruby continued to grow, until it was the size we know it as now, and the first of the wild magic folk used it as a conduit to travel from their realm to ours. We know this as the first golden age, when all five kingdoms were formed, and the races all lived in harmony.

"It is said that the dragons were protective of mortals and our varying longevity. Humans having but brief lives, dwarves and half-elves twice as long, farells twice as that, and full elves even longer, but still only a fraction of how long a dragon lives, or those of wild magic.

"Ashmedai could tell you all this, though he rarely speaks of those times. His people, learning the ways of mankind, grew more like us too, and realized that with their power, they could be like gods to us, rather than just wise watchmen like the dragons. So, they siphoned more and more from the gemstones, pulling power from their old world that became corrupted when it reached this one and corrupted them too.

"The corruption spread, and the kingdoms began fighting. The dragons got pulled into it, forcing some of the wild magic folk back home, destroying others, and others still, like Ash, chose to leave on their own, ashamed of what they'd let happen. But with the wild magic folk gone, the wars didn't stop. It grew worse, the kingdoms became more divided, and the dragons chose to leave too.

"We were worse than the corrupted wild magic folk who'd made demons of themselves because some of them realized their folly and retreated, while mortals refused to admit that we might be at fault too.

"The part of that history less seldom told is that some of the dragons thought it better to exterminate us, forcing us to rise up against them. Or, if they were found slumbering, they'd devour whoever disturbed them and wreak havoc on nearby lands. Eventually, they were all killed, had long since left, or were asleep in places we couldn't reach.

"Except for the platinum dragon of Ruby. He cherished the riches of our kingdom so much, he refused to go."

"Then… he was causing trouble?" Bertram asked. "He was a threat to the people of Ruby?"

"The legend certainly paints my ancestor as a hero who saved us from a threat." Enzo gestured to the tapestries. "But it's said he took pity on the dragon for being the last of its kind. The banner showing an audience around them is meant to indicate the dragon was imprisoned in our coliseum. There are records of Dragonbane triumphing again and again in feats of combat there, both against other warriors, and hoping to subdue the dragon rather than slay it. It seems the dragon eventually escaped, however, but he still spared it and merely drove it into the caverns."

"Maybe because… the dragon hadn't meant to cause trouble? Maybe it had been subdued."

"Maybe. Though there are elemental scorch marks in places along the border stones of our city that are supposedly from their last battle, far from the safety of the coliseum."

"Then your ancestor was a powerful mage as well as a fighter?"

"I don't think so. The stories only talk of him using a maul, not magic."

"But he's a dragon!" Bertram realized how emphatically he'd spoken. "*Was* a dragon. Surely, one man with a hammer would be no match against that, especially trapped in a coliseum together. A platinum dragon could have eaten him in a gulp. Erased him to nothing."

"Why do you think it became a legend?" Enzo smiled. "I'm afraid, without anyone left who witnessed those events in person, we'll never know what the dragon wanted, what his relationship might have been to Dolgar Dragonbane, or whether it was really a mercy to drive him away."

"It seems you have a newfound interest in dragons." Cullen fingered the dragon brooch holding Bertram's short cloak in place.

"Yes, perhaps I do." The brooch still had the white flower in it. The bloom had just been so beautiful, given new life from a real dragon's touch, that he'd tucked it back into place when he dressed that morning.

"Oh!" Cullen's attention turned toward a candle clock down the corridor. "It's later than I thought. We really should be going. Come with us, Bertie? You couldn't have experienced all Amethyst has to offer before nightfall."

"I… I might stay and visit for a bit, but you go. Enjoy the festival and say hello to Ashmedai and Levi for me." Who might reveal that Bertram had been there with a *dragon*, but by the time any revelations surfaced, he hoped to be long gone.

"If you explore, you might run into some familiar faces in the streets who plan to head to the festival themselves." Cullen grinned cryptically, which intrigued Bertram, but he was distracted, knowing he likely wouldn't learn the truth unless Pax told him.

One thing was certain—if Pax was the dragon from the story and this Dolgar was really just a man with a maul, then Pax allowed himself to be driven away. He'd allowed himself to be buried.

Why?

Cullen didn't need nearby shadows to travel. He and Enzo embraced Bertram again, said their goodbyes, and then with an eruption of closely woven shadows from Cullen's very being, they were gone. Somehow, Cullen doing that never unnerved Bertram the way seeing Ashmedai in full form did.

Maybe it was the teeth.

Bertram studied the tapestries a while longer but eventually strolled back through the castle and out into the courtyard, which opened to an area with shops, taverns, and a theater. Where once a large statue of Dolgar Dragonbane had stood was now one of the rulers of each kingdom when this new golden age had been ushered in. Mavis, Ashmedai, Jack, Reardon, and Enzo each gripped the handle of a great magical maul in unity.

Only now, what they'd built together was poised to crumble.

"Bertram?"

Bertram turned toward Chadwick's Pub, where a trio of men were poised to enter but had stopped upon seeing him. Among them was Wynn, his father's friend, the half-elf who'd left Sapphire for Ruby. But as pleased as Bertram was to see him, the pair with Wynn were a greater surprise.

Human in appearance, similar in height and build, and older than Bertram remembered, maybe as though in their forties now, one had green eyes and auburn hair, the other's eyes blue with his long hair snowy white.

"Uncle Jack? Reardon?"

"SO, WE figured we'd meet up with Wynn for a pint and then head to Amethyst to join the others," Reardon finished.

The four sat at a table in the pub, all with pints in front of them. The former kings of Emerald and Sapphire weren't dressed in any finery, but as simple travelers, who most people might not even recognize as two of the very monarchs portrayed in the statue outside.

"Only Zephyr and Nigel know we're headed home," Jack said. "We wanted it to be a surprise. I'm sure your mother will scold us terribly for not warning her in our last letter."

"She will." Bertram chuckled. "But she'll be happy to see you. *I'm* happy to see you."

"Agreed!" Wynn raised his mug in a toast.

They brought their mugs together and drank.

"It's only been a year since we last visited," Reardon said after downing a few gulps.

That eased Bertram, knowing it hadn't been the whole decade, but that they must pass through the kingdoms regularly. It might still be a year before he'd see them again in his time, but he couldn't rely on them to save the day. He had to solve Emerald's problems on his own.

And he did have to solve them, didn't he? If nothing else, his wish had proved he couldn't walk away, and he felt a sting of shame that in this version of the world... he had.

"We'll head to Sapphire before it gets late," Jack said. "Although, I think Zephyr and Nigel might try to coax your parents to join the festival and meet us there. I know Josie hasn't wanted to leave the kingdom unattended for too long given all that's happening in Emerald."

"Thirty years." Reardon scowled and didn't finish the gulp he'd been about to take. "Thirty years, and in a decade, they reverted to even worse than my childhood. Of course we had to come home."

"And many people will be happy for it." Wynn patted Reardon's shoulder. "But you're still enjoying retirement, I trust?"

Reardon leaned in toward Jack, and the pair grinned and shared a kiss. "Very much. I never thought I'd see even one other kingdom, and now we've been to other lands that feel like other worlds. Some of it is as backwards as Emerald has returned to, but there's always something good to be found, something wondrous that I am thankful to share with my true love rather than having remained stagnant and unhappy in a life that would have been uneventful and far shorter."

"And I am pleased to share those things with you, my little king, that are eventful and *longer* than expected."

"Jack!" Reardon shoved him.

Like Cullen and Enzo, they had always been a beacon of what to strive for in Bertram's eyes, both as leaders and as companions. It eased Bertram further to see that they hadn't lost a step, even older, having traveled through un-immortal lands, and burdened by their return being to face an unwelcome change in one of their kingdoms.

Jack even still called Reardon his "little king" despite Reardon being taller and neither being kings anymore.

"Were you... disappointed in me for deciding to not take up the crown in Emerald?"

They turned to Bertram with a start, and Jack reached over to take his hand.

"Wipe that sorrow away right now," he commanded. "We've had enough regret in this family, centuries worth, for you to carry your own."

"The important thing is that you're happy," Reardon said. "We would never be disappointed in you."

"Even with Emerald in such a sorry state?"

"There is no guarantee you could have changed that," Jack said.

No, but he hadn't even tried.

"I need to go." Bertram squeezed Jack's hand but pushed from the table.

"You just got here," Wynn protested.

"And we've missed you," Reardon urged. "We want to hear what you've been up to."

"And I shall tell you," Bertram promised. "Next time I see you."

He raced from the pub with them still calling after him, but he wouldn't be stopped. It didn't matter what Pax was hiding. It *did*, but he could wait to learn it. He needed to return to Pax, return home, and end this wish at last.

When he returned to the castle foyer, he saw guards starting to shut the doors into the throne room, closing off travel through the Veil Curtain for the night.

"Wait!" Bertram waved and ran faster, grateful that one of the guards halted the other, and they allowed him to be the last person to escape inside, shutting the doors behind him.

"See, horrible here."

Bertram gazed down the long expanse of the hall, panting and breathless, to see Pax draped over the Ruby throne. He doubted Pax had been there a moment ago, where the guards might have seen him and scolded his insolence.

But he'd come after Bertram. He'd followed him, even though he clearly detested the idea of returning to this kingdom.

That loathing was present in the tightness of his shoulders, despite his attempt to look casual. It was in the creases in the corners of his eyes too, betraying his smile as false. It hurt him to be here, and that made Bertram certain that Pax was the dragon from the story, even if his depictions weren't always right and the truth of what happened remained untold.

He also looked unfairly attractive sprawled across the throne like that.

Pax seemed to be waiting for Bertram to ask about his past, and oh, Bertram was curious, but there was something he needed to say first.

"I'm ready to go home now."

CHAPTER 12

TEN YEARS AGO

ONLY A moment had passed since Pax and Bertram left this room. *Days* had passed for them, but only a moment here, where the royal chambers belonged to Bertram, and the kingdom was not yet in turmoil.

Pax could see the weariness from what they'd experienced on Bertram's face, as he gasped at the change in location and looked around in relieved wonder. He raced to his window and threw it open to see the sun beginning to set like it already had in the time they'd come from.

The streets were quiet and calm.

He paused at his desk on his way back to Pax. It was covered in crumpled pieces of parchment, and he gathered them all up and dumped them into his rubbish bin. Pax wondered what had been written on them but imagined it didn't much matter now.

"Thank you," Bertram said when he returned to Pax, showing a swirl of emotions in his *emerald* eyes. He wore that fetching green, blue, and turquoise doublet as well—though he didn't have his crown, since Pax kept that. "And I'm sorry."

Sorry? Had he learned something? Did he know? If he did, he didn't say more or ask any questions, merely waited for Pax's response.

Pax had no intention of offering anything. It had already felt strange and invasive being back inside the Ruby castle, but then, he'd never spent much time there, and Gar never sat on that throne. That had made it easier than venturing out of the throne room might have been.

"Mortals have notoriously short tempers." Pax shrugged.

Bertram snorted but nodded, like that was all he'd been apologizing for.

"I… was perhaps being a selfish ass," Pax admitted, "but you did need to learn more than one lesson from that wish."

"Yes. One I must believe I can fix, and the other… I don't want to forget."

He reached for Pax, brushing his palm along Pax's cheek, and drew him down to his height for a kiss. It began tentative but deepened with passionate abandon that urged Pax to wrap his arms around Bertram and hold him tight.

The aftermath left Pax unable to speak.

"I… can't imagine anything you found in Ruby was an aphrodisiac," he finally said.

"No." Bertram snorted again. "But maybe indulgence on occasion is a good thing."

"You mean distraction?"

"That too." Bertram pressed both hands to Pax's chest and started to push him back toward the bed. "I have so much ahead of me to figure out. And I will. I will do my duty. But tonight, I want you. If there is still something appealing in a king who almost ran from everything."

He'd accused Pax of running too. And he wasn't wrong about that. Pax had run, he'd skulked away, but he hadn't abandoned anything. He was the one….

Pax pushed those traitorous thoughts from his mind. Never again. But indulgence and distraction he could provide. He lifted Bertram around the waist and tossed him onto the bed to land softly with a playful bounce. Then he leapt after Bertram, achieving a height almost as if he'd unfurled his wings before he landed upon him with a predatory prowl.

Bertram laughed. It was clear he'd set aside his guilt, his uncertainty, and was resolved to do what he could in this time to change his fate and the fate of his kingdom. That was what a dragon's wish was for, and if Pax got something out of it too, all the better.

The kiss he initiated started as passionate as the first had become. He straddled Bertram, settling in comfortably with Bertram between his thighs, and began a slow rolling thrust. Returned to where they'd been interrupted behind that stall in Amethyst, Pax intended to spur them back to arousal without losing a step of momentum.

"I am going to tongue your sac, mouth your shaft, and tease your tip with my fangs," Pax husked, undoing Bertram's doublet to get at his chest and the soft sprinkling of hair there, "before slithering my tongue back inside your slit—"

"*Pax*." Bertram bucked upward, already hard in his trousers against Pax's hip.

"Or… shall I glide my tongue along the walls of your true entrance and tickle your insides until you're trembling for my cock?" He had one hand in Bertram's doublet, pulling open his undershirt, while the other shoved down Bertram's front. He palmed him, stroked him, while Pax's own cock sprang free from the skimpy confines of his undergarment, leaking wetness that he smeared against Bertram's thigh.

The angle was too constricting, so Pax willed his covering to vanish and pulled free the ties of Bertram's trousers. He yanked them down Bertram's hips to rut against skin, shifting positions until it was cock against cock.

"Yes…." Bertram thrusted up harder. "All of it… *all* of it… but…."

"But?" Pax dragged his teeth beneath Bertram's ear and down his neck. "Are my promises not enough for you, sweet king?"

"They are," Bertram groaned, "but please… please… let me see your scales. All of them."

Clothing was but a construct of magic and the mind for Pax. He need only will the rest away and his outfit melted, almost as if it formed his scales and other metallic aspects that replaced it.

He sat upright, still thrusting their cocks together, and took them in hand, his taloned hand, as Bertram lay in a tangle of messily untucked and half-removed clothing. Pax was his glorious dragonkind self, scales sparkling, and shot his wings outward behind him, letting Bertram take in the full radiant sight of him.

"What perverted acts do you have in mind for this form, Bertie?"

"For now, only to look at you."

Pax stuttered in the rhythm of his hips, words and thoughts lost. How did Bertram keep doing that to him? How did he want without selfish whims and only see Pax as a wonder?

The way he touched Pax's face, his horns, and splayed his hands across Pax's chest to feather down both sides of his delicately scaled rib cage was as if he truly saw Pax without wanting anything but Pax himself.

No. Pax couldn't think like that. Not again. He was glad Bertram was no longer upset with him, he wanted fun and adventure for them, not bickering, but this was too familiar. This was becoming something, somewhere, that Pax might not want to leave, and he knew the folly of that wish. That was why he gave wishes to others and had been a fool to ever make one of his own.

Pax dropped onto Bertram to pin him in place until he gasped from the weight. Then he licked between Bertram's parted lips, kissing him roughly, with fangs grazing Bertram's tongue. Pax didn't make wishes. He granted them. And when he wanted something, he took it.

Once Pax released Bertram, the pinned king fought to recapture lost breath. Pax flapped his wings to lift off Bertram's hips, and while airborne, he hooked his tail into Bertram's trousers and dragged them off to fling them aside. He coiled his tail around one of Bertram's thighs then and wrenched it up to part his legs, making room to land back between them.

Bertram panted up at him in excited awe.

"My tail's not nearly as dexterous as my tongue but can be quite useful." Pax unwound the tail from Bertram's thigh slower than it had pried his legs apart, replacing it with both hands spreading the legs wider, and careful with his talons, but not shying from letting them gently scratch. He rocked Bertram backward, and his tail dropped down between Bertram's cheeks. "If I open the way a little first, I think you might be able to handle its softer tip, hm?"

Bertram's eyes widened, and he shuddered when Pax's tail circled the pucker of his hole. The very end of it didn't have a fin yet or as rough of scales, but the softer, thinner ones like those on Pax's ribs and cheeks and cock.

"You can be the judge, of course." Pax leaned lower to breathe in Bertram's musk and moved his tail up Bertram's body near his mouth with a playful wave in front of his face. "It is its own level of sensitive and does so enjoy attention."

Wonder danced in Bertram's gemstone-touched eyes, but he smiled wickedly as he took the tail in hand. His gaze slid to meet Pax's and held steady as he brought the tip to his lips the same way he'd boldly devoured Pax's cock the night before.

This was what Pax wanted. Not wishes for himself. Not attachment. Not forever.

And to never again....

Fall in love.

BERTRAM SUCKED Pax's tail into his mouth, running his tongue along the soft scales, while Pax descended lower to drag his fangs up Bertram's shaft as promised.

A garbled moan left him as he continued to suck. The scales here were like the ones on Pax's prick, thin but lightly textured. At a point half the length of Pax's cock, the scales grew thicker and less pliable, yet even if the tail wouldn't be able to penetrate Bertram as deeply, it was twice the width, even there at its tip. The thought of it fucking inside him made him suck harder to moisten it.

He'd been so angry, wounded, and unsure. But with that possible but hopefully not certain future behind him, all he'd wanted was to know Pax better, to see and feel him in this form again and surrender. Bertram had a duty to this kingdom, but also to himself, to never become no more than a title, with a name long lost to regret. Whatever Pax's past might be, it must be a sad story to put him to sleep for centuries. It could wait.

"Ah!" Bertram pulled off Pax's tail with a snap of his head back. Pax had been sucking his cock in matched rhythm to Bertram on his tail with little teases of fangs, but now… he'd slid lower and was flicking his forked tongue over Bertram's hole.

It plunged in, and Bertram felt it lick so deep inside him that he quivered head to toe and could have come right that moment. Thin but impossibly long, it licked with an ever-widening spiral, stretching him open with slick perfection that made his breath stutter.

He had always enjoyed sex, but he could go without, tend to himself when the need arose, and focus on more important things. *Had* been able to. But with Pax, it seemed different, like food, water, and sleep, both craved and necessary for survival. Maybe because it was new, because it had been so long for him, because Pax's tongue was forked, and he had a tail and wings, and Bertram was ever in awe of him.

But also because Pax was all the things Bertram lacked, a balance that made him feel whole like no other partner in his bed or someone he'd spent time with ever had. And for as long as he had more wishes to make, this magical creature was his.

Pax's talons couldn't aid in stretching him, but the tail could, and it slithered down Bertram's body, dragging its wetted tip along Bertram's skin. The ties of his doublet and undershirt were undone, chest exposed, but the garments were still on him, in decadent disarray that made him look especially debauched. Though perhaps not as much as when Pax raised his silvery eyes from tonguing Bertram's hole, and the tip of the tail pushed in to replace it.

Bertram's mouth dropped open in a cry that couldn't be voiced. It was such a great pressured burn that he almost squirmed away, but the moment he was about to, Pax eased off. Then pressed his tail there again. And eased off. Then again, breaching a little further, out and in, widening Bertram's hole with a thickness not even the bulb of Pax's sizable cock could match. Bertram took it regardless, more and more on each go, until the burn was but a pleasant heat building and coiling up inside him like Pax's tongue.

His tongue....

"P-Pax...."

The tip of one fork was entering his slit again, and Pax's mouth followed with a hot suction up Bertram's shaft. It was so much at once, that when Pax's fangs grazed the skin again, Bertram went limp. His body was a weightless heap, being thrust up the bed with every slam of Pax's tail.

But it wasn't deep enough, and when it tried to go farther, the sharper graze of firmer scales made Bertram hiss.

"Mm...." Pax hummed, as tail and tongue drew away and he popped his mouth off Bertram's cock. "Ready for more?" The offer came with the faint circling of a talon around the sensitive and gaping edges of Bertram's hole.

"*Please.*" Bertram trembled, nodding in desperate petition.

Pax lined up his cock and slowly pushed in, rocking like their first time, in just a little, then a little more, echoing the tail's depth until he finally pushed deeper. "You might be the most erotic man I've ever been with, Bertie."

"Me?" Bertram laughed.

"You. And you've doubted and denied yourself for so long. You want to remember this lesson as much as the other one, don't you?" Pax pulled all the way out in wait of his answer.

"Yes."

"Then I will ingrain it upon you with such passion that you never forget."

"Ah!"

Pax slammed his hips forward, dragging his scales along Bertram's tender walls, and began pumping with a steady vigor. He watched Bertram's body move up and down the bed with each successive slam, seemingly enraptured by him, as if Bertram was truly the more erotic between them. Though how anything could be as seductive as the *dragon* fucking Bertram with wings spread and horns adorning him like a gleaming crown, he couldn't imagine.

"As much as I adore the unkempt look…." Pax paused after a few more glorious slams. "I want you bare this time."

He hefted Bertram from the bed and tore the shirt and doublet off him. The almost upright position drove Pax deeper inside him, and Bertram yelped. He didn't want it to lessen, though, and clung to Pax's neck, clenching around his cock to let him know he liked it. Pax helped him stay vertical, held him close, and flapped his wings once more to right their position.

As Bertram gazed on the wings in amazement, air suddenly swept over him as they beat forward, surrounding him and Pax like a cocoon, while Pax continued to bounce Bertram on his prick. The wings were so beautiful. Even where they weren't scaled or metallic-looking, they shimmered, and the insides appeared so soft that Bertram had to feel them for himself.

"*Oh*," Pax grunted, picking up his rhythm at the first gentle brush.

"Do you like having your wings touched, Pax?"

He growled in fervid affirmation.

Bertram stretched both arms outward to caress up and down each side.

"*F-fuck.*" Pax dropped his forehead to Bertram's chest with a shudder.

With the wings enclosing them in their own little world, Bertram gave over to the sensations taking hold of him. He dragged his hands up and down the inside of Pax's wings the same way his insides were being dragged against by scales. They were both panting, murmuring nonsense, as they clung to each other and increased the speed of their hips.

How Bertram had lasted this long, he couldn't say, and stranger still was when Pax burst first with an eruption of heat inside him, spilling a magnitude of come to coat his insides. The squelching of Bertram continuing to pump and thrust and bounce to impale himself only spurred him on more.

More.

More.

Pax raked the tips of his talons up Bertram's back, and finally Bertram came, head lolling wantonly in the aftermath with his arms dropping limp to his sides.

"Yes... oh yes," Pax purred, bringing a hand to Bertram's chin and teasing a talon across his lips to keep them parted. "*You* are the erotic one, Bertie, and you should never forget it."

He wouldn't. He couldn't.

Even if he didn't believe Pax, he would never forget this.

The wings unfurled with a fresh gust of air coming in, and Bertram shivered from the release of heat. He touched Pax's horns again, the outward stretching ones, and then the pair that reached straight up, and tugged them to tilt Pax's face toward his for a kiss.

It was a slow kiss, and Bertram wriggled his hips against the remaining plumpness of Pax's cock in him. Only when they pulled apart did he realize how dark the room had become with the sun setting, but with a wink and snap of Pax's fingers, all the candles and torches in the room burst alight.

Gently, Pax pulled Bertram from his spent cock, and the ooze of come that spilled out made Bertram aware of how gaping he was. He could have taken more of that tail now if it weren't for the sharper scales up from the tip.

Pax laid him back and bent to lick some of Bertram's come off his stomach with a playful leer. He snatched up the discarded undershirt to wipe away the rest and tossed the bundle of clothing to the floor. He didn't change out of his dragonkind form as he tugged at the covers so they could climb beneath, though he did dismiss his wings to make it easier to lie back. It was too early to sleep, but not to lounge and enjoy a few breaths of naked bliss.

When Pax pulled the covers over them with use of his tail, Bertram laughed. He wanted to touch every place where Pax had scales, but he reached first for the ones along his cheekbones and kissed him again.

"Well then," Pax said, grinning and seeming quite content with a lick at his lips with his forked tongue. "Now that that's done—but hopefully only a precursor to more...." He lifted one hand out of the sheets, and between two talons was a freshly plucked scale. He handed it to Bertram. "When you're ready for your second wish."

Bertram had no idea what he would ask for, but he frowned as he looked at it, because once his wishes were up... what then?

Cries sounded from the streets below, and they both sat up abruptly.

"Your Majesty!" David's voice came only seconds before he threw open Bertram's door.

Bertram darted his eyes to Pax—who was blessedly elven-looking, fast enough with his magic to hide his scales. "What is it?" He returned to David, trying to act as though he wasn't mortified to be caught with someone in his bed by his royal guard.

To David's credit, he only looked flustered for a moment. "It was just spotted, Your Majesty. The people are panicking again."

"What was just spotted?"

"The dragon."

Bertram and Pax spoke at the same time. "*What?*"

CHAPTER 13

PAX WILLED himself to be wearing trousers, since a tunic manifesting, when the elf who'd entered could already see his bare chest, might raise questions about his magical prowess. He leapt from the bed to reach the window, with Bertram following at a slower pace, given he had to put trousers on the normal way.

Another dragon? Could it be?

The streets were indeed in a flurry, and the moment Pax's eyes darted down from watching the skies, he saw a shadow fall upon the scattering citizens. He looked skyward again and saw—

"It *is* a dragon!" Bertram exclaimed.

"No, it isn't."

"It isn't?" Bertram and the guard gaped in unison.

"It's illusion magic. I can see right through it."

The guard eyed Pax with no small amount of suspicion, but at least Bertram took him at his word.

"An illusion? But why?" Bertram questioned.

It was true that the dragon soaring past in the darkened sky looked like Pax—identical, in fact, which had been another giveaway—but while any mortal might be fooled, Pax knew the difference between illusion magic and his own brethren. He had no answer, however, for why someone would be foolish or brave enough to make a copy of him.

"It must be a diversion…." Bertram started backing away from the window, his face contorting into a different sort of worry. "To purposefully cause another panic and…. David!" He spun toward the guard. "What of the other guards on duty?"

"They've all gone out to quell the unrest, Your Majesty, as we assumed you'd want." He tensed, as this answer prompted Bertram to fly over to his wardrobe and seek a new undershirt. "A small contingent stayed behind to protect you, of course, but we thought—"

"We need to call back as many as we can," Bertram ordered, only just getting the shirt over his head, "*without* leaving, and—"

Louder voices erupted from inside the castle than what were ringing with terror in the streets. David whirled around on the defensive, aiming his spear, as the cries grew closer. With a few steps forward to see outside the doors, Pax saw a handful of guards being overtaken by a group of mostly humans with meager weapons but far greater numbers.

And the young woman who'd been queen in the future led them.

"Don't!" Bertram called before Pax had even lifted a hand or betrayed a shimmer of his scales. When David turned at the exclamation, Bertram pretended his words were for him, but Pax knew he spoke to them both. "I know you wish to protect me, but I don't want bloodshed. We can't let it be proven that the sources of magic they fear are the enemy. We need to find another way."

"But Majesty…," David protested, and Pax held Bertram's stare, also wanting to be certain if this was what he wanted.

"If it's gotten to this point, then I've failed them already. I must find another way."

David faltered as much as Pax and answered in the same way he would have too. "As you wish."

He dropped his spear, and as the insurgency flooded into the chambers, all three of them stood still to let themselves be captured.

"PRISONERS TOGETHER. This is a new one for me," Pax said, tapping his foot as he leaned against the cell wall.

It smelled of such muskiness, it had clearly not been swept out or cleaned in decades. It was cramped and cold and had only one barred door and a similarly barred window looking out into the castle courtyard above, for of course they were in a dungeon below normal ground level. Their captors hadn't chained them, but they hadn't been very gentle either, seen in the scrape along Bertram's forearm from being thrown into the cell, which had nearly made Pax shed his guise and attack despite Bertram's wishes.

Still in his feigned undress of only trousers, and Bertram in only trousers and undershirt, they were barefoot and tousled. Under different circumstances that might have prompted Pax toward a little prisoner role-play, but he doubted Bertram would be up for it, even if it was just the two of them, with David having been taken elsewhere to be stripped of his armor.

Faint voices could be heard, likely guards in other cells, but none close enough to truly communicate with, given the thick stone walls and placement of the different cells down the long dungeon's corridor. The leader of the anti-magic group had overseen Bertram being deposited into the cell herself, saying she'd be back when he'd had time to rethink what side was right, even if they were long past being willing to bow.

To Pax, it was a lost cause to sway them, but he saw Bertram's refusal to believe so in the frantic patter of his bare feet along the floor. He spoke as if not having heard Pax at all.

"There must be a way. There must be."

"I don't appreciate their rough treatment of you," Pax said louder, pushing from the wall to gently grasp Bertram's injured arm and halt his pacing.

"It's only a scratch." Bertram tried to tug his arm back, but Pax held fast.

"For now. You've seen what these people become."

"Because they're scared. Isn't it always fear that leads to such things?" Bertram's eyes darted down with a cringe in his brow. "Fear and regret...."

Pax cringed too and fought to banish it before Bertram saw. He knew something about regret, but he didn't think Bertram had brought it up as a connecting thread or barb. Pax had hoped to be done thinking of such things, but they'd barely spent another night together before Pax's chosen perch for this adventure turned on them.

He wanted to wipe it all away, for Bertram and for him, and summoned a breath of earth magic to start on Bertram's wound. It really was only a scratch, but he pushed up the sleeve regardless, bent down, and pressed his open lips to the edges of the cut to heal it with a kiss. The area was smooth in moments, and Bertram met the raise of Pax's eyes with a calmed smile.

"Thank you."

"My pleasure. Now, shall I break us free from this insult, or do you need more time to think about how to handle your enemies?"

"They are not my enemies," Bertram insisted, pulling his sleeve back down. "They're my citizens, my people. You were there. Penelope felt remorse for her actions in the end."

"After a decade. It's easy to regret something when you see how wrong it becomes." Pax almost cringed again. He hadn't meant to say it like *that*. He never meant to keep reminding himself of his own past.

"She's scared and angry and thinks she knows what she wants," Bertram said. "The people on the pro-magic side aren't any different. They just fear different things. And maybe they'll never agree completely on how to weather those fears, but there must be some compromise where they'll recognize that peace is better than eradicating each other. That's what I was taught. That's what I have seen from the other kingdoms."

"Kingdoms with more magic than this one," Pax reminded him. "It's mostly humans here. Even the wars of old started because this kingdom grew afraid first, believe me. From what you've said of the history I missed, that persisted up until just before you were born. Maybe this return to that way of thinking is inevitable—"

"No. I won't believe that. I refuse to believe that the people of Emerald are doomed to repeat the past. If the same fears keep returning, then it is up to those in power, up to *me*, to find a balance."

"What about that fascinating potion the wizard brewed in Sapphire?" Pax suggested.

"Ten years from now. I could offer up the idea, but it's not immediate."

"Again, you could always wish—"

Bertram held up a hand to halt that idea, but then he paused, seeming contemplative. He reached into his trousers' pocket and pulled out two scales—one with slightly less shimmer to it that had granted his first wish, and the other, the still brilliant one that Pax had given him only minutes ago.

"You know your next wish, then?"

"No." Bertram turned for the window. "I can't rely on you to fix this, Pax. I need to be sure I can lead my people even when… you're gone."

The sting of those words made Pax's nose wrinkle in a far worse cringe than before, and he was thankful Bertram's back was to him. It shouldn't sting at all. He had always planned to leave.

"All I need to escape one of these cells is a hard edge." At that, Bertram began using the scales in tandem to whittle away the mortar where the cross-section of bars met the stone. "The people forget, these cells haven't been used in thirty years and were already old and weathered then. I'll barely need to scrape off some of this crumbling mortar and…." He paused to shake the bars, proving they were laughably loose.

"You'll never fit through that window," Pax noted as Bertram continued carving away. "Not with those fine shoulders and hips."

"I don't need to."

It took a handful of minutes for the bars to be pried free, and while the opening would have been tight even for Pax's teenage form, Bertram moved on to the mortar around the nearest stones, removing them one by one to widen their means of escape.

Pax tried to not let on how much he was impressed.

"And what will we do once we're free?" he asked.

"Find Dain, the leader of those in favor of magic."

"I thought you weren't choosing a side."

"I'm not, but after one side acted, once word spreads about what's happened, it's only a matter of time before the other side acts in retaliation. People could die. I need to convince Dain to try something else."

"What?"

"I… I don't know yet, but I'll find an answer. I have to," he finished in a quiet mutter, just as he pulled a final brick free. He turned to Pax with an expectant look.

"Technically…." Pax sauntered over with a nod at the scales in Bertram's hands. "I still helped get us out of here."

Bertram chuckled, pocketing the spent scale in one side of his trousers and the yet to be wished upon one in the other. "Technically, if you hadn't shown up at all, Penelope's side might not have been prompted to act this soon. And even if they had, I would have been properly dressed for this insurrection and could have used the stiff edges of my brocade doublet to do the same thing. It might have taken longer, but it still would have worked."

Pax could tell by Bertram's expression and voice that there wasn't accusation in the words, even if it might have been a little bit Pax's fault for pushing things to erupt now. Despite that, he looked at Pax the same, hoisted himself out the window, and turned back to reach out a hand to offer Pax help as well.

This was the man Pax had seen while soaring over the city, a glittering crowned king ushering his people to safety and going to the aid of citizens in need, regardless of the dangers to himself. He was ready to be that man again. He was ready to do all within his power to save his kingdom.

Pax might have felt a swell of pride at what his first granted wish had wrought, but... no. He'd helped, certainly, but Bertram had always been capable. He'd simply needed to be reminded. And Pax was maybe relieved to not have a second wish made just yet, which would have shortened their time together.

"Lead on, Your Majesty," he said and grasped Bertram's hand.

OUTSIDE THE dungeon, Bertram glanced up at the night sky, but the illusion of a Pax-like dragon could no longer be seen, the ruse given up.

The falling darkness made it easier to sneak from the courtyard into the streets. The castle gate was locked, leaving the tricked guards outside, who hovered in wait, demanding to be shown that the king still lived. Penelope was making them sweat—or maybe she didn't know what to do now that her plan had succeeded.

Her people were many, but not so many that Bertram and Pax couldn't find a portion of the wall to sneak over where there weren't as many eyes. They didn't even need to use Pax's magic.

"Any thoughts on where to go next?" Pax whispered as Bertram hurried them not toward his guards but deeper into the city.

"Our alley."

"*Our* alley?"

Bertram flushed, even gladder for the fall of night to hide it. It *was* their alley, though, where they'd met, where they'd ended up again in that dark future, and where they needed to go now. "It's likely Dain is there and might even be using Jafari's as his faction's home base. He's a Jafari too. It's his brother's shop."

And as Bertram well knew, having made this same trek backward what was only hours ago but a decade's time by the power of a wish, Jafari's wasn't far. The streets were quiet now, besides the distant yelling of the locked-out guards. Whether people hid in their homes from the dragon or the troubling development of the castle being seized, it seemed few, if any, remained outside.

Just once, Bertram would have liked to show Pax his real kingdom, the way he knew and loved it when not running clandestine through alleyways. Like the inn they passed, Emerald's smallest, but that's why Bertram liked it best when he wanted a drink or to enjoy some music at a tavern. Sans crown and dressed in simpler attire didn't make him unrecognizable, but the people at that inn tended to let him pretend he was any other patron.

There were also grand gardens lining the interior of most of the city wall. It kept being night when they snuck around in near enough places to have seen any, but plants always thrived here, inside the city walls, probably because of proximity to the Emerald gemstone beneath the castle and their closeness to Aurora Wood. There weren't plants with quite the same iridescent colors as Aurora, but some flowers, fruits, and vegetables grew here that could be found nowhere else, not even in the surrounding farmlands.

Bertram would have shown Pax Jafari's under better circumstances too. The family were artists at their core, with wonderful handmade crafts. He would have shown Pax the monuments to all that had been changed in this kingdom since ancient days, one of which had been an inspiration for him. Not statues of Reardon and Jack, but representations of them, as a pillar of ice being surrounded by vines that bloomed with roses, a sign that curses could be overcome, magic could unite with non-magic, and life could blossom all the better for it.

That's what Bertram needed to remind his people of too, and he would have shown all that to Pax if things were different.

Would have.

Would have.

He still could when this was over. He could. Besides Ruby, Emerald was the only other city they hadn't gotten to explore together. So maybe... he'd save one wish to ask for that.

The front door into Jafari's might have been safe with how calm the streets were, but Bertram didn't risk it. He ducked down the alley to the side entrance and knocked. While they waited, he glanced at Pax and saw that he'd morphed into his teenage form, clothed like usual, and less intimidating than his towering adult self.

Bertram readied to knock again when a voice barked, "We're closed!"

"Please!" Bertram called back. "I'm looking for Dain. This is your king speaking. I escaped the castle, and I need your help."

There was a pause, likely skepticism, but then the door opened. "King Bertram?"

It wasn't Dain who appeared, but Leslie, Levi's brother, younger and less weary-looking than when Bertram had last seen him.

Leslie ushered them inside, where Bertram's guess that the shop might be a hub for Dain's people was proven right, with Dain and his extended family among a large crowd, taking up every bit of space in the small shop. Filled with knickknacks, décor items, and gifts, like beautifully crafted music boxes, the shop was three floors tall, with the second floor an extension of the shop and the third living quarters. The number of people was enough that some spilled up the stairs.

"Your Majesty!"

"King Bertram!"

The cries echoed through the people as they recognized him, and everyone who could kneel did so, others bowing low or at least lowering their heads.

"You're barefoot!" a woman announced, once they'd all raised their eyes again. "Quickly, someone get him some boots!"

It wasn't just any woman, Bertram saw, but Leslie's wife, more obviously ten years younger, since she was human, and very pregnant with what must be their first child.

Bertram would have dismissed any fuss being made over him, but he really did need a pair of boots to ease and cover his sore feet after trekking over cobblestones. "Thank you," he said when he was handed a stray pair that he didn't ask the source of. He put them on, while the people made room for him and Pax, and Dain came forward looking like he'd won some great blessing.

"It is so good to see you, Your Majesty. How did you escape?"

"I know my castle well and have a trick or two in me," Bertram said, causing a smattering of laughter through the crowd.

"I wish it hadn't come to this for you to see reason." Dain clapped a hand on his shoulder. "But I'm glad you understand now which side to be on."

"You misunderstand, Dain. I won't choose sides, no matter how misguided Penelope's actions."

"You can't be serious. They took the castle. It's rebellion. Treason! They even had a magic user cast an illusion spell to get what they wanted, yet they don't think themselves hypocrites."

At least it had spread that the dragon wasn't real—at least not that one.

Pax had blended in with the crowd, leaving Bertram to handle this his way as he'd asked.

"They seek peace of mind," Bertram said, "and some people with magic agree—"

"You're siding with them?" someone asked from the crowd.

"No. No sides. Please listen to me," Bertram beseeched. "There is a way through this that does not end in civil war."

"Agreed," Dain said, raising his voice to address the shop in full. "There is a real dragon out there, somewhere. It wouldn't simply vanish. We've been combining knowledge and abilities to find the right magic to identify it, even if it's hiding amongst us in mortal form."

Bertram did his best to not slide his eyes toward Pax.

"Word is it's a platinum dragon, and we are close to knowing how to track it down."

"Then what?" Bertram asked. "You'll request its aid?"

"We'll demand it or pluck out its scales to wish our demands true."

"What…?" Bertram's eyes widened at the horror of those words.

"It is said in some of the oldest tomes that a dragon's scales—"

"You can't do that!"

Several people, many with children at their sides, flinched at Bertram's outburst, but were they mad? Even if they could track Pax and point him out in a crowd, how could they possibly expect to steal scales? How could they think such an act anything but foolhardy and barbaric?

But Dain didn't look troubled by his declaration. "This dragon terrified our citizens and is likely hiding amongst us having a laugh while people panic in the streets. And I, for one, believe it is worth doing anything to keep our people safe. Sides or not, I thought you felt the same."

Bertram's eyes did slide to Pax then, finding him cooing at some of the children nearest him, doing playful sleight of hand with a wooden flute he'd swiped from a display that would likely end up in his hoard.

Was he even listening?

"Not that," Bertram said. "I can't believe you'd skip straight to demands over even trying to talk to him."

"If you would like to talk and make requests once we've captured the dragon, by all means, but I won't take the risk that it'll simply fly off and be lost to us."

"And what would you wish for? You can't change Penelope and her people's minds. You can't wish them out of existence. So what? Wish them from the city? Wish for everyone to have magic, despite their side already counting magic users amongst them? None of that would make a difference."

Dain looked troubled, disappointed, but if he did have a wish in mind, he didn't speak it. "Penelope is going to realize you're gone soon. She'll know something's coming. We need to get back to tracking the dragon. What I want, Your Majesty, is to get you your castle back. I hope once we do, you'll use your authority wisely."

It was a thinly veiled threat, goading Bertram to dare command Dain and his people to stop their attempts to find the dragon, which would make him look even more like he was on Penelope's side. There was no answer yet that Bertram could give, no suggestions that would make them see reason without losing their faith in him.

So, he said no more as Dain moved through the crowd to a corner of the shop, where his family and several other more powerful magic users were poring over books and fussing with magical artifacts in their attempts to find Pax.

The people, while trying to remain respectful of their king, looked uncertain, and Bertram hated that he didn't know how to ease them.

"I thank you for the boots, but I need air and to gather my thoughts." He moved back to the side door to exit into the alley.

Bertram sagged against the wall, the narrow alley lit only by that lone lamplight with Jafari's sign that Pax had once dangled from. He still didn't know the answer. He'd thought it might come to him once he met up with Dain, but the divide between his people was a crater he couldn't fill. Part of him still wanted to believe that if he could just find the right materials, he could build a bridge, a way for them to calm down and see each other's points of view long enough to meet in the middle.

But how? With what? Time was short and growing shorter. Bertram knew that him never having become king wasn't the way out, but what was? Was this kingdom truly destined to keep reliving the past?

"Why so glum, Bertie?" Pax appeared from nowhere, not having come out the door—though possibly *through* it or through the wall of the shop. He was still in teenage form, which made his playful tone even more infuriating.

"Did you not hear what they're planning?"

"Good luck getting any of my scales," Pax snorted.

"This is serious. It doesn't matter if they're capable. It's still all unraveling. I don't know if I can stop that future from happening. Or another just as bad with the other side in power."

"You'll sort it out." Pax nudged him. "There's always your next wish."

"Another wish? You'd still suggest that?" Like in that other world, Bertram felt his temper flare at Pax's flippantness. "I need to think about the future, Pax. I need to think about what to do when you're not here. I told you I can't rely on the easy way out. That is what all of them want, too, instead of thinking through things rationally. Instead of considering compromise!"

"Calm down, Bertie. You're taking it all too seriously. We—"

"And you're not taking it seriously at all!" Bertram bellowed. "At least in my wish, that was only a possibility. This is now. This is real. This matters to me! Yes, indulgence is important for living, but so is balance. It can't all be… sex and merriment and soaring through the skies."

"It can if you wish it to be."

He wasn't listening, and it made his apology from before seem hollow. "Then you are constantly running from anything real. Just like I was."

Pax's good humor fell from his expression. Bertram found some vindication in seeing that, but Pax pushed from the wall as if Bertram was the one trying *his* patience. "See, this is why I had a rule about never getting attached to mortals. You always spoil my fun eventually."

"Is that all I am to you? Just another mortal? Passing fun, who's no longer worth your time once things get difficult?" Deep down, Bertram had known that. Pax had made it very clear on a number of occasions. But it still hurt. "You are truly nothing like the platinum dragons from the tomes."

"Tomes?" Pax scoffed, and his teenage form fell away to the larger one, back in his short, open-chested tunic, looming over Bertram with his sudden extra height. "Do you want to know what the other platinum dragons were like? Pretentious killjoys. None of my brethren would have deigned to even drink with a mortal, let alone bed one. No, that was for the lesser dragons," he said in mocking tones. "I alone saw your potential and worth."

Bertram was reminded of just how powerful and terrifying Pax could be if he wanted to be, but he refused to be cowed by him now. "You still scorn us if you refuse to get attached. Is it truly all because some dwarf from Ruby drove you into the caves?"

Pax's eye twitched in a telling flash of anger. "You don't know that story."

"Then tell me. I know that's who you are. The last of the dragons, a platinum dragon, was said to have been buried in the Ruby Mountains, where *you* came from."

Pax seemed to deflate, almost in the magical way he could shrink, yet it was just a slump of his shoulders. "The caverns of Ruby are where I slumbered, yes." He didn't say more and clearly had no intention of expanding or telling Bertram the truth.

"Your hoard of trinkets is near there too, in Aurora Wood?"

"They're not *trinkets*, but yes."

"Show me that, then."

"What?" Pax sputtered. "Is that your next wish?"

"If it must be." It wasn't quite what Bertram wanted, but it might be a start.

Pax looked more uncertain and flustered than Bertram had seen him, clearly unsure what answer was best to meet Bertram's challenge. In the end, he steeled his expression with a bitter smile and said, "Fine, if you're going to be such a brat about it, you can have this one for free."

He snapped his fingers.

CHAPTER 14

HIS HOARD. His treasure vault. His collection.

Pax had only ever allowed one other person here before.

Just one.

He hadn't been here himself since he woke up, though he'd sent back plenty to add to its stores. To some, he supposed this little pocket out of time and space and the normal realm resembled a manor home, just a bit more cluttered than most would have preferred. And ten times as large.

The room they appeared in first was mostly made of dark wood with a marble floor, and items from across the ages were on tables, stands, displayed like the treasures they were, or set neatly onto shelves as tall as the high ceiling. The ceiling itself was glass, so clear it might have appeared as if open to the arching branches of the uniquely colored trees of Aurora Wood. If Pax willed it, falling petals could breach the glass and rain down on them like in a dream. He'd done that for someone once too.

"Oh...." Bertram gasped as he turned to take it all in.

Some items were valuable in the mortal sense, some not at all. Time was halted here, so even things that might have decayed with the years remained intact, like the matching flower to the one he'd given Bertram in Diamond that would never lose its bloom.

Pax saw the continued awe on Bertram's face, that familiar marveling as he strolled around the room—this *first* room—and realized there were many, many more, each a little different. What might appear disorganized was quite meticulous actually. Though Pax couldn't necessarily say *how* in some cases. But he knew it all made sense why a silver teapot was in a room that looked like a solarium, a straw hat was in his library, and a drum was amongst what was otherwise mostly an armory.

"I was right," Bertram said, gingerly touching an ornate lantern, which sat on a shelf beside a child's stuffed toy in the likeness of a lamb. "None of it matches. There's no cohesion. It's all just—"

"*Don't* say junk. I cherish every item."

"Normal," Bertram finished.

"Well, of course. My hoard is experiences, and I collect items to remind me of them."

He followed Bertram to a tucked-away nook where his most recent possessions had been sent, from his last adventure to this one, like the bottle from the potion, that book on dragons, and the cathom's red ball. Bertram seemed to be drawn by something specific, and only when he reached toward a pair of familiar leather boots did Pax cringe. But Bertram's hand kept going, reaching for the shelf above, where his own undergarment from Diamond sat.

And his crown.

"You collect... experiences," Bertram repeated, dropping his hand before he'd completed the touch to glittering gold and emeralds.

"Yes."

"And the people who were part of those experiences are just passing memories captured in a trinket?"

"They're *not* trinkets." Pax's chest flared with heat.

"Aren't they?" Bertram turned slowly, his face hard as stone. "Those beautiful words you said in Diamond, about mortals teaching you to live each moment to the fullest, like with the wonder of a child? It's a lie. If you get attached to things, but not people, it's all just a lie. Because when it comes to us mortals, you throw us away."

"Careful...."

"Is that the real reason you have a younger form, so you can pretend you're a child and take no responsibility for your actions?"

"I am the wise sage giving advice," Pax growled, "not some thirty-year-old mortal who has barely lived."

"And what wisdom have you imparted so far, other than to not be like you?"

Pax slammed Bertram back, catching his shoulders and head on the edges of the shelving. Bertram hissed and his eyes widened in fright. Pax hadn't meant to. Nor had he meant for his hands to be claws, but they were, his talons gripped tight around Bertram's shoulders, which scratched too closely to the skin with him only in an undershirt.

Shaking off his dragonkind features, Pax drew back. "What if I was the one who was thrown away?"

"Tell me," Bertram pleaded.

"I can't. There is no experience worth the answer to that question."

"But there could be a wish." Bertram pulled the still active scale from his pocket.

"No."

"Yes. Because you won't tell me any other way, and I think you need to tell someone." Bertram stalked forward, and how pathetic Pax was in the face of this wish being asked of him, because he actually stumbled back. "You said I could have anything but death, resurrection, or a changed heart. Then I wish to know the truth of what happened between you and Dolgar Dragonbane."

"Dragonbane?" Pax scoffed with a wince he couldn't hide. "How apt a name change...." And how cruel. Bertram was being cruel too. But no wish from a dragon's scale that fit the rules had ever been denied. "Fine. But believe me...." Pax's voice caught on a surge of emotion as he raised his hand to snap his fingers again. "My heart was changed."

PAX DIDN'T always know how his wishes would play out. The magic had a mind of its own sometimes, and so he was curious, if otherwise filled with dread, how this might manifest.

How it did was by taking them to a long white hall with doorways looking in on different scenes, different... memories, frozen like a picture, the first starting the day that Pax met Gar.

"What is this?" Bertram asked as he stared upon the first memory. "It's almost like the tapestries."

"Tapestries?"

The scene showed Pax in his true dragon form curled up for a nap in the main room of his hoard. It was large enough to fit him, but only just barely. He liked to sleep among his possessions, comforted by their presence. It was one thing he had in common with other dragons, some who hoarded gold, others books, others items imbued with magic. He'd even known a blue dragon who kept the whittled-away wood chips from an artist's carvings.

He'd never really understood that one, but hoards were personal.

"In Ruby, they... there's a set of tapestries telling the story of how Dragonbane forced the last dragon into the caves. That's him?" Bertram stepped closer, indicating a small figure at the edge of the room, just daring to begin entering and disturb the sleeping beast.

Pax had left little magical doorways all over the Gemstone
Kingdoms that could lead someone brave enough into his hoard. It was
a game he'd decided to play to distract himself from his mother having
left. From *everyone* having left and Pax being alone. He thought surely
the right mortal would find him, if they be worthy, and whether they tried
to steal from him, rouse him, or *arouse*, so long as they didn't run, Pax
would grant them three wishes.

"Yes," he said, and as Bertram stepped nearer to the scene, what
had been still began to move, "but to me, he was Gar."

THE SOFT footfalls woke Pax immediately, but he continued to feign
sleep. At last, someone had found one of his doorways and wasn't
immediately sprinting away in fear at finding a slumbering dragon.

With a thought, Pax banished the other doorways. It would do him
no good to have another find him while he was engaged with this daring
mortal. But perhaps, he hoped, a new adventure would prove he'd made
the right decision by staying, and he could continue adventure after
adventure, with mortal after mortal, and nothing needed to change.

A hand grazed the scales of his right side. Daring indeed.

"Beautiful…," a low voice said.

Good taste too. Pax peeked an eye open to look upon the intruder,
and oh… he was beautiful. A dwarf, squat in build and strong-looking,
a hard worker with finely muscled arms exquisitely displayed through
the sleeveless tunic he wore. He had ruddy skin, long auburn hair, and a
matching beard tamed into a single braid.

The impressive facial hair didn't hide his youth, however. He was
of age, but only by a few years, in his early twenties. His eyes matched
his hair in color, a warm reddish brown, and they sparkled with wonder
as he continued to touch Pax.

"My scales are quite beautiful," Pax said, and the young dwarf snapped
his hand away with a start, "as is the man who dares touch them." Unfurling,
not quite able to stand to his full height in this chamber, Pax could still make
himself more presentable than being curled up like a cat.

The dwarf backed away, but there was no fear on his face. "You
think I am beautiful, sir dragon?"

"Pax. And yes, I do. I am quite particular about who I find attractive,
and who I permit to enter my most coveted of spaces."

"There was a door in the caves near the Ruby—"

"Yes. And you walked through it."

"I thought I'd found some hidden treasure cache." The dwarf took a cautious step back toward Pax. "Then the real treasure presented itself."

Oh, Pax liked this one. "Am I to have your name in return?"

"Dolgar Laster, the cobbler's son," he greeted with a bow of his head. "Were I a blacksmith, at least I would have some armor and a weapon to face my fate before a dragon, but alas, all I have is some finely adorned feet."

Indeed, while the young man's outfit was simple, he wore some of the most finely crafted boots Pax had ever seen, with intricately designed stitching patterns and a perfect curl at the toes. As Pax regarded them, the dwarf continued closer, reaching again for his scales. "You're not afraid?"

"Should I be?" the dwarf stroked the platinum and held Pax's gaze without blinking.

Pax liked this one a great deal indeed. "Not today, little Gar."

Pax shrunk in a blink, and Gar's daring hand was pressed against an elven-like chest instead of a single scale. Pax kept his dragonkind appearance, so his horns and tail and wings still evoked the awe he so enjoyed seeing, but while he expected another flinch, Gar splayed his hand, thumb and pinky grazing where Pax's scales began along his ribs.

"Tell me, Gar, am I still beautiful like this, or not your type?"

Gar grinned. "I have never seen your equal."

Yes. He was perfect.

If only Pax had realized then that the hunger he saw on Gar's face wasn't for what he thought.

PAX FEIGNED the swing of the hammer striking true and roared to the delight of the crowd. Gar fell upon him with another vicious thwack— not even risking a dent in any of Pax's scales, but the onlookers didn't need to know that.

After the onslaught, Pax slunk away, snorting a brief billow of fire that made those watching gasp in fear that he might unleash his great breath attack, only for a rune to glow on his throat, symbolizing it had been disabled. It was the rune for Water, so people assumed it caused his fire to go out, only Pax didn't breathe fire; he breathed whatever he wished to, and no rune was going to change that.

They didn't need to know that either.

Cheers and applause erupted through the coliseum for their favorite fighter, the mighty Dolgar, who'd captured a dragon and kept it cowed and controlled with weekly thrashings. A series of tournament battles between fighters showing off their prowess each week culminated in Gar's continued victories over the dragon, who almost—but never quite fully—escaped to seek its revenge. It was marvelous fun.

The gates of the cage where Pax was "kept" slammed down as he was once again defeated, the crowd still cheering as Gar urged them on and spoke of how he would never let the fearsome beast break free. Even before the shouting and stomps in Gar's honor diminished, Pax was morphing to his elven form, laughing to himself at their display today, and slipping seamlessly out of the cavern to await Gar outside.

That rune did quench his thirst but made him ravenously hungry. He'd request they head straight to the tavern today for a spot of lunch. Gar liked that anyway since many of the patrons from the fighting ring would end up there too and buy him a round, praising him further.

Renown was a common enough wish, but since Pax couldn't grant that anyone's hearts or minds be changed, he couldn't make Gar famous overnight, but he could provide the means to get him there. Gar's actual wish had been for the proper armor and weapon to "slay" the dragon before a crowd. It was a fabulous story he'd concocted, about finding the armor in the caves where he'd also found Pax, no doubt belonging to some wayward warrior who'd failed to defend himself against the beast that had gone mad as the only dragon left in the kingdoms. Gar had taken pity on the poor creature and decided to not slay it after all unless his hand was forced. Got the crowd going every time.

He looked good in that armor too. Pax didn't hide his perusal of Gar when he finally appeared, strolling up to where they met after each show ended, winged helm tucked under his arm. It was winged like feathers, meant to contrast the leathery wings of the dragon he fought, and each piece of armor was inlaid with designs that Pax had purposely crafted to remind him of the stitching of Gar's leather boots—which he'd long since sent to his hoard.

"The mighty warrior, victorious again!" Pax bowed.

Gar laughed and fell into step beside Pax, following him toward the tavern without question. "For now. Is it really only three wishes?"

"Only? Many of my brethren would grant *only* one, you realize."

"Ah, but you are so much greater than any of them."

"Nice try." Pax leaned down and kissed the top of Gar's head. "But it's three. Why worry anyway? You've only made one so far. Plenty to go."

A few passing patrons from the coliseum stopped to congratulate Gar on his bravery and fortitude against the dragon. He accepted it as humbly as one might expect. Who they thought Pax was never seemed to come up—a friend, a manager, a lover, all of which were true, so they could think what they liked.

They were ushered to a prime table in the center of the tavern, and it was a good several minutes before they were left alone long enough to continue the conversation.

"I shall have to make my wishes count," Gar said over his first free round of the day. "I wouldn't want to have them wasted or have you disappear from my side too quickly."

"It is a lovely side to be near," Pax said, enjoying his own mug of ale.

"He's no warrior," a passing man sneered, before claiming a table beside theirs, not even attempting to keep his voice low. Those with him snickered. "It's an act. That dragon's more pet than threat to us."

"Really?" Pax turned with a grin, tempted to let his fangs grow or to loom over the man and scratch a talon under his chin just firm enough for him to feel its point.

"*Pax*," Gar hissed. "Don't."

Pax obeyed, but only because the man was smart enough to not push once challenged.

"They'll figure it out if you're not careful," Gar said.

"And what if they do? You're still a grand showman."

"But a showman's fame is fleeting." Gar sagged, like he was already worried about his downfall when he'd barely been on top for more than a few weeks. "Pity there are no wars anymore for me to prove I'm more than that. Only true warriors are so revered that they never need cobble a shoe or sing for their supper."

"Oh, there's still some song and dance to it," Pax said.

"I suppose. All the best ones have songs and stories about them."

"Is that your second wish, Gar? A song?"

Gar perked up, like he'd thought of something far better. "Not quite. But I may have a few ideas to get there."

"How CAN you possibly not want to see more of the kingdoms?" Pax asked.

"I *am* seeing them—from the best view possible."

It was a lovely view, up in the clouds so high they'd look like a passing bird more than a dragon and rider to anyone spotting them.

"Besides, I like my home." Gar patted the scales of Pax's head. He didn't hang on anymore, certain that Pax would catch him if he fell—which, of course, he would—and sat with his feet kicked forward, lounging between Pax's horns. "There are different ways to enjoy adventure."

He stroked the scales around one horn with purposeful teasing, more comfortable doing so than most others when Pax was in this form. Others had found it too strange, but Gar could coax Pax to quite the high level of arousal before requesting he change to a form better suited to complete the act.

"I know what my second wish is, Pax."

"At last? You've been putting off making it for weeks."

"Maybe I've been thinking carefully. Maybe I don't want you slipping away too soon."

"Mm, and would you wish to have me stay?"

"If I had to wish it, then no."

Pax laughed. Indeed, if someone ever wished for him to stay, he couldn't grant it, since it would break the rules of a changed heart.

Although, with Gar, it was the first time he'd ever wanted to stay on his own.

"But I do have my next wish ready. I'm tired of that rented room so near my father's shop. I want a place of my own. I wish for the grandest villa in town, large enough that you could take any form you want in it." He laid down and stroked again around Pax's horn. "And Pax? I'd like you to take *me* in it right now."

"Now that is a wish I can get behind."

Pax soared out of the clouds toward the mountains below, already willing the villa to be built into the caverns on the edge of the Ruby

Kingdom's grand city, where any eyes that spotted it would wonder if it had always been there.

IT COULD be uncomfortable lying on his wings, but Pax didn't mind when in bed with Gar, wrapping them around him while they basked in the afterglow of another evening well spent. Gar had only grown more handsome to him as the weeks stretched into months, more muscled and stronger from their play-fighting in the coliseum, with longer hair, and his braided beard fuller too.

Pax held Gar close and laced their hands together, talons gently curling between Gar's softer fingers. "I think we have now officially christened every room in this villa. Twice. Funny how we saved the bedroom for last."

Gar chuckled and leaned up for a kiss.

It had been another successful bout of the dragon being subdued—and then Pax had done some subduing of his own. But the crowd was becoming sparser each week, and he could tell they were less convinced of the dragon as a threat. Many had probably guessed Pax's identity by now, but Gar was still quite beloved, just like he'd wanted.

Beloved by the people.

Beloved by... Pax.

"Still no third wish?" Pax asked, like he did most days now. He'd been gearing up to tell Gar that using up the last wish didn't mean he'd leave. He never thought he'd feel that way about anyone. Never wanted to entertain the idea. It was a rule he'd maintained his entire life to never get attached. And this was supposed to be the start of a new age of adventures, not a final hurrah before settling down with one miraculous mortal, but he found that he didn't want to leave these arms, possibly ever.

"I have so many things now that I always wanted," Gar said. "Money and notoriety, so I never need to take over my father's shop or waste away into obscurity. A manor worthy of me and the partner in my bed."

"All true." Pax held him tighter. "So, what's left?"

"*Infamy*. From one last show."

"That's your wish? To retire?"

Gar shifted to look at Pax. "A real show this time, Pax. Something they'll never forget. But what I *wish*," he finally said it, "is for it to play out exactly as I want, and you need to follow my lead."

"Then… no more? Back to the villa? Maybe christen the rooms all over again?"

"And wait for the songs and stories."

"Gar…." Just once, *just once* Pax wanted to say it. To tell him. But after.

He'd say "I love you" after.

"I will follow your lead wherever you wish to take me."

IT WAS quite the spectacle that Gar wanted to make of this final fight between warrior and dragon. For one, it wasn't starting in the coliseum or on the usual day, but in the middle of the week in the streets of the city, as if the vile beast had escaped captivity at last. Pax could play that up fine. After all, if this was to be their final fight, it needed to be a grand one.

He'd slipped into an alley, and at the appointed time, grew to his full size and burst free as if appearing from nothing, upsetting some of the stone on either side of him until he flapped upward to be sure all saw him when he roared to announce himself.

Some people shrieked and scattered in fear, but others looked merely inconvenienced. They really didn't take him seriously anymore, but he could fix that. Gar had asked him to make this as real as possible, so he soared through the streets, right over people's heads, and landed on a building he knew to be empty, crushing the stone of its roof with his talons and baring his neck to the watching citizens so all saw when the rune shattered.

He turned and spewed fire on the tops of buildings that didn't have any people nearby to get caught by the flames. It didn't do anything to the stone but looked terribly frightening.

"Get back! Everyone, hurry! It's free!"

And there came the brave warrior to save the day.

Gar was sprinting through the streets to reach Pax, winged helm in place and hammer swinging to let fly toward its mark. Pax leapt from the building and smacked the hammer from the sky, flinging it back toward Gar to slam into the ground with a crack of the stone. Just like they'd practiced.

Gar snarled and snatched up the hammer without slowing, a true vision, with a warrior's cry, and spun the hammer to unleash it again. Several times, Pax struck it down like before. A few times, he let it hit him right when he looked ready to spew his breath attack upon Gar. Finally, a few other times, he let it knock him backward or down to the ground and feigned having to struggle to take flight again. It was brilliant, inspired, more fun than any performance before it.

Until the explosions started.

Pax tumbled into a building without meaning to, caught by debris from the part of another building that had burst apart.

"It's real! It's really attacking!" someone screamed, and he realized they thought the explosion was from him. Which, well done, great idea, but why hadn't Gar warned him?

The hammer hit Pax when he wasn't looking, an actual, unexpected strike, and he stumbled again, knocking into another building.

Where another explosion rained down debris.

"Why turn on us now?" Gar accused, racing forward to retrieve his hammer with a wildness in his eyes that Pax wasn't used to, not even from their best performances.

Pax took to the air to get his bearings, but another explosion sent a gust of wind beneath his wings and pushed him farther backward. They were at the edge of the city to avoid anyone getting hurt, but this was too much. The people believed it enough that guards were gathering, and others were starting to grab weapons to join Gar in the fight.

"Stay back! It's gone mad!" Gar outstretched an arm to keep the crowd from approaching and looked to Pax with hinting eyes. He wanted this to look real, and it was certainly starting to.

Pax could work with that. It made sense to surprise him with the explosions so his reactions would be real. And, after all, he'd not only promised to follow Gar's lead....

He'd granted it as a wish.

Roaring and lashing out toward Gar, who continued to swing and throw his hammer, Pax realized he was being herded toward the caves. Of course! What better place for the fearsome dragon to be banished once and for all.

After a few more explosions with Pax spitting fire toward them to increase the illusion, the crowd forming behind Gar seemed intent on aiding him rather than listening about staying out of the way. Shrinking to the size he needed to fit, Pax gave one final roar and dove into the opening he'd backed against.

He hurried through the caverns toward the Ruby gemstone, knowing Gar would be close on his tail.

"Sick of games, beast? You can't escape me!" Gar's cry preceded him racing in after Pax. He was well ahead of the others, but by the sounds of it, half the city was chasing them.

"Gar!" Pax went to him, shifting into an elf. "What's the end game here? How—"

"What are you doing?" Gar snarled. "Change back!"

Pax startled, never having known Gar to snarl like that, even when acting. "Just… trying to understand the script."

Gar downturned his brows in apology but his fierceness didn't fade. He tugged Pax down for a kiss. "You're doing beautifully. Just remember my wish. You follow my lead. Now change back, before they get in here."

"At your command," Pax said, kissed Gar again, and retreated to give room for him to grow, as large as his dragon form could be while hunched from the height of the caves.

Gar lifted one of Pax's talons and slashed himself in the leg with it, right between his armor plates.

"Gar!"

He threw himself to the ground as if Pax had sent him there, just as the people poured in. "Stay back! It's too dangerous!" he shouted, and then snarled at Pax once more. "I will not let you harm anyone!" He hefted himself upright and slammed his maul into Pax's heel without the restraint of their usual playacting.

It hurt, a rare spot that Gar knew to be tender. Of course it didn't really *hurt* Pax, no real threat to him, but the sting made him stumble backward, just as a new explosion discharged overhead and a whole section of the cavern started crumbling.

"Back, beast! You want chaos, then be buried by your choices!"

Pax withdrew to get out from under the falling rocks, as more and more tumbled between them. He was being cut off from Gar, the barrage not slowing, and Gar didn't look like he wanted it to.

He wanted… *this*?

He didn't want Pax?

"Go!" Gar met his eyes between raining debris, and there was no uncertainty there, as he finished cruelly, "And never return."

He almost looked elated when he pivoted to face the cheering crowd, turning his back on Pax and leaving him in darkness as the last rock fell.

THE FINAL room that looked upon those ancient memories seemed unnecessary. All it showed was Pax in that deeply buried chamber, walking farther in until he found a large enough space to curl up and go to sleep.

"But... surely, you could have broken out," Bertram said. "The wish had been fulfilled. You'd played the scene the way he wanted. Afterward, you could have left."

"I could have. I could have gone to my hoard at least and slept there. I just... didn't have the will to do so."

With Bertram's wish over, the white hall and its painful scenes faded, bringing them not to the hoard, for Pax didn't want to see any more memories today, but to the alley.

"He chose glory," Pax said, returning to how he'd been leaning against the wall of Jafari's, only as an adult now instead of a teenager. "So I went to sleep."

"I am so sorry, Pax," Bertram said, facing him. "You broke your rule for him."

"I broke my rule. He broke my heart."

"But... now that you're awake again, do you truly want to go back to pretending you don't crave the deeper connection you thought you had with him?"

"That's rich coming from a man who'd been doing the same thing."

Bertram didn't look away but met Pax's stare with a somber nod. "I kept telling myself there was time, that there were more important things. I don't want to do away with my responsibilities. They matter too. I care about the work. I want to be a good king. But I want more than only duty in my life, and I thank you for showing me that, Pax. And your past." He gently tugged Pax's tightly crossed arms and drew them down to take hold of his hands.

He was too kind, too good a man for Pax to keep the bitterness in his voice. Though he still muttered, "You did sort of make me."

Bertram snorted. "I did. Maybe I was being the selfish ass this time. I do truly think you needed to see all that again. Just like I needed to see a future where I made my worst mistakes. I don't want it to be ten years from now, and I'm worse off than I was, lonely, distant, sleepwalking through life. I can have both, do right by duty and have what my heart craves. Just like you can without fearing that someone else will break it."

Heat prickled Pax's eyes. He'd managed so well to not let that happen while watching Gar betray him again, yet a few words from Bertram and….

Pax tried for levity to hide the tears he couldn't shake.

"That's quite the proposal."

"It doesn't have to be me!" Bertram's lovely brown cheeks flushed darker, but he squeezed Pax's hands more firmly. "Gar fooled you for weeks before he decided on the right wishes to get his true desires, and we've only known each other for a few days, so you've no reason to trust me. But if I've learned something from all this, I hope you have too. You weren't wrong to want what you did, to risk what you did, it just ended up being the wrong partner."

Learned something? Had he?

He'd learned it was just as pathetic to watch oneself make mistakes as having made them.

He'd learned he maybe liked having someone around who he didn't want to leave once their wishes were up.

He'd learned he might have been done with purely dallying with mortals all the way back when he met Gar, and he'd liked entertaining the idea of having more.

Which meant the blue half-elf from Amethyst was probably right about him being lonely, and that was pretty irritating actually.

Most of what he'd learned, maybe all of what he'd learned, he'd learned from Bertram, and since when had a mortal taught him something? Other than betrayal.

"You continue to amaze me, Bertie," Pax said, smiling through the pesky tears that spilled free. "That's difficult. And I've been around a while."

"Well, I still have a kingdom to save. We'll see if I can do that. But while I try to figure out my crisis, please promise me you'll be careful. We don't know—"

"Oh, please, as if they could possibly—"

The door opened, and before even a person was made known, a pair of manacles with the glow of magical limiters were clapped onto Pax's outstretched wrists.

He instantly began to grow, changing shape into his dragon form without willing it.

"Pax!" Bertram cried, but he had to go; he had to escape the alley before he grew too large to spare Bertram from being crushed.

CHAPTER 15

PAX'S TAIL swung as it tripled in size, and Bertram barely ducked out of the way to avoid being smacked to the back of the alley. Pax was growing and *growing*, clearing the alley just as his full size overtook him and causing the edges of the buildings on either side to bow from his mass. He loosened more stones as he wiggled free and finally collapsed in the larger street beyond.

"Pax!" Bertram chased after him, trying to get around to where the limiters had been placed on his wrists. They had the same red glow as the ones on Leslie's family but were imbued with an extra rune for Giant, allowing them to change size with their captive.

Pax's eyes were closed, and he was panting, as if the energy had been sucked right out of him.

"Your Majesty, we did it!"

Bertram spun to see Dain and several followers rushing from the alley to join him.

"Did you know? Or had the dragon tricked you as well?" Dain asked.

They thought he was in the dark about Pax, and he had to pretend he was. He couldn't risk them turning on him and clapping him in irons too. He had to find a way to get Pax free without making things worse. "I… suspected. But please, I can't condone this. You can't strip a dragon of its scales and force it into servitude. You don't know his purpose, his intent. No one has been harmed by him."

Dain's earlier look of disapproval was patient now, probably because he thought he had what he needed. "Talk to him, then." He placed a hand on Bertram's shoulder like before. "But we will be attempting to remove at least one scale. I hope there is a way out of this besides civil war as well, Your Majesty, but I won't sit around waiting for that decision to be made for me."

"Even if ordered by your king?" Bertram shrugged his hand aside.

"I hope that is an order you do not make." Dain held his stare and then turned to the people who'd followed him, commanding them back toward Pax's haunches to try removing a scale there.

Dain was giving him privacy to talk to Pax, which was something at least, but if Bertram wanted to resolve this with a wish or request from a dragon, he would have done so with the scales he'd been gifted already.

He didn't even have a new one yet, and Pax hardly looked capable of plucking one free.

"Pax…?" Bertram said quietly, moving around in front of his large head. Riding him was not the same as seeing him up close from the front with Pax's chin on the cobblestones, his nostrils gently flaring as he breathed, and eyes twitching as if dreaming.

His scales were so beautiful, as were the tufts of fur beneath and between them, his platinum horns, and how the streetlamps made him glimmer in a whole new way compared to sunlight. Bertram caressed the curve of Pax's chin and up along his cheekbones that were all scaled, unlike only a few lining them when he was dragonkind with the base of an elf.

"Pax? Are you all right?"

A bit of air puffed from his nose. "Bit sleepy, to be honest," he grumbled and peeked one eye open.

Bertram hugged as much of him as the span of his arms could reach and pressed his forehead to Pax's snout. "Does it hurt?"

"More like a gentle throbbing. The anti-magic side uses magic, and the pro-magic side uses limiters. At least they're even."

"I'm so sorry." Bertram moved to where Pax's front claws were splayed forward, the enlarged manacles glowing as they contained his magic. Bertram had no idea how to remove them, and he reached up in further sympathy to stroke the edge of one of Pax's wings that was curled forward.

"Mm," Pax hummed. "That feels lovely, Bertie. You know if you'd like to move around back and go a bit lower—" He flinched, and Bertram peered around at where Dain and his people were focusing on a single scale on his leg that they were trying to pull free using force and spells. "Though I ask that you be a bit gentler than they are."

"This is serious, Pax."

"And it's a serious request. Not the least bit interested?"

"In a prick as large as me?" Bertram tried to play along despite his heart sinking. "And what would I do with that?"

"You could give it some attention. Maybe kiss it—"

"*Pax.*" Bertram's voice cracked. "I don't know what to do."

His other eye opened, and he looked at Bertram with steadier breath. "You could slay the dragon, Your Majesty, or command it, depending on which side you choose."

"I don't want to choose sides. I don't want either of those options."

"Even if you could have the peace you want for your kingdom?"

"If those are the only ways to achieve peace, then damn this kingdom." Bertram never thought he'd feel that way, even when he'd wondered if a future without him ruling might be the answer. But as much as he thought he would do anything to change that future, to save Emerald from a repeat of the past, he wouldn't trade his soul for it.

He wouldn't trade Pax.

"If it means harming or using you like that, then damn this kingdom forever." He returned to Pax's snout and gently kissed the center of a scale on his chin.

"Well then...."

Smooth, cool metal was suddenly the press of soft lips.

Bertram snapped backward. Pax was elven, holding the manacles in unchained hands, right before they burst into a shower of red sparks like he'd done for Leslie's family.

"What would you have us do instead?"

"You... you could get out of those the entire time?"

"The first few seconds were a bit rough, but by the tenth—"

"Pax!" Bertram shoved him.

"Brilliant invention, truly! Would work on just about anyone, but really, Bertie, I'm a dragon." Pax swept forward and kissed Bertram firmly, forked tongue and all with a wondrous heat that flooded Bertram's belly from the passion in it and the feel of Pax's arms wrapping tight around him.

Damn him. But praise him, too, because Bertram couldn't possibly resist kissing back.

"Your Majesty!"

Dain and the others were running up from where the rest of the dragon had disappeared.

"I've half a mind to put limiters on *you*," Pax called back at them, and they stuttered in their progress forward. "That'd teach you. Not that I'm confident you'd actually learn something. All Bertie has been trying to do—"

"Wait." Bertram patted Pax's arm to halt his scolding, amusing as it was for him to be the one doing it. "I think you gave me an idea."

"I did?"

"Teaching. *Learning* something. Dain!" Bertram waved him closer. "Please, it's all right. I didn't remove the limiters. I wouldn't have known how. But they weren't enough to hold him. He's a platinum dragon—of course they weren't. He was merely being kind by not reacting in anger after your cruelty."

"Which could very quickly change," Pax warned them.

The others held back, but Dain continued to approach.

"He is on our side," Bertram said, "all our sides, but only if we treat him like more than a tool. I need you to trust me. To listen and allow for some compromise with Penelope."

"Like she and her people are willing to compromise?"

"I am hoping they'll listen too. I think I have a plan." In truth, one that harkened back to the compromise he'd managed as a boy when he got two arguing neighbors to share a tree until a second one grew. "But I need you to follow my lead. All of you." He looked at Pax, recognizing that those words might carry a sting. "Not wish. I don't wish it. Just need."

A stillness hung in the air, the empty streets too quiet and tense, though at least that meant few if anyone had seen Pax transform.

Eventually, Dain nodded, and when Bertram looked to Pax again, he nodded too.

"I'm listening," Pax said.

IT WAS a brilliant plan. And just shy of being a painful reminder of the last time Pax was asked to perform for the sake of a companion he'd fallen for.

And he had fallen. It was all Bertram's fault, really.

He was easy to fall for.

"And now you steal the castle from its rightful king! Do you not see your folly?" Pax thundered, filling the streets of Emerald as he walked, not flew, down the main road toward the castle gates, crunching menacingly into cobblestones and prompting everyone who dared look out their windows to tremble in fear at the sight of him.

He did so enjoy making a spectacle.

At least when no unexpected explosions occurred, just the occasional impact of paltry spells thrown at him by Dain's people, who were in on the ruse.

"Magic? You argue over magic as if my kind, the first to inhabit these lands, are a joke or mere story to be forgotten?"

He spat a breath of earth magic at a guard who turned from the castle gates to run at him, binding him in vines that suctioned him to the ground and held him immobile.

"How it wounds me when the balance of magic was my people's greatest pride. I wept in my slumber over how this kingdom treated elves and those with magic for so many years, but you recovered, you thrived and became better." Or so Bertram had told him since Pax hadn't been keeping an ear to the kingdoms while sleeping. "That you would risk falling to those ways again woke me from my long sleep."

At another guard, Pax blew a stream of ice that froze his feet to the ground.

At one of Dain's people, he covered her in shadows, so she appeared to vanish—but was actually transported to another side street.

At one of Penelope's people, who must think himself safe behind the gates as he and others exited the castle to see the commotion, Pax shot a bolt of lightning over his head, so that his hair stood up from the static.

Pax snorted fire from his nostrils, and finally opened his mouth to show a collecting ball of prismatic force, combining all his elements together. He really wished he could see how striking he must look right now.

"Please, great dragon, understand!" Bertram took his cue, racing in front of the gates where Pax had come to a stop, and all the remaining guards scattered. Bertram looked ragged, humbled, in borrowed boots and simple shirt and trousers, which Pax imagined caught the attention of the onlookers even more. "Some of the people, those with lesser or no magic, are afraid. We are still working toward a compromise."

"*This* is compromise?" Pax swallowed the magic he'd had no intention of unleashing and flapped his wings to billow back those still trying to stop him with spells. The wind knocked them to the ground, while those hiding behind the gates trembled, Penelope included. "One side steals my likeness to stir fear and dissent, another tries to clap me in irons to steal my scales. No limiters can hold me. Such things to dampen magic should be used to train and temper, not enslave."

"Then might I offer a final plea to my people?" Betram stood tall, playing the role of bold king, for that was what he was. "If they agree, we can end this feud and form a council of civil and open-minded citizens to prevent such unrest from happening again."

Pax stomped the ground, no one else daring to try attacking or confronting the fearsome dragon, but seeing their leader, their rightful monarch, standing up to him despite the danger. "One final plea," Pax rumbled. "You seem a decent king. Address your people."

A brilliant plan indeed, but still one that both sides needed to see the logic in.

"This dragon, a symbol of the very source of magic," Bertram called to all who were listening—guards, scared citizens in their homes, Dain's people who'd played along but were still wary, and Penelope's who'd taken his castle and imprisoned him out of fear, "makes the very point I have wanted you all to understand. Compromise. Balance. And maybe what he said can be how we achieve that. Perhaps the distribution of limiters could be a temporary answer to safeguarding the city against unintentional and underage magic—"

"You mean to shackle us!" someone cried from their window.

"No. To train and temper, like the dragon said. So many families hid themselves for so long in decades past, pretending they had no magic. Can you truly say that didn't stunt proper training and use of it? Weren't *you* teaching your children once to hide it yourselves? And no, I do not mean for any of you to do that again, but training is needed.

"What I propose is that we build a school with volunteers to be the first teachers." He looked to Dain's people especially. "And we use limiters not as shackles but as training tools. I have it on good authority that the people of Sapphire have an idea for a potion that isn't as, well, limiting, and once ready, we would never need real limiters again. But we do need something in the meantime. You must look beyond the now, beyond the fears and inconveniences of today, and allow for where we can go.

"Magic should be allowed freely, but not foolishly. If someone uses it in a barfight, it is the same as if they pulled a dagger, and such an offender should be punished the same too. We can't pretend that magic isn't part of us, but we can teach the next generation, we can teach those who don't have a handle on their powers as they should, how to use it well. There will be accidents." He turned to Penelope, who stood nearest him through the gate. "There will be people who go against the rules. But that is true with or without magic, for even decent people can become brutes and thieves if they think themselves capable."

Pax held back from snorting, wondering if those would-be thieves from the day he met Bertram were in the wings somewhere, shaking in their boots.

"Please," Bertram continued, holding Penelope's stare, "if both sides can calm themselves enough to agree, I will pardon everyone who acted against another today, even those who committed *treason*, and we can start anew. A school, limiters used but only justly, only temporarily, and a council voted on without its beginning having its members at each other's throats.

"What say you to that?"

His final words rang through the streets with a fading echo, followed by several beats of strained silence. The suspense was thrilling, and Pax hoped he didn't look too much like he was smiling.

"That doesn't answer every concern," Penelope said.

"I don't think anything could." Dain stepped forward. He might have only seen reason because the dragon he'd wronged had promised not to filet him, but he'd listened, nonetheless. "Perhaps this can be enough. To anger someone who speaks for the earth." He gestured at Pax. "Not only for magic, but for our very world... I don't want to be what this dissention has made of me or see more of what it has done to our city."

It wasn't too much damage, of course, for Pax had been careful to only crush and scuff a few buildings, but the real damage was in the people's hearts, and only they could fix it.

Penelope, like any good leader, looked to her people gathered in the courtyard behind her, who had taken the castle by force only hours ago. When what she saw was agreement and nods of hope—and maybe a little fear of Pax—she turned forward again. "It's a start."

"And you, great dragon?" Bertram addressed Pax while Penelope opened the gates behind him. "To prove we will do as we've said, will you stay and help lead us in learning to appreciate the balance of magic?"

What? That wasn't part of the plan. Bertram hadn't mentioned….

But Pax could see a subtle smile peeking through Bertram's expression.

He wanted him to stay.

"For a time," Pax answered, trying to keep the true emotion from his voice, "so long as I find you worthy." He'd been meant to wing away now, but given the invitation, Pax shrank his form instead, becoming his dragonkind self that made the fear on most people's faces turn to awe. "It seems you might be worthy indeed. And that is why…." He produced Bertram's crown as if it had merely been hiding behind his back rather than plucked out of space and time from a shelf in Pax's hoard.

He was keeping the undergarment, though.

"You are the rightful king."

Pax placed the crown where it belonged on Bertram's head, and an eruption of applause and cheering began, with Bertram basking in it, facing Pax, with gratitude and a broad smile.

"May I ask?" One of the guards came forward from within the castle, released from the dungeons, or possibly having escaped during the commotion. He wasn't in armor, but Pax recognized the elf as David—who was definitely not fooled, seeing as how he'd seen Pax in Bertram's bed. "What would you have done, great dragon, if we had failed to agree with our king's ruling?"

"Well, I certainly wouldn't have eaten anyone," Pax said, and any remaining fear of him seemed to dissipate. "Mortals are far too stringy. But let's say, considering you have agreed, I help fix up some of this mess?"

He snapped his fingers and the disturbed stones and slight damage to walkways and buildings from his playacting began to repair themselves. People who'd stayed in their homes began peeking out to get a look at this "great dragon." It was a different sort of feeling to be looked on as the savior instead of the enemy after a performance. Especially in one form, to another, and finally, to just his elven self so no one had to stare at him in wonder for too long.

As Bertram led the way through the gates into the castle, with Dain and some of his people, Penelope and some of hers, David and the other guards, and Pax tailing the lot of them with Bertram's request that he stay, he thought some of him might be repairing itself too.

CHAPTER 16

"ARE YOU sure about this?"

"As long as you can truly change the size and texture of that tail like you promised."

"I can magic away scales, the start of fins, and make it any size you desire."

"Yet you didn't mention that the first time you prodded me with it?"

"I dare say I didn't hear any complaints." Pax squeezed Bertram's hips, where he hovered above him. The sturdy and well-muscled but petite young king was bronze perfection when bare of anything but his crown and necklace.

The necklace was a simple thing, a thin golden chain with two dimmed but still dazzling scales threaded onto it. Pax had been rather touched by the request to have it made, since usually he was the one keeping reminders.

He did still sometimes steal Bertram's crown, but fucking the king of Emerald was more fun when he was properly adorned.

Although at the moment, Bertram was angling his fine, thick cock to fuck Pax.

The ripe and weeping head breached Pax with a slide along the tender ring of scales that circled his entrance. Within, Pax was warm, wet flesh like anyone else, and he clenched in agreement of Bertram's intrusion with frequent squeezes at every push.

Lying on his wings could be a pain, but not like this, spread wide beneath him, and reaching far enough to stretch over either side of the bed. While Bertram rocked him backward to push in deep, Pax likewise petted Bertram's hole with little flicks of his tail. He willed it smaller, just a bit at the end, vanished some of the scales or made them thinner and soft where they became too sharp, and did away with that first fin.

He waved it over Bertram's shoulder so he could see just how much they had to work with now, and Bertram laughed, falling forward to push himself deeper inside of Pax.

"Oh!" Pax arched his head back—and returned his tail to Bertram's hole.

"*Ohhh....*" Bertram's moan was lower as Pax pushed in, with a puff of breath on Pax's chest where his head had fallen. He looked up, rolled Pax farther backward to sink in even deeper, and brought his face in alignment for a kiss.

He started rocking while their tongues tangled, and Pax met his rhythm with matching thrusts of his tail. Pax's tongue was as thick as any mortal's at the meat of it, but the thinner points where it forked made it longer, and he coiled it around Bertram's tongue with firm strokes as if fellating him.

Bertram moaned between their mouths and kissed Pax harder, thrusting deeper too, but at a slow, sensuous pace. Pax's tail was at the point where, the last time they did this, it couldn't have gone farther, but it could now, its girth a little less thick and the way inside smoother. Pax thrust in a little more, a little *more*, letting it deeply drag inside Bertram as far as its new form could go.

"*Pax....*" Bertram's head snapped up from their kiss, and Pax latched on to his neck, grazing his fangs and flicking the tiny points of his tongue. He licked up Bertram's neck to tease the lobe of his ear, around the edges, and the inner grooves. "P-Pax...."

"Yes, Bertie?" Pax breathed hotly where he'd licked.

"H-have you ever... made love in the air?"

"Thinking about that *you*-sized prick?"

"N-no." Bertram laughed. "I just... wondered... what you flying might look like." He didn't cease his rhythmic rocking, which also rocked him back to take in Pax's tail, but he slowed. And slowed. And slid his hands from how they'd been hooked beneath Pax's knees, bending him even more in half, to touch the tender skin of Pax's wings.

"Oh!" Pax shuddered. "You... want to see my wings in action, do you? While stuffed full and stuffing me? I'm afraid it's difficult to get the right *friction* while airborne. However...." He thrust them upward with a push of his wings and flapped hard to send them soaring across the room.

"Pax!" Bertram's eyes went wide from the shock of hitting the wall, but then he marveled at how they *were* airborne, just properly anchored to make him howl when Pax rocked atop him with the wall as their bracing point—and he didn't even disturb his crown.

Pax didn't need to constantly flap to stay inflight, but he let his wings flutter as he kept them afloat and skillfully rode Bertram. He continued to thrust into him with the tip of his tail, and then deeper than just the tip, *deeper*, leaving Bertram little more than a writhing captive.

But as much of a vision as Bertram made like this, it was Pax he looked at as if *he* was the true wonder.

"Y-you are so… beautiful. Worthy of every song… and love story. Every wish granted… that you granted another."

"Bertie…." How did he always do that, prompting moisture to fill Pax's eyes?

He seemed to realize the effect his words had on Pax, maybe for the first time, and took his cheeks in hand. The look he gave Pax before he pulled them together for a kiss was… it wasn't hunger. Not wonder either, not really, not the way others looked at Pax, thinking about what it meant to have a dragon near them—and what that dragon could do for them. It was amazement for Pax purely as himself and just wanting to be with him.

No one else had ever looked at Pax like that.

"Ah!" Bertram's lips tore from their kiss.

Pax's tail was especially deep inside him, and Bertram's cock pulsed within Pax, a throb that made Pax feel so wonderfully full. It warmed his insides, dragging along his walls, slick with bubbling pre-release, while his tail was swallowed up inside Bertram.

Then Bertram's fingers feathered over Pax's cock between them, smoothing Pax's own pre-release down his softer scales with a fervent pump.

"Bertie!" Pax came, hard and unexpected, and it made him thrust his tail into Bertram faster like an echo of his release spurting.

He rocked harder on Bertram's cock too; Bertram, who was pinned and barely able to move or risk falling down the wall, yet he'd coaxed Pax to spill first. He'd held *him* captive, and kissed Pax with another plunge of his tongue just as he finally spilled too.

It would have been easy for Pax to let his fluttering wings slowly lower them to the floor, but not nearly as entertaining as making Bertram yelp and clutch at him tightly when he flapped to push them away from the wall again and returned them to bed with a gentle bounce.

"Pax!"

The crown had been disturbed this time, and Pax plucked it from the pillow to put on his own head instead. "Now *that* was something." He wrapped Bertram up in his wings, refusing to be reminded of anyone else he'd ever held like this.

Bertram was different.

Oh, Pax hoped he was right that Bertram was different.

"You might have slayed the dragon but chose to lay him instead. Smart call."

Bertram snorted and snuggled against Pax. They were sticky, but it was mostly Pax covered and filled with come. He didn't mind. Before long, they'd need to be up anyway, and he planned to lay there for as long as he could.

Although, there was one thing they kept putting off, and Pax couldn't help how it uneased him to have that unfinished.

"So… still one wish to go, sweet king."

Bertram lifted his head and glanced out of the canopy of Pax's wings to the table beside them, where a lone gleaming scale rested. When Bertram shifted toward it, Pax dropped his wings to allow him to retrieve the scale. Pax had given it to him after the first round of successful talks between Penelope and Dain's people, but two days later, he had yet to make a wish.

"Know what you want, then?" Pax asked, since Bertram was studying it intently.

"I think I do."

Pax swallowed, uncertain what he wanted to hear. He hadn't worried about a companion's final wish in a long time.

"I wish… for you to stay, and for longer than just 'a time.'"

PAX LOOKED troubled by Bertram's request, which he'd expected.

"I can't change the hearts of people, Bertie. Not even my own."

"I know, so your heart will have to want to stay on its own." Bertram handed the scale to Pax and closed it in his taloned grasp. "No magic required, just a wish from one heart to another."

"You're giving it back? You don't want a third wish?"

"I know we haven't known each other for long, and if someday we are meant to part, so be it, but I don't need wishes to know I want you to stay with me, Pax."

Wetness filled Pax's eyes like it had while they were against the wall. To Bertram, it seemed such an impossible thing that no one had ever asked this of Pax before. That no one had ever wanted to keep him, at least no one who Pax wanted to stay with.

That Pax nodded, squeezed the scale in his hand, and kissed Bertram deeply was more impossible still, because it meant Pax did want to stay with him.

"Can't imagine anywhere else I'd rather be," Pax said.

"Are you two up yet!" Several knocks sounded at the door. "I thought we were heading to Festival Day early!"

"Oh dear…." Bertram glanced at the candle clock that was definitely lower than he'd realized. "Coming, Raya! Just a few minutes!"

After all, they weren't in Bertram's chambers in Emerald, but in his old room in Sapphire.

It had been a few days before the yearly festival in Amethyst when Bertram first met Pax, meaning they could attend the event all over again in this time. Once things had been settled in Emerald, he'd allowed himself to spend a night at home, so they could wake up here and spend today at the festival with all those dear to him.

"Hurry up, then!" Raya called, quite reminiscent of her mother from what seemed like a lifetime ago but was actually ten years from now and likely an event that wouldn't happen. "Just because you're courting a dragon doesn't mean you're exempt from common decency," she muttered as she left.

Bertram flushed, and Pax let out a laugh.

They hurried to get ready, which, for Pax, meant a simple will to be presentable—although what he willed onto himself was the outfit he'd donned in Diamond with a gold cord and adornments, holding in place very meager amounts of teal and white silk. He'd warned he might do that, but dammit, Bertram could not walk around in something similar around his parents!

Instead, he wore the royal doublet his mother had made him and the short cloak that, like the outfits from Diamond—including Bertram's undergarment—Pax had made a point to bring back with them from out of time.

Bertram noticed Pax also wore a new necklace, very like his own, but with only one scale, the one never used that glittered like the most precious of metal.

"Shall we?" Pax held out his arm once Bertram was ready. He was elven now, for his wings, tail, and talons could get in the way at times, but as soon as they stepped foot on Amethyst's lands, he'd be dragonkind again.

Bertram was enamored with him no matter which form he took. "We shall."

It was strange being back in Sapphire, when last he'd walked these halls, so much had been different, with children older, new ones born, and some people having left for other kingdoms.

The people here had also not known Pax was a dragon—and he'd looked like a teenager. His larger self commanded more attention, and most people who saw him gazed in wonder. Once Pax talked with someone, the novelty usually wore off, for he was a jovial and direct man, not at all stoic or humble like in the tomes and stories.

The real thing was far better than any story.

"Oh! Now there's an outfit," Josie proclaimed upon seeing Pax when he and Bertram entered the throne room, where the Veil Curtain awaited those planning to leave for Amethyst.

"Mother!" Bertram chided.

She immediately slid her eyes to Barclay beside her, who flushed at the insinuation that she wouldn't mind seeing him in something similar.

Definitely best that Bertram hadn't worn his own skimpy attire. He could save that for later, in private.

They weren't the last to arrive, so no one was using the Veil Curtain yet. Pax got dragged off by Nigel and Zephyr before he could comment on Josie's perusal of him, having immediately befriended the pair again and showing off his thieving prowess.

"We were worried you might not bother with the festival this year," Barclay said, "given how busy you've been. You hadn't even written to us yet."

"I… wanted to solve a few things before I updated you. But even new monarchs need to take time for themselves."

"About time you loosened up," Raya said in passing, accompanied by her sister. "I was afraid you'd become a complete bore before long, drowning in duty."

"So was I."

"That is a lovely flower, darling," Josie said of the White Dragon tucked within the actual dragon broach of Bertram's cloak.

"Yes. A very special one."

"Oh! I almost forgot!" she exclaimed anew, pulling a piece of parchment from a pocket in her skirt. "Guess what arrived this morning? Letters from Reardon and Jack! They had one enclosed for you, of course." She handed it to him, and Bertram was almost afraid to touch it for its aptly timed arrival.

> *Dear Bertram,*
>
> *Jack says I should be the one to pen our letters, since my handwriting is better. A convenient excuse, I think!*
>
> *We are having a marvelous time though, and I hope things are going well in Emerald. Should you ever need anything, do not hesitate to message us. We will return to the Gemstone Kingdoms and reach you through the nearest Veil Curtain at a moment's notice. But I know you won't need us to become a good king. The people don't always know what they want, but a good leader can help them discover the answers through community and often merely by listening.*
>
> *And other times with a kick in the rear.*
>
> *We know you will be amazing at it, carrying on not only our legacies but generations' worth, or we wouldn't have asked you to try.*
>
> *We will visit soon, but in the meantime, don't be afraid to seek your own adventures, even while delving into the duties of being king. Above all else, remember: Curses can be broken. Hearts healed. Minds changed. And love can be found in even the most unexpected of places.*
>
> *Love you always,*
> *Your Uncles Reardon and Jack*

"But where do you have room to stick it?" Nigel was hemming and hawing over whatever newest item Pax had swiped from him.

"I'm afraid to do that search, my friend, you'll need to consult my companion." Pax winked at Bertram, and Bertram had to shake his head.

His gaze found Ambrose then, one of the stragglers coming in to join them. Their eyes met, and Ambrose gave what Bertram thought might be a somber smile. He must be rather surprised about Pax and maybe disappointed, because in this time, they'd been an *almost* not too long ago.

Among a cluster of others, gazing on Ambrose as though the broad, blond man was the most beautiful thing he'd ever seen, was the very half-elf Bertram remembered seeing with Ambrose at that other Festival Day, and at his side in the dining hall here in Emerald. His future husband.

"Mother, do you know that elf?"

"Hm? Oh, Hylan? He's a recent addition from Diamond. Learning from Oliver, I believe, to be an archer. Oliver goes too easy on the young recruits these days. Just wait until Hylan has his first lesson with Rosie. He's far stricter."

"Yes."

"Are you all right, Bertie?" Barclay grasped his shoulder, bringing Bertram's attention back to his parents. "Oh. It seems you are."

Bertram nearly forgot that his father… *knew*, whatever his visions might have shown him of the adventures Bertram would have. He didn't need to ask for specifics. He'd seen enough of the future himself. "Yes, I think I am. One moment."

Pocketing the letter, which he felt far more equipped to take to heart than he might have a week ago, Bertram went to join Ambrose, who seemed fidgety and uncertain, a look that did not befit the burly man at all.

"Ambrose."

"Hello, Bertram."

Bertram. Not steward.

Definitely better.

"But I should say Your Majesty now, shouldn't I?" Ambrose inclined his head in a bow.

"Bertram is fine. Have you met Hylan?" Bertram waved the watching half-elf over. "Mother was just telling me he's been training with your father."

"Is that right?" Ambrose turned to the startled and suddenly blushing young elf.

"Are we going to get going or what?" Raya called over the din, for it seemed all who they'd been waiting for had arrived.

Pax rejoined Bertram as they fell in line for the Veil Curtain, groups of people blinking away in clusters of half a dozen or so.

"Am I going to get to see your monstrous side this time?" Pax asked.

"Perhaps."

"You need only will the change, you said, but what you become is a mystery? I think you'll be a… centaur. Or a sphinx!"

Bertram laughed. "We'll have to see."

What they did see when they arrived in the Amethyst market square was Ashmedai and Levi with fellow monarchs Cullen and Enzo, greeting people as they arrived. They'd all been informed about Pax, so this time, Ashmedai was not startled to see a dragon waltzing into his kingdom.

"I better not hear any I told you so's from you," Pax said to Levi, who looked thoroughly confused, given they hadn't technically met yet.

Bertram didn't know what Pax meant either, though he had some guesses.

Mavis, the Fairy Queen, was there too, with her husband, Finn, neither of whom Bertram had seen on his adventure. They were always a grand pair, dressed in indigo and violet that matched well with Amethyst's celebration, and wearing their antlered crowns. Mavis was a dark beauty, with Finn a flaxen contrast.

She smiled knowingly at Bertram. She always had that smile, like she knew more of the future than most, even more than Bertram's father. Bertram didn't envy either of them if they knew what came next. He preferred to be surprised.

But then, he realized, there was one couple whose fate remained a mystery that he couldn't help being curious about.

"I have a good idea of the future for the other kingdoms and all the important people that helped shape our unification, except for one pair," Bertram said to Pax as they strolled in search of pastries for breakfast, admiring the stalls and violet-colored decorations among the glittering black buildings. "Janskoller the bard and his Fairy Prince. I've only met them once or twice. They traveled much, never rulers themselves."

"But they went through the Diamond, you said, beyond the veil?" Pax asked. "Time works a bit differently there, but I'd bet they'll be back someday."

"You think so?"

"Is that a question in exchange for an experience, Bertie?" Pax grinned.

"I will join in any experience you ask of me."

"Well then! I'll answer anyway. I do think so. With the Gemstone Kingdoms at peace and to remain so for the next decade and hopefully longer, you might be surprised how many others find their way back."

"Like you did?"

"I never really left. And I am special." Pax paused to sweep Bertram close and kissed him right in the middle of the market path. He smelled even more like bergamot and leather in his dragonkind form.

"Yes." Bertram giggled. "You are special."

He reached to tug the freshly sprouted horns upon Pax's head and pulled him down for another kiss.

TEN YEARS LATER

IF THEY'D timed things right, it should be Festival Day in Amethyst, but of course, since they'd entered the world beyond the veil through the Diamond gemstone, that was where they had to return first.

Janskoller shook off the flood of magic that passing through such a nexus of power left in him. When they'd originally gone through, it had knocked him on his ass, but this time, it felt like coming home.

"What a pleasant and quiet evening, my love," he said to his companion, since the Diamond rested in a picturesque park, and there were no onlookers to have witnessed their return.

"It won't stay quiet for long," Nemirac snorted.

He was as beautiful as the day Janskoller met him, with his long silver braid, golden eyes, elegantly pointed ears, and dark skin. Their initial adventures beyond the Gemstone Kingdoms had left Janskoller with a few fresh grays in his hair and beard, but in the lands of wild magic, no more had sprouted, and he was fairly certain a few had returned to brown.

Glancing about, Janskoller spotted what he had hoped to find here, lying in wait for his inevitable return—the cap he'd left on the dais of the gemstone, black with gold trim and a white feather, which Jason, the former bard who'd borne the Janskoller name before him, had gifted him the night he won Nemirac's heart.

He cleared his throat as he plucked it from its place of honor and twirled it around a finger until Nemirac noticed. "Your meal, my dear. Shall we find some salt? Or perhaps just a glass of water to help wash it down?"

"Very funny." Nemirac hopped down from the dais into the grass, balancing himself with use of his diamond-topped staff.

"It was you who said: if dragons are next, I'll eat your hat."

Janskoller had long since replaced that cap with a new one, given to him by the original Janskoller, who he'd had the pleasure of meeting beyond the veil. This one was a hat of many colors and could be whatever hue he wished it. Tonight, it was turquoise.

He plopped the white cap on Nemirac's head, since he wouldn't be eating it. "After all, we are here to see a king about a dragon—and all his brethren who plan to visit very, very soon."

Nemirac tilted the hat up from having fallen over his eyes and smirked. "Best we get going, then."

"Indeed." Janskoller removed the lute from being slung over his back and began a simple strum. "I think this calls for a song. I cannot wait to see everyone again."

But that is another story.

Not yet written.

THE END

Keep reading for an excerpt from
Coming Up for Air
by Amanda Meuwissen

CHAPTER 1

IF HIS life had gone differently, maybe Leigh Hurley would have been an engineer working toward his master's in thermodynamics by now instead of sinking to the bottom of the river.

At least he couldn't tell how filthy the water was since it was midnight and he was plummeting fast into the dark depths, the glimmer of moonlight above him quickly disappearing. He was a good swimmer, not that it mattered with twenty-pound weights attached to his ankles. He had about two minutes before he passed out, and then it would be curtains.

Fighting against the panic clawing at his chest the same way his lungs begged for air, he forced his body to curl downward in a frantic attempt to reach the weights. They were cinder blocks attached with actual shackles. Under normal circumstances, he might have been able to remove them using one of his lockpicks, but he couldn't see. A bitter mantra of "if only" followed his path downward like the bubbles of air escaping as he tried to think of some other way, any way to get out of this.

If only he wasn't a criminal. If only he hadn't been so damn opportunistic. If only he hadn't gotten caught.

It had been a smart plan. The streets by the docks where Leigh lived were split in half between the Moretti brothers and Arthur Sweeney, who might have been Irish to their Italian, but that wasn't the root of their animosity. Everything revolved around power in Cove City. At the end of the night, what mattered was which family had the most territory, like some old-fashioned trade of land equaling wealth, which was always true, and Leigh owned nothing, not even the apartment he could barely pay the rent on.

Since his best friend was Alvin Sweeney, Arthur's son, Leigh played for their side, hoping to rise in the ranks on more than nepotism. Looking good to Sweeney Senior meant making a splash on the scene, so Leigh had been working overtime for months on small thefts that caused an increasing decline in how much the Morettis brought in from their protection racket.

Leigh gave most of what he stole to Sweeney, but some he returned to the neighboring mom-and-pop stores as a good Samaritan, and a little he kept for himself. This made the Morettis look weak, like they couldn't protect their own. It was all about the long game and how it would make things easier for Sweeney to claim those streets in the months and years to come.

It would have worked, too, if they hadn't been waiting for Leigh tonight.

"Nobody crosses the Morettis," Leo, younger brother to Vincent and in charge of their muscle, had said before his goons dropped Leigh over the side of the docks.

Now he was going to drown with no one to remember him other than Alvin and maybe the handful of people in his building who relied on his technical talents and didn't care if he was a runner for a mobster as long as their TVs and dishwashers worked.

It was such a waste, pushing him to struggle harder to swim upward after he gave up on the shackles, vainly trying to beat back fate, even though he knew he wasn't strong enough and barely made an inch of headway before he continued to sink.

Soon he'd disappear, another good riddance that he doubted even his parole officer would miss for how often she sighed and told him to make something of himself instead of falling back into bad habits. But what was there to make of a life without privilege? Leigh had no prospects, no family, no education, only honed skills of survival. He'd been a thief since he could fit his hand inside a passing pocket. With his record, even at only twenty-five, there was no hope for him in this city that didn't lean on Arthur Sweeney, and now he'd lost that opportunity too.

The water was cold even in spring since this part of the river was wider. The docks wouldn't see any activity until morning, and not much then either at this location, though with a few shortcuts, it wasn't far to Leigh's apartment. He'd die close to home, if that meant anything. He just wished he'd been smarter, faster, and had another chance to do things better.

Those two minutes had to be up, because it was getting harder to fight, his mind sluggish and unable to think of a solution to save him. He was even starting to hallucinate, maybe dreaming, maybe already dead and fading away. A light shone in the blackness as he hit bottom. More like a glimmer of bare skin, because he'd swear he saw a face approaching as his mind grew hazier and his vision dimmed.

Somehow the face became clearer, though, beautiful too, like something ethereal—flawless features, concerned eyes, dark hair swaying in the water. If he was real, he would have been the exact sort of man who would have made Leigh take notice. Maybe the man was an angel, and Leigh's passing wouldn't be as painful or as terrifying as he'd feared, despite his lungs burning with the struggle to breathe.

But he didn't deserve an angel. He wasn't good in any sense of the word or worthy of heaven. He didn't believe in love, not even in saying the words, because that was more damaging and hollower than being hated if it came from somewhere fake or turned into rubbish along the way. His father had taught him that early, and life only reaffirmed the dangers of love and trust over the years.

Scared as Leigh was, part of him believed he had this coming, but the angel in the water didn't snarl or fade away. He came close enough that Leigh could make out every detail of his face, including occasional freckles and a wide smile. Then the beautiful man floated closer, looking back at Leigh in wonder, and captured his lips in a cold kiss.

A song filled his mind like when one got stuck in his head, playing distantly and sweet like he imagined this man's voice might be—lovely but understated, just a tune without words.

Leigh was dying. He should have been filled with terror, but in his last moments, he felt calm to have had such a pleasant final dream.

The next moment, he was gasping for breath, somehow on shore, on the riverbank far enough from where he'd been dropped that Leo and his goons couldn't see him, but still close enough to walk home. It didn't make sense. The man in the water couldn't be real. Cove City didn't produce unknown saviors, yet when Leigh looked down at his ankles, the cinder blocks were gone.

Coughing into the sand and dirt, unsure how he'd been saved or if he'd been touched by some miracle, all Leigh knew was that he had to get home, and after he rested, he'd have precious little time to prevent this same fate from befalling him again tomorrow night.

With a mighty push, he thrust up onto his knees, staggered to his feet, and began the slow trek back to his apartment, trying to banish the vision of that lovely face from overriding what he knew could only have been a trick of the mind.

LEIGH DIDN'T mean to fall asleep when he reached home and shed his soaked clothing. He only planned to rest his eyes for a moment, but he'd underestimated how exhausted he was, and when he roused it was to a loud knock at his door, with the clock on his nightstand blinking 7:00 a.m.

He didn't have time to be tired. That could already be Moretti goons or Sweeney himself, furious at Leigh for failing. It didn't help that he didn't feel as though he'd slept. His dreams had been filled with the face he imagined in the water. He didn't think he'd ever seen a man like that before, but his mind had conjured such a perfect specimen for his final moments.

The kiss had been nice too.

Leigh couldn't get distracted by phantoms, though. While he had no idea how the weights had come loose from his ankles or how he'd ended up on shore, it couldn't have been some mystery man.

"I'm coming!" Leigh called when the knocking refused to cease. It wasn't the Morettis or Sweeney or they would have kicked down the door by now. It had to be Miss Maggie. Only she ever got this uppity before 9:00 a.m.

Yanking the door open, Leigh stood in his sweats and long-sleeved T-shirt, barefoot and still chilled from his time in the river, but clean after a shower when he'd arrived home. He rubbed the sleep from his eyes and scrubbed at the closely shorn length of his hair.

"What?"

Miss Maggie was indeed the person on the other side of his door, but she looked particularly surly this morning. "William," she said sharply, using his given name, which he despised. "About time. I might be an old woman, but that does not mean I want to see some young man walking buck naked through my halls at all hours just because you had a wild night."

"Excuse me?" Leigh took a moment to process what she was complaining about. He hadn't started to undress while still in the hall last night, had he? He was out of it when he returned home, but not that disoriented.

"You know I support your lifestyle, whatever it may be, just so long as you keep the volume down after 11:00 p.m. and act respectfully, but this was just vulgar. Are you playing some game with the boy?"

"Game? Miss Maggie, I have no idea what you're—"

But before he could finish, she yanked someone else into view, who was wearing what appeared to be one of her housecoats and nothing else, not even shoes, though that wasn't what stopped Leigh short.

It was the man from the river. Same hair, same eyes, same everything.

Leigh really had died last night.

"William."

Which meant he was in hell if he was still dealing with Maggie's temper.

"Keep your evening activities confined to your apartment. Now, mind yourself, young man," she said to the flesh and blood figure who'd saved Leigh's life, "because I expect that nightgown returned at some point, preferably washed."

She shoved the man into Leigh's arms, and he had barely a second to register the full form of him, slim and tall, maybe half an inch taller than Leigh, and just as beautiful as he remembered, before Maggie hurried down the hall in a huff.

Leigh stumbled backward, causing the man to stumble with him, and pushed the door closed more on reflex than conscious choice. The man was real. Leigh hadn't imagined him. But if he'd saved Leigh's life, why was he only showing himself now?

And why the hell wasn't he wearing any clothes?

"I found you," he said in a breathless voice, as if in awe of Leigh, immediately evoking the memory of that same voice singing. "I knew I would, but still, I found you."

Carefully Leigh pushed at the man to hold him in front of him so they could get their bearings. He didn't seem very stable on his feet. Had he been drunk last night? Was that why he was swimming in the river at midnight naked and wandered all the way here in the same state? His eyes, large and almond-shaped, didn't look intoxicated. With olive skin, a reddish tint to his black hair, and freckles, he looked as likely to be of South Pacific descent as Greek or Jewish, maybe all three.

"You are even more handsome than when I saw you in the water," he said, with an intensity to how he stared that made Leigh shiver. The peek of long legs out of the housecoat was not helping his straying thoughts.

Leigh's generally fair looks with blond hair and blue eyes had gotten him out of sticky situations before. He knew what he had and how to use it, but he didn't think he compared with this lithe elfish beauty before him with a smile that lit up the whole apartment.

"It's you," he said, unable to articulate anything more than that. He pulled his hands from the man's shoulders, thinking it too intimate considering he was wearing nothing more than a nightgown.

"Yes." The man stepped into his space as if beckoned by a magnetic pull.

"You saved me. You found me."

"My apologies it took so long. I hesitated to follow, and once I decided to, I had trouble finding my feet, as they say. I knew the Breath of Life would lead me to you, though. Our souls are intertwined now, William. Ah, but you prefer Leigh, don't you?"

How…? "How do you know that?" And what was he talking about?

"You know my name as well."

"No, I…. Tolomeo. Tolly," he said before he could finish denying it. Had they met on the shore after all and Leigh simply didn't remember?

"Yes," Tolly said, smiling wider still.

This was too strange. Leigh's head was pounding, he was exhausted, and he still had to worry about Sweeney and the Morettis. He could not get caught up with some weird nudist—flower child—whatever this man was—when his life was in shambles.

"Look, I don't remember everything from last night, so if you explained this before, who you are, I'm sorry. I appreciate what you did. You saved my life, but it won't stay saved for long—"

"Those people who tried to drown you will continue to wish you harm," Tolly said.

"Yes. So if you came here expecting something more than my thanks, I hate to disappoint you, but I don't have much to offer."

"Oh, I am not like my brethren, I swear to you. I wish for no boon or life debt."

Okay. Was this guy a method actor or something? Maybe he was just crazy. "What do you want from me, then?"

"I wish to stay with you," Tolly said as matter-of-factly as asking for cab fare. "Forever."

Definitely crazy.

Holding up his hands to ward off whatever reaction might come next, Leigh chose his words very carefully. "Tolly, I will give you something to wear and then maybe there's someone we can call, okay? Or a hospital you came from?"

"I came from the sea," Tolly said, unfazed by Leigh's line of questioning. "Well, the river in this case, but all water is connected in my world. We can transport between depths through magic. I like bodies of water close to cities. The rest of my kin stay away, which I prefer, and I get to experience more of the human world."

"Human world? Your... kin?"

"Merfolk."

Leigh curtailed his reactions as best he could. "Tolly, is there anyone I can call to come get you?"

At last, a bit of that sunshine disposition flickered. "I have no one. No family or friends to speak of. That is why I chose to follow you. I was drawn to you, Leigh"—he stepped forward, making Leigh step back—"in the water, in your last moments, like I have never been drawn to anything. Others of my kin would have let you die, drowned you themselves, or forced a more self-serving pact, but I knew I had finally found the one who could give me legs."

If this guy snapped, Leigh was fairly certain he could take him, but he hoped it wouldn't come to that. "You are not a mermaid. You're a man. You're on legs right now. You did not have a tail last night."

"You only saw my face."

"You didn't have a tail because mermaids don't exist!"

"I shall prove it to you. I need only to submerge in water to call out my tail. Then will you believe me? Your bathroom should have what I need." Without waiting for an answer, he glanced around the apartment and pushed past Leigh, deeper inside.

Leigh needed to get this guy out of his home, even if he had saved him last night.

Merfolk? Seriously?

Tolly found the bathroom quick enough and proceeded to turn on the taps to the tub before Leigh could organize his thoughts for a proper protest.

He tried anyway. "Listen, I don't have time for this."

"I am used to cold water, but perhaps I shall try something warmer," Tolly said as he held his hand under the water and adjusted the taps accordingly. "Is warm water nice?"

"I... yeah, usually. Can we please just talk about this—"

Tolly disrobed without shame, right there in front of Leigh, just shed the housecoat and stood there nude. He was even more beautiful bare, entirely hairless below the neck, thin like a swimmer but well-muscled, without a single scar or imperfection other than the sunspots that Leigh thought only enhanced how beautiful he was.

Being gorgeous and naked in Leigh's bathroom did not change that he was clearly insane, however.

"Tolly, you can't just…. We need to talk about this." Leigh turned to stare at the wall. He was a hardened criminal. Sort of. Sometimes. It should not be this difficult to throw someone out of his home!

"Not until you believe me. Our conversation will go nowhere if you think me mad."

He was a smart crazy person at least, but that didn't help the situation. Leigh had to focus on the Morettis, on what to say when he saw Sweeney, on how to get himself out of this mess so he didn't end up dead some other way tonight, without having to flee the city. He'd break parole if he did that, and the money he'd saved so far wouldn't last him long on the run.

Maybe the Morettis didn't know where he lived. If they did, surely they would have sent someone to rummage through his things, looking for that extra cash. Maybe they did know and someone was on their way now. No point in rushing over when they thought him dead.

"Tolly, just put the housecoat back on or grab a towel. I'll get you some clothes—"

"Do you not find my form pleasing?"

Out of the corner of Leigh's eye, he could tell Tolly stood facing him, hands running down his hips and thighs like he really was unused to legs. "It is very pleasing, but it's not…. I hardly know you."

"Ah yes, human decorum. I might fail at that on occasion, but I will try my best. I know so much of your world, but I have not experienced it firsthand. Still, you know me better than you think through our connection. The Breath of Life is a powerful bond. I am yours now. You are welcome to look at me."

Leigh was certain some of the porn he'd watched over the years had lines like that. "Tolly…."

"I do not wish to make you uncomfortable. I will get into the tub to conceal myself until the water is high enough. Hopefully you will not find my tail displeasing."

Tolly lowered himself into the tub, and Leigh allowed a glance in his direction. Even mostly hidden, he was enchanting to look at. Despite having come from the water last night, his hair had perfect body and poof to it. Why did someone so gorgeous and who had saved Leigh's life have to be nuts?

"I have to figure out how to handle those men who tried to kill me. Do you understand?"

"Of course. I will help you."

"No offense, but you're a little skinny to be a bodyguard. This is going to take strategic planning."

"I am an excellent planner. I often have to dodge others of my kin. I am not popular, as I do not conform to the merfolk ways. Kill or be killed—it loses all the magic of life, even when magic surrounds me in the water. How can one live like that?"

Leigh almost took the words as an attack, though he knew Tolly didn't mean it that way. He'd never killed anyone before, but his plans to rise in the ranks with Sweeney meant one day he would. Kill or be killed was the only way he could survive in this city.

"You were right, warm water is nice, though the cold can be pleasant too." Tolly tilted his head back and sank lower into the tub.

Scrubbing a hand down his face, Leigh was thinking of how to get this naked delusional poet out of his apartment without drawing the attention of his neighbors when he heard a strange wet slap and a contented sigh.

"There, you see? I am merfolk, but you gave me legs, and now, I am yours."

The red glimmer in Leigh's periphery before he looked up had to be an illusion because of how tired he was. There was no way it could be anything else.

But when his gaze focused on Tolly in the tub once more, it wasn't a pair of feet propped on the edge but the unfurling of the most beautiful deep red tailfin he had ever laid eyes on, trimmed in gold-tipped scales.

"Holy shit."

AMANDA MEUWISSEN is a queer author with a primary focus on M/M romance. She has a Bachelor of Arts in a personally designed Creative Writing major from St. Olaf College and is an avid consumer of fiction through film, prose, and video games. As the author of LGBTQ+ Fantasy #1 Best Seller, *Coming Up for Air*, LGBTQ+ Horror #1 Best Seller and #1 New Release, *A Delicious Descent*, and several other titles through various publishers, Amanda regularly attends local comic conventions for fun and to meet with fans, where she will often be seen in costume as one of her favorite fictional characters. She lives in Minneapolis, Minnesota, with her husband, John, and their cat, Helga, and can be found at https://linktr.ee/amandameuwissen.

THE PRINCE
AND THE
ICE KING

A Tale from the Gemstone Kingdoms

AMANDA MEUWISSEN

Tales from the Gemstone Kingdoms: Book One

Every Winter Solstice, the Emerald Kingdom sends the dreaded Ice King a sacrifice—a corrupt soul, a criminal, a deviant, or someone touched by magic. Prince Reardon has always loathed this tradition, partly because he dreams of love with another man instead of a future queen.

Then Reardon's best friend is discovered as a witch and sent to the Frozen Kingdom as tribute.

Reardon sets out to rescue him, willing to battle and kill the Ice King if that's what it takes. But nothing could prepare him for what he finds in the Frozen Kingdom—a cursed land filled with magic… and a camaraderie Reardon has never known. Over this strange, warm community presides the enigmatic Ice King himself, a man his subjects call Jack. A man with skin made of ice, whose very touch can stop a beating heart.

A man Reardon finds himself inexplicably drawn to.

Jack doesn't trust Reardon. But when Reardon begins spending long days with him, vowing to prove himself and break the curse, Jack begins to hope. Can love and forgiveness melt the ice around Jack's heart?

www.dreamspinnerpress.com

STITCHES

A Tale from the Gemstone Kingdoms

AMANDA MEUWISSEN

Tales from the Gemstone Kingdoms: Book Two

Created by the alchemist Braxton, Levi was "born" fully grown and spends his early days learning about the monster-filled kingdom he calls home.

Even though he is just a construct pieced together from cloned parts, Levi longs to fit in with his mythical neighbors, but more than that, he wishes he could say two words to the Shadow King without stuttering.

Ashmedai has been king of what was once the Amethyst Kingdom since it was cursed a thousand years ago. Only he and Braxton know what truly happened the night of the curse, and Ash's secret makes walking among his beloved people painful, so he rarely leaves his castle. However, with Festival Day approaching, Ash wouldn't mind going out more often… if it means seeing more of Levi.

Ash wishes he deserved the longing looks from those strangely familiar violet eyes. He knows no one could love him after learning the truth of the curse. But if anyone can change his mind, it is the sweetly stitched young man who looks at him like he hung the moon.

www.dreamspinnerpress.com

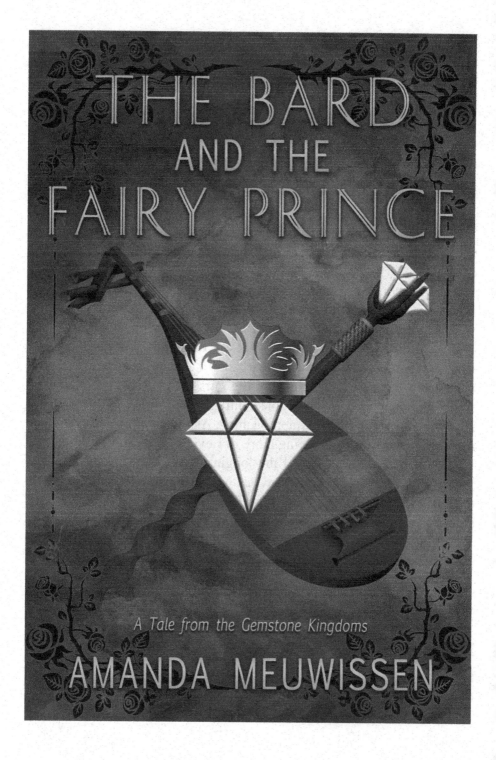

THE BARD
AND THE
FAIRY PRINCE

A Tale from the Gemstone Kingdoms

AMANDA MEUWISSEN

Tales from the Gemstone Kingdoms: Book Three

When Prince Nemirac learns of his heritage, he vows to become the most powerful demon in history. But he can't do it alone.

Feeling betrayed by his parents' lies about his true lineage, Nemirac embarks on a quest to visit all five Gemstone Kingdoms and drain the stones of their power to ascend as a new being. But until he obtains that magic, he's vulnerable.

Enter Janskoller the warrior bard.

Janskoller has just returned to the Gemstone Kingdoms, drawn by stories of broken curses and lands open for travel. He doesn't expect a pretty young mage to hire him as a bodyguard, but it's a good gig for a bard—lots of adventure to fuel his stories, and plenty of travel to spread his fame. Besides, Nemirac's passion and obvious secrets intrigue him. But soon Janskoller realizes the peril of Nemirac's goal—an end that puts the five kingdoms at risk and corrupts Nemirac into a darker, twisted version of the man Janskoller has come to care about. As the two grow closer, can Janskoller convince Nemirac to abandon his pursuit of power in favor of the deeper, more lasting magic of love?

www.dreamspinnerpress.com

VOID DANCER

A Tale from the Gemstone Kingdoms

AMANDA MEUWISSEN

Tales from the Gemstone Kingdoms: Book Four

A brilliant inventor, Enzo Dragonbane has plenty to hide, including his secret identity as the recently deceased king's bastard son. But he's not half as mysterious as Cullen, the man he finds in the caverns. Cullen has no memories at all.

Cullen doesn't know who he is or how he got there, and he certainly doesn't know anything about his strange shadow powers. But he soon learns that memories or not, magic or not, the Ruby Kingdom stands on the brink of civil war. A lower-class group called the Ashen is poised to take advantage of the power vacuum caused by the king's death to fight for equality.

Soon Enzo and Cullen find themselves in the midst of a revolution. As they untangle Cullen's past, they discover they have much in common. But if they're to have any hope of a peaceful life together, they'll have to discover the secret of controlling Cullen's abilities, take sides in the coming fight, and face up to the truth of who they really are.

www.dreamspinnerpress.com